SMASH AND GRAB

CALLAHAN SECURITY, BOOK 2

LORI MATTHEWS

WILD COYOTE PRESS

ABOUT SMASH AND GRAB

Logan Callahan knows he's out of his depth. As CEO of Callahan Security, he thrives on balance sheets and bottom lines. But there's a huge different between running a company and running for your life. Unfortunately he doesn't have a choice. The woman he came to the Bahamas to investigate was kidnapped and he was taken right along with her. He knew the sexy lady lawyer was trouble. He just had no idea how much.

Taken again. Lacy Carmichael was not new to the Kidnap and Ransom game but usually she managed to talk or fight her way out of it. After all, when your father was one of the largest arms dealers in the world danger comes with the territory. Since Logan was grabbed with her, she'll have to reveal all her secrets in order to save their asses.

Logan is hesitant to trust Lacy but a power grab by her father's enemies removes his choice. If only she wasn't so damned smart and sexy, staying neutral would be easier. Searching for a way out of the mess, and fighting their mutual attraction to each other, will take all of Logan's and

Lacy's skills. Unfortunately, deception and betrayal by those they trust the most has changed the rules of the game, and they find themselves battling for their lives and their love.

Smash And Grab

Copyright © 2020 Lori Matthews

Disclaimer:

This is a work of fiction. Names, characters, places, and incidents are products of the author's imagination, or the author has used them fictitiously.

For Joan Matthews
Thanks for teaching me about the importance of fun!

ACKNOWLEDGMENTS

Thanks once again to all the inhabitants of my city – the one it takes to bring this book into the world. My deepest gratitude my editors, Corinne DeMaagd and Heidi Senesac for making me appear much more coherent than I actually am; my cover artist, Llewellen Designs for making my story come alive: my virtual assistant who is a social media guru and all round dynamo, Susan Poirier. My personal cheer squad which I could not survive without: Janna MacGregor, Suzanne Burke, Angi Morgan, and Stacey Wilk. Thank you all for talking me off the ledge more than once. My mother and my sisters who told me to dream big. My husband and my children who make my life complete. You all are my world. A special heartfelt thanks goes out to you, the reader. The fact you are reading this means my dreams have come true.

CHAPTER ONE

"I'm not going, Markus," Lacy Carmichael hissed as she tugged her arm from the large man's grasp.

She took a step back and glanced around the party to see if anyone had noticed. It was packed, and the beat from the music was vibrating in her chest. "Like I told you when you called, I'll meet my father on Monday. He expressly told me not to come to see him before then. If he wants me to come now, he's going to have to call me and tell me himself. I'm only following orders."

She straightened her dress. "Now," she said above the noise, "I'm on this yacht to enjoy myself, not to discuss business." With that, she turned on her heel and disappeared into the crowd. She glanced over her shoulder to see if Markus followed and smashed right into someone, a man's chest to be accurate.

Looking up, she almost choked on her champagne. "Logan, what are you doing here?" she sputtered. Of all the people she could have run into on a yacht party in the Bahamas, this was about the worst-case scenario.

"It's nice to see you too, Lacy." A small smile played at

the corners of his mouth as he wiped champagne from his chest.

He looked amazing. His dark hair was a little long, and the moist Caribbean air was making it curl more than usual. One lock tumbled over his forehead, and she started to raise her hand to push it back but caught herself.

"Is everything OK?" His blue eyes, so piercing, glanced over the top of her head, but when she whipped around, there was no sign of Markus. Thank God.

She should have been ready for his next question, delivered seconds after the first one, but somehow she wasn't.

"Who was that man you were fighting with?"

This time she did choke. She coughed and coughed. Logan, concern written on his face, drew closer, but she waved him off.

"Sorry," she croaked. "Went down the wrong pipe." She coughed a bit more. "Ah, nobody." She ran a hand over her own hair, smoothing down any wayward strands. "It's nice to see you, Logan. I'm just surprised you're here in Nassau. I didn't know Callahan Security had clients in the Bahamas... unless you're on vacation? Being the CEO of your own company has some perks, eh? Are your brothers with you?"

She bit the inside of her cheek to stop herself from rambling and tried to make her expression as neutral as possible, but she'd always felt Logan could see right through her. It wasn't something she was willing to admit to anyone else. She knew his former associates had nicknamed him "Lucifer" for that very stare which, rumor had it, could see right into a person's soul. Not to mention he was a devil in the courtroom if the case ever got that far.

"Callahan Security doesn't have clients here, and I left Gage and Mitch in charge in New York. A bit of a risk, I admit." He smiled. "Actually, I have some business to attend to for my old law firm. They flew me down."

He had finished wiping his chest, and now he gave her the once over, even studying her arm where Markus had grabbed her. "You sure you're all right?"

"Um, yes. Fine." She started to bring her hand up to fix her hair again but stopped herself. No need to let him know how much he rattled her.

"What about you?" he asked. "What are you doing in the Bahamas and, more specifically, at this party? Do you know the Dobsons?"

"The who?" She had been distracted by his cool blue eyes checking her out. The smile was back, threatening the corners of his mouth again.

"The Dobsons. This is their party. They own the yacht."

"Right. The Dobsons. Well, actually, I was invited by an old college friend who's here in town. He asked me to drop by."

Logan glanced around as if looking for the person in question.

"Oh, he's around here somewhere." She pretended to look for him. In reality, she had been invited by a woman she met by the pool at her hotel. She wouldn't normally say yes to something like this, but life had been stressful of late, and she just wanted a chance to dress up and go to a party without the hassle of having to talk to anyone. Now she very much regretted her decision to party crash.

She saw Markus coming up from below. He was talking on his cell. Holding up her empty champagne glass, she said, "You know, I think I'll go find some water. Great to see you!" She quickly turned and fled. The last thing she wanted was for Logan and his super-stare to see her and Markus arguing again.

She made her way through the crowd to the railing and leaned over the side of the yacht. It was a perfect Caribbean night. The breeze was warm but not hot. The boat was decorated with twinkly lights along the railings and lanterns hung high up across the decks. They had even turned on the lights by the water so the hull was illuminated. She saw a fish swim alongside the yacht and then disappear into the inky water.

She peered up at the night sky. The bright light on the yacht made it difficult to see the stars. She made a mental note to look up once she left the yacht. The pier and the parking lot weren't well lit so she might be able to see the brilliant white dots in the heavens, if there were any visible.

Rolling her shoulders, she tried to ease some of the tension in her neck. Some vacation. She wanted a weekend to decompress from work, which had sucked lately. Well, it always sucked. The truth was, she wanted out. Out of being a lawyer. She had enough clients to make a good living, but she just found the whole thing boring. And there was her father…but she wasn't going to think about that. This was her weekend off. She wanted to enjoy it.

She glanced up, spotted Markus again, and then breathed a small sigh of relief when he disappeared around the bow of the yacht. She wasn't surprised he found her at the party. Her father had eyes everywhere. It was weird though, that her father hadn't contacted her directly to tell her he wanted her to come home. Why send one of his henchmen? He knew she wouldn't go with Markus unless he called her. She was following his instructions. The whole thing was off somehow. Come to think of it, Markus was acting weird, too. Nervous.

She exchanged her empty glass of champagne for a full one from a passing waiter and took a large sip. One for the road. It was time to abandon ship. This wasn't the way she'd wanted to kick off her weekend break.

She caught a glimpse of Logan through the crowd. Logan Callahan. The man who always had made her knees weak. From the moment she saw him across a boardroom table, she'd been hyper aware of him. She'd been a newly minted lawyer and thought she knew a thing or two. He quickly ground her into dust.

She'd never forgotten him, or forgiven him for that matter. Still, their interactions had made her a better lawyer. She had been much better prepared the next time they'd met. She even scored a point or two on him.

Since then, she'd improved greatly, and now she was pretty sure he saw her as a worthy adversary. Or at least he had until he quit and started running Callahan Security with his brothers. She didn't want to think about her weekend with Callahan Security. It was part of the reason she needed this weekend off.

She prided herself on being a very capable and strong woman. She knew she couldn't have gotten far in life—her life, specifically—if she didn't have her shit together. But Logan always threw her for a loop. She'd gotten better at hiding it but, still, the moment she saw him, she turned into an idiot. Case in point. She'd just spilled her drink all over him.

Keeping one eye out for Markus, she worked her way across the length of the yacht and down the stairs to the deck below. As she neared the gangplank to get off the boat, she heard a splash and then a scream. The world seemed frozen for a second before people rushed to the railing. The party-goers were yelling, pushing, and shoving, and someone yelled, "Call for an ambulance!"

Dread washed over her as she elbowed her way to the rail. Her stomach lurched at the sight of what lay below.

A body bobbing in the water.

No need for lights and sirens. Markus floated face up, giving her a perfect view of the hole in the middle of his forehead.

Panic engulfed her, and she white-knuckled the railing. *Just breathe. Just breathe.* She kept repeating the mantra until everything stopped spinning. She scanned the crowd. Most people were still peering down at the body in shock, but some were already making their way off the yacht. That seemed like a grand idea to her. While she and Markus had been acquaintances and she was sorry he was dead, it wouldn't do her any good if she got caught up in whatever mess he was leaving behind.

As she turned, something caught her eye, so she stopped to scrutinize the deck above. Logan was standing there watching her. Their eyes met. A shiver ran down her spine. Then some panicked partygoer slammed into her, and the spell was broken. By the time she righted herself and looked up again, Logan was gone.

Sirens in the distance made goose bumps raise on her arms. She made her way to the gangplank, pushing through the crowd. Being gone by the time the cops arrived would be best. It was never good to chat with the cops with her father on the wrong side of the law.

As she hit the pier, the mass exodus created a logjam of bodies heading the same direction as she was going…to the parking lot. Strobing lights on the arriving cop cars lit the sky, rendering any chance of seeing stars moot.

Glancing around, it appeared the best way out of there was to walk left and back down the pier along the side of the warehouse, away from the parking lot. The pier extended maybe twenty feet past the end of the warehouse.

She tried to pull up a mental map of the area. Wasn't there a boardwalk on the far side of the warehouse by the other end of the parking lot? If she traveled around the warehouse, she should be able to get to the boardwalk. She would only be exposed as she covered the last bit of parking lot. There were a couple of hotels if she remembered correctly. She could grab a cab.

Changing direction, she worked her way through the

crowd. She finally broke free and hustled down the pier, sticking close to the warehouse so she would be in the shadows the whole way. The shock of seeing Markus floating lifeless in the water was starting to wear off, leaving dozens of questions in its wake.

Behind her, cops were ordering people back onto the yacht, so she picked up her pace. There would be plenty of time later to theorize about what had happened. She rounded the corner and broke into a light jog along the far end of the warehouse. Not easy to do in high heels, but desperate times called for desperate measures.

It was dark, and she stumbled, but caught herself. She glanced upward and realized there were no stars. So much for the perfect Caribbean night.

Coming to the next corner, she peered around it, making sure there were no cops. She stuck close to the warehouse as she worked her way back down the pier. She was almost halfway down the side when a cop came around the corner of the warehouse from the parking lot. She stopped jogging and quickly hid behind some pallets that were stacked on the pier next to the warehouse. The cop walked directly toward her, and she shrank back into the shadows.

A hand covered her mouth. All the air left her lungs. Struggling to breathe, she started to fight off her attacker.

"Stop struggling, or the cop will find us," a voice breathed in her ear. She froze. Logan took his hand away from her mouth and pulled her deeper behind the stack of pallets. Her pulse skyrocketed. Being pressed against Logan wasn't helping. Electricity danced across her skin.

They stood frozen as the cop came closer. He took out a flashlight and moved the beam around the pier. The light didn't penetrate the pallets, and the officer walked back the way he'd come.

As soon as he was out of earshot, Lacy turned to face Logan. "You scared the shit out of me!"

"I didn't want you to yell and let the cop know where we were."

She couldn't see his face in the shadows, but she had a sneaking suspicion he was laughing at her again. "Whatever. I need to get out of here." When she took a step forward, Logan followed her. She glanced at him, "What are you—?"

"Looks like we both want to get out of here, so why don't we talk later and just keep moving now, hmm?"

It was tempting to argue, but she nodded and started walking toward the end of the warehouse. Logan was the last person she'd expected to find hiding out on the pier. He was a top-notch lawyer. Squeaky clean. The fact that he was lurking in the shadows tonight was interesting. Very interesting.

When they came to the end, Logan glanced toward the yacht. "The cops have the area cordoned off. Looks like they're questioning people."

Lacy took a quick look and confirmed what he'd said. She immediately swore.

"What?" he asked.

"Peter Trenthom."

"Who?"

"The guy in the suit standing next to the gangplank. He's probably the lead detective on the case."

He cocked an eyebrow. "And how do you know so much about the police in the Bahamas?"

"It's a long story. Let's just say, my employer has had some legal issues in town." She peeked around the corner again, trying to figure out her best move.

If Trenthom saw her, it would be game over for sure. He knew both she and Markus worked for Armand Fontaine. She would be questioned. If he found out she had been arguing with Markus, she might have to spend the night at the station. She wanted no part of that. Very few people knew that Armand Fontaine was also her father, and she'd prefer to keep it that way.

Logan eyed her. "What are you thinking?"

She turned her head toward him. It was hard to see his features in the small bit of ambient light, but she the intensity of his gaze warmed her.

She licked her lips. "The boardwalk is just over there, so I think we should make a break for it and hustle toward the hotels that are down the beach." She started forward, but he grabbed her arm and hauled her back.

"Let's take a moment to think about it." He held her arm as he scanned the area, the contact making the butterflies in her stomach take flight. She tried to pull away gently, but he held fast. Her heart started to beat a bit faster.

"If we walk across the parking lot to the boardwalk entrance, we're bound to be seen," he murmured, more to himself than to her.

The scent of Logan carried on the breeze, surrounding Lacy. He smelled distinctly male, mixed with citrus and a hint of salt air. The heady aroma was clouding her thinking and making her conjure up all kinds of inappropriate thoughts. She swallowed hard. "Well, do you have a better plan?" she asked as she tugged her arm again, anxious to be free of his touch. This man was friggin' kryptonite, and she was losing the ability to concentrate.

"As a matter of fact, I do." He let go of her arm and wrapped his arm around her shoulders, pulling her close. Startled, she gasped and glared up at him.

"Just follow my lead." He walked them out from behind the building and turned *toward* the yacht.

"What are you doing?" she asked in a fierce whisper. *Was*

he crazy? She heard someone yell, but Logan didn't pause. He lowered his head closer to hers. "Keep walking."

The yell came a second time. Logan whipped her around, placing himself between her and the police by the yacht. He bent down and swiftly captured her mouth with his. She opened her mouth in surprise, and he deepened the kiss. She put her hands on his chest, ostensibly to push him away, but they had a life of their own. They fisted his shirt and pulled him closer. She was so wrapped up in him, she barely noticed someone was still yelling at them.

He suddenly broke away from her and turned his head. She was trying to get her bearings. Was he talking to someone? The world snapped into focus. There was a uniformed officer standing just to her right.

"Sorry, officer," Logan said. "We didn't hear you." His aw-shucks smile was almost convincing enough to fool her. "What's going on over there? Did someone get hurt?"

Her heart was pounding so hard she was sure he could feel it. That kiss had been so amazing and crazy and *ohmygod* good. Her body was still crushed against his, and the closeness was killing her concentration.

The officer hesitated and then took in her cocktail dress and his suit. "You need to come with me."

"We'd be happy to come, officer. We were just walking over to the party when we saw all the commotion. We took a bit longer getting ready than we'd planned." He winked at the cop.

Heat crawled up Lacy's neck. Was he for real? Did he just wink? Mortified didn't begin to cover her consternation.

"You haven't been to the party?" the cop asked.

"No, we were on our way. What happened? Are the Dobsons alright?"

The officer gave Logan the once over. "Do you know the Dobsons?"

"Yes. I went to law school with their son, Peter." He turned to Lacy. "Maybe I should go and see if Peter needs help."

Just then a second police officer arrived.

"What's going on?" the new cop asked.

"These two say they were just going to the party," the first officer said.

"Yes, officer," Logan agreed. "We were late getting here. I understand there's been a problem. As I was telling this officer, Peter Dobson and I went to law school together. I thought I might go over and offer my services."

"Ah…" The second cop hesitated. "I don't think that will be necessary, sir. It's better if you leave. I'm sure the Dobsons will be in touch if they require your assistance."

"If you're sure," Logan said. "I'd feel badly leaving Peter in the lurch. Maybe I—"

"No, sir. I'm afraid I'm going to have to ask you to leave." The officer pointed to the boardwalk behind them.

Logan turned himself and Lacy slowly as he said, "OK. We'll go."

"Thank you, sir. Have a good evening."

Lacy let out the breath she'd been holding. That had been close. Too close.

CHAPTER TWO

"Where are you staying?" Logan asked. They had walked down the boardwalk without speaking and, as if by silent agreement, were now waiting for a taxi outside the nearest hotel.

"Ocean Beach Resort. You?"

"Same." *Of course, because I'm following you.* If he could kill his brother Gage right now, he would. His brothers, Gage and Mitch, were the ex-Spec Ops guys. He was a lawyer and a damn good one. When they'd agreed to take over their father's security company, Callahan Security, he never counted on being in the field. Skulking around warehouses in the dark and trying to get one over on the police was not his thing.

Well, the police thing had been kind of fun. He hadn't pulled a stunt like that since his teen years, but following Lacy around and spying on her was outside his comfort zone. Hell, everything about Lacy Carmichael was outside his comfort zone. He could still feel her lips on his, her body pressed against him. Not good. Better if that didn't happen again.

He'd promised Gage and Mitch he would follow up on this lead. Lacy was hiding something, and he had to find out if it had anything to do with Jameson Drake and the prototype he and his brothers had been hired to protect. Still, he hated lying to Lacy about why he was there. He hated lying period.

The fact that she'd been hiding from the law and arguing with the dead guy made him nervous. When he'd agreed to this, he'd thought the chances of Lacy Carmichael being involved in corporate espionage were slim to none. He should have known better. His days as a JAG lawyer had taught him that everybody was capable of committing a crime given the right circumstances. He wondered what those circumstances were for Lacy.

Mentally sighing, he said, "We can share a cab back to the hotel, and you can fill me in on your connection to the dead guy. Including why you were fighting with him."

Lacy's back went ramrod straight. He'd hit a nerve there, no question.

"Look, I appreciate your help with the police back there, but I did have the situation under control. And I don't think it's any of your business, so I won't be explaining anything to you."

As they approached the front of the line, the attendant asked where they were going. As Logan was giving him the address, Lacy hurried forward and climbed into the next cab, closing the door quickly. Apparently, she didn't want to share a cab. *Well, too bad.* Logan hustled to the opposite side of the cab, opened the door, and slid in next to her before the cab could leave. Lacy gave the driver the name of the resort and then leaned back in the seat and closed her eyes.

The driver started on his way. Logan was having a hard time relaxing. Lacy's scent, ocean breeze mixed with some sort of flower, haunted him. It floated around him, bringing back memories of their kiss. He was getting hard just thinking about it. Gage had been right about one thing; he needed to get laid.

"So, are you through pouting yet?" he asked quietly. He needed to distract himself somehow. Maybe he could get the information he needed and then leave Lacy alone. There was a bar somewhere calling his name, and he'd like to spend some time there in peace.

"I am not pouting," she retorted.

"Would you prefer it if I called it a 'hissy fit'?" He did his best to suppress a smile. He was baiting her on purpose. He could see she was getting frustrated with him. It was fun to annoy her. She was cute when she was ticked off. Sexy was more the word for her tonight. The dress was killer and clung to every curve. Her chestnut hair had shone in the lights on the yacht and he'd delighted in the super-soft texture when he had been holding her close. He cleared his throat. "I think we should discuss this further back at the hotel."

"I don't wish to discuss it," she said through her teeth. "It's none of your concern. I have everything under control."

"Then how come you were hiding from the cops? Makes you look guilty."

"I don't look guilty!" she retorted indignantly.

He continued to goad her. "You had an argument with the dead guy seconds before someone shot him and sent him over the side of the ship."

"I. DID. NOT. Shoot Markus Spires!" she screeched.

He was so caught up in pissing off Lacy, he was totally unprepared when she was suddenly pitched face down into his lap. She yelped in surprise as he wrapped his arms around her and held her tight. The tires of the taxi screamed in protest to the sudden turn and braking. The vehicle came to an abrupt halt.

"Hey—" She didn't get to finish the sentence before

gunfire broke out and glass flew all around them. The sound was deafening.

Logan pushed her down on his legs and covered her as best he could with the top half of his body. "Stay down," he commanded.

Suddenly, it was silent, eerily so. Logan lifted his head a bit. The front windshield no longer existed, and the driver was slumped over the wheel, blood soaking his shirt. Lacy was reaching out an arm toward the driver when the passenger door was wrenched open.

Logan instinctively tightened his grip on her when two men pointed assault rifles at them. The men were both dressed in black fatigues, and dark bandanas concealed the bottom half of their faces. The first guy, a bald man, gestured with his rifle for them to get out of the taxi. Logan raised his hands in a gesture of peace, nodded, and gave Lacy a look that he hoped clearly conveyed an order. *Move.*

AS LACY STARTED SITTING BACK UP, her fingers knocked against something sharp. She glanced down to see a small, sharp piece of plastic. Part of the cab must have been destroyed in all the shooting. She closed her hand around it and slowly sat upright and moved out of the vehicle.

Once standing, she turned to face the men, willing herself to memorize what she could see of their faces so she'd be able to describe them if the opportunity arose. It was hard with the lower halves of their faces covered, which was undoubtedly the point of the disguise. Her father had spent years preparing her for this sort of thing, and now that her shock had eased, fear started to make way for anger. Taking a deep breath, she tried to calm herself and focus.

"Move," the bald man said, gesturing with his gun for her

to step aside. The other guy was pointing his gun at her. He had long black curly hair and cold eyes. At least they seemed that way to her.

When Lacy took a step toward the trunk of the taxi, Logan emerged beside her.

They edged closer together, but neither of them said a word. He was so still. She knew without looking at him that he was watching every detail just like she was. Looking for weaknesses that could be exploited. He had been in the Navy, even if it was the JAG Corps, so she assumed he wouldn't be totally useless in a fight.

A third man came around the side of the cab. He was taller and slimmer than the first two and dressed in a light-colored suit with an open-collared white shirt. He nodded to the other men, and they stepped back. So, this was the man in charge. He didn't bother to cover his face. Not a good sign.

He had pale skin, cold black eyes, and an ugly scar bisected his right cheek. Fresh panic threatened to close up her throat.

"Good evening, Ms. Carmichael," Scar said as if they'd crossed paths while out for an evening stroll. "I am sorry for the"—he paused and waved his hands at the scene—"dramatics." He shrugged. "It couldn't be helped. This was the most expedient way for me to get what I wanted."

"Which is what?" Logan's voice rumbled out of his chest. Scar turned his head and focused his cold gaze on Logan. He ran his eyes quickly up and down, assessing what he saw, and then dismissed him.

He turned back to Lacy. "Why, Ms. Carmichael, of course. We have a date with history, you and I." He smiled, which was more a baring of teeth.

Lacy found her voice. "I'm afraid I don't understand." She had a sinking feeling in the pit of her stomach. She was pretty sure she *did* understand, but she was really hoping to be wrong. "Why do you want me?"

"Oh, I think you know exactly why I want you." The smile, such as it was, disappeared as Scar turned back to Logan. "The question is, what do I do with you?"

He gave Logan another once over, and this time his eyes lingered on his suit. "You are a business man. Does he work with you?" he asked, turning back toward Lacy. "I wasn't informed about him, so I tend to think not."

"Yes—"

"No—"

Logan and Lacy spoke simultaneously. Scar laughed. "Shall I give you a minute to get your stories straight?"

Lacy tried to clear her throat, but it was Sahara dry. "He does not work with me. We're friends." She took a deep breath and continued, "And since I am the one you seem to want, you can let him go." She held her breath. If she said the wrong thing, it was conceivable that Scar would kill Logan.

"I don't think I can let him go." Scar shook his head. "He's seen too much. He'll tell your father things before I am ready for him to find out. No. Letting him go is out of the question." He gestured to the bald gunman to come closer.

"Wait." Glancing around, she saw dilapidated, abandoned buildings with boarded up windows. There was a stripped car on the side of the road that had been burnt at some point in the past.

"We're not in the best area, and there aren't any sirens after all that gunfire, so I'm guessing you made some sort of deal to keep the cops away." She gestured to Logan. "It's a long walk back to the center of town, through some not-so-great neighborhoods. We'll be far away before he can alert anyone, if he makes it back at all. The crime rate is pretty high these days on New Providence Island. And he doesn't even know my father." She knew she was babbling, but she was getting desperate. If they killed Logan in front of her... well, she didn't know what she'd do.

"What is your name?" Scar took a step toward Logan, careful to make sure he wasn't blocking his gunman's shot. Logan said nothing. Without issuing a warning, Scar punched him in the stomach, making him double over. Logan grunted, but then straightened up again. "Frisk them," Scar commanded. Lacy still had the sharp piece of plastic in her hand. She quickly brought her hand behind her back and dropped the plastic piece. It hit the ground next to her shoe. She immediately nudged it back under the cab with her foot. The gunman came toward her and then gave her a brisk but rough search. She couldn't hide much in an evening gown, and her purse with her cell and wallet was in the cab. He stepped away again.

She used the opportunity to pretend her heel gave out, causing her to stumble. She turned sideways and squatted down. She rubbed her ankle with one hand. With the other, she reached under the cab for the plastic piece. Once she found it, she stood up again. She said a small prayer of thanks that no one noticed.

The gunman took more time with Logan, taking his cell, but coming up empty on the wallet.

She caught Logan's eye and raised an eyebrow in a silent question. He shrugged slightly.

Scar demanded. "Where's your wallet?"

Logan said nothing. He hit Logan a second time, and once again Logan doubled over before standing back up.

"You take a punch well, my friend, but let us see how you take a bullet." Scar nodded to his gunman.

"No!" Lacy stepped in front of Logan. He grabbed her and tried to move her aside, but she fought back. *What the hell was she doing?* her brain screamed at her. But she knew if

Logan was shot, she wouldn't be able to forgive herself. "No," she said in a calmer voice. "There's no need to kill him. I will come with you peacefully if you let him go." Logan's hands tightened on her arms.

"You'll come with me regardless. I don't care if it's peaceful or not. As you said, no one cares, so scream all you want." Scar's eyes narrowed. "But"—he turned to Logan —"the lady seems to care for you, so perhaps you will come in handy."

Scar turned to his men and said something in a language she didn't understand. There was a flurry of activity, and then more men materialized out of the darkness. They started searching the cab. One of the men grabbed Logan's wallet from the floor where it must have fallen during the commotion. He handed it to Scar. That answered what had happened to Logan's wallet. She had been hoping he had hidden it somehow.

"Well," Scar said, "Mr. Callahan, looks like you are coming with us. But let's make sure you don't get any ideas…"

The bald guy grabbed Lacy's arms, his hands digging in so hard it hurt, and then flung her at a new guy that came around the side of the cab. He grabbed Lacy and marched her over to a large square delivery truck. It most likely had been white at one point, but it was hard to tell from all the dents in the side.

There was another man waiting next to the truck. The two men each took an arm and hoisted Lacy up and pushed her into the back of the truck. She landed hard on her knees and fell forward onto her hands. She slowly turned so she was sitting on her butt. Blood was oozing out of the cuts on her knees, and her palms were scraped. One of the men followed her into the truck and bound her hands together in front of her.

The whack of a fist hitting skin made her feel ill. The corresponding grunts made her shiver. The two men stood at the end of the truck. One faced outward and one watched her, each holding an AK-47. She desperately wanted to help Logan, but there was nothing she could do.

She waited in the box truck for an eternity, feeling more and more ill with every passing second. She'd managed to hide the wedge of plastic in her bra, but she couldn't get to it with the armed man staring at her and with her hands shackled the way they were.

Finally, Logan appeared at the back of the truck. Lacy swore soundly when she saw him. There were a couple of cuts on his face, and a slice on his lip was sending a thin trickle of blood down his chin. His hands were tied in front of him, too. They pushed him toward the truck, and then hoisted him up as they had done with Lacy.

When they gave him a huge shove and, Logan lost his footing and fell, twisting at the last minute so he landed on his shoulder. The kidnappers jumped down and pulled the door closed after them. Lacy heard the lock click into place.

Left in total darkness, she didn't move until the truck started to roll. "Logan." Silence. "Logan." Desperation leeched into her voice.

"Shit. Yeah?"

"Thank God. Are you OK?""

"Other than a few cuts and bruises, I'm fine," he said.

She let out the breath she had been holding.

"So," Logan said, "want to tell me what the fuck is going on? I hope you have an idea, cause I sure as hell don't."

She sighed. "I think they're trying to get to my father."

"Why? Is he rich or something? Are they looking for a big payday?" He coughed a bit as he rolled onto his back.

"No. At least I don't think that's what this is about." She paused. She really didn't want to tell Logan the truth.

"Then what the fuck *is* it about?" Logan snarled.

She didn't blame him. He was obviously angry, deservedly so, but as soon as she told him the truth, he was going to be furious.

She swallowed. "I think my father refused to sell to them, and they're trying to force his hand."

"Just what the hell does your father sell?"

She tried to moisten her lips, but her mouth was dry. "My father is an arms dealer."

CHAPTER THREE

Logan froze. "Are you fucking serious? An arms dealer? As in guns?"

"Shhh! Quiet down. And to answer your question, yes, but more like RPGs, that sort of thing." Lacy said it so quickly the words had fallen over one another.

"Whoever these men are, I suspect my father turned them down. I only know about the deals that go through, and not even all of those. Just the ones that he needs logistics help with." She sighed. "It's not the first time someone has become...upset at my father and tried to take it out on me. Although this is the first time they have somewhat succeeded."

"Somewhat," Logan growled. "We're tied up in the back of a box truck, kidnapped by some trigger-happy lunatic. I would say 'somewhat' is out the window, lady!" He grunted as he moved into a sitting position.

Go to the Bahamas Gage had said. *Catch some sun, get laid. You need a break. It won't be hard, just keep an eye on her. We don't really think she's involved. This is just a precaution.* Precaution, his ass. Logan winced when his ribs throbbed.

"Wait. You help your father? You're an arms dealer?" It took a minute for what she'd said to sink in. Could this get worse? Apparently so.

Her voice was quiet. "More like an occasional assistant."

Logan grunted again as he shifted, trying to find a position that hurt less, but it was a losing battle. He leaned back against the wall of the truck and swore loudly.

"Are you all right?" she asked anxiously.

"Fine," he breathed. He was anything but fine. He was tied up in the back of a truck with an *assistant* arms dealer, and his ribs and kidneys were killing him. But he wasn't about to tell her that. It was obvious he didn't have a clue about the real Lacy Carmichael.

He should have listened to his gut and said no to his brother, been more forceful, but he'd been intrigued by Lacy from the moment he'd seen her across the boardroom table. When his brother told him about this job, he was thinking of getting laid, alright.. He'd been picturing Lacy wearing a string bikini, lying on a beach towel next to him.

He should have... Shoulda, coulda, woulda, it didn't matter now. Regrets weren't getting him out of this mess. If he hadn't of come, then Lacy would be trussed up in this truck by herself. The mere thought of that made his stomach clench. Logan cursed softly as he shifted again, trying to get comfortable.

"So," he said in a calmer voice, "any idea where we are going? Or what the plan is? It sounds like you've been down this road before."

"No idea. I'm guessing Scar will try to do some sort of exchange. Us for whatever equipment this guy wants. My father won't make a deal with them if we're hurt, so we're probably physically safe."

Logan snorted. "Scar. Fitting. But there's a problem with your theory. First of all, he was quite willing to kill me back there. The only reason I'm alive is because he thinks he can use me as leverage against you. So, why does he need leverage if he's just going to trade us?"

"I…I don't know." The sound of a gear grinding filled the truck.

"Well, I'm sure we're going to find out." When he moved, pain radiated up his ribs. He clamped his jaws together and waited until the pain receded. "Did you happen to notice anything usable in this truck? Anything that might come in handy?"

"No, it's totally empty." He could hear her moving closer to him. When the truck hit a bump, she grunted and fell onto his shins. She shoved upright, steadied herself with a hand on his leg then settled next to him. She whispered, "I have this, though."

Sticking out his hands, he turned to face her as best he could, which was when his fingers brushed against her breast. It was firm and soft at the same time.

She gasped.

"Sorry." He wasn't the least bit sorry. Feeling her up could be the last bit of action he was ever gonna get. Besides she'd just rubbed her hand up his leg and he'd enjoyed every minute of it. He was glad she couldn't see his grin in the dark.

"No problem. Just keep still, and I'll find you." A hand touched his, passing something sharp to him. "I think part of the console was blown off in the gunfight. I grabbed it on the way out of the cab."

"Nice. Can you tuck it back into wherever it came from? Chances are better they'll miss it on you." He felt her take the piece and then he heard rustling. In his mind's eye, he pictured several possible hiding spots for the piece of plastic. He started to feel warm at the thought. Touching her breast had killed his focus. Now all he could think about was how good she felt. He shook his head, trying to get rid of the image of Lacy naked. *So not the time.*

"We should make a plan," Lacy stated and then promptly fell into him as the truck took a sharp turn.

Logan grimaced in pain. He would normally welcome the chance to have her lean on him, but it hurt too much at the moment. He gently used his shoulder to help push her upright again. "Hard to make a plan when we have no clue where we are going or what Scar wants."

"You have a better idea?" she asked in a sarcastic tone.

"Let's just see what happens when we get to wherever it is we're going. We don't have a lot to work with at the moment. We need a better advantage than what we've got."

"You think we'll be OK once we get to wherever they're bringing us?" she scoffed.

"No. But we don't have a choice. We've got nothing to work with but one piece of plastic. I'm a little sore and you..." He paused. "Did your father teach you anything about being in situations like this? You said something similar happened before."

"Not similar exactly. Someone made a grab for me, but he wasn't a professional and he bungled it. I ended up breaking his nose and several of his toes."

"Nice."

"Hey, it worked. My father taught me to pay attention and always be prepared."

"Great. You're a boy scout. Not exactly helpful." Logan knew his tone was bitter but he couldn't help it. The pain was getting to him.

"Who found the plastic?" she asked in a biting tone. "It may not be much, but it's more than you've got."

"Touché." He hated that a hint of annoyance had crept into his voice. Not that he was annoyed at her, just annoyed she was right. He didn't have anything that could help. The darkness was making him slightly claustrophobic. He tried to figure out their next move.

He had no idea of how they were going to get out of this mess. Certainly not the best situation to be in as the head of a security company. If word got out, this little incident could be very damaging. They were walking a fine line as it was. His brother Mitch's foray into personal security had already dented their reputation. Although, truth be told, it wasn't really his fault. Still, if this situation became public, he and his brothers were done for in the security business. It wasn't helping his ego any either.

The noise of the truck engine changed. They were slowing down. It was a good thing because the smell of the truck and the swaying in the darkness was making him nauseous. Last thing he needed was to puke his guts out.

The truck turned to the right and then rolled to a halt. Logan heard Lacy's quick intake of breath. He reached out blindly and managed to put a hand on her leg to comfort her. He didn't need a hysterical woman on his hands. But he grudgingly admitted she'd handled herself well so far. Except for almost getting him killed, of course. Still, all in all, not bad.

The sound of the cab door closing clattered through their little space, and voices faded in and out. Then the back of the truck opened. Logan blinked in the sudden light. They were parked next to a shed with security lighting in some sort of boat yard. The bald guy and the guy with all the hair were at the back of the truck, waving them out with guns.

Logan struggled to his feet and turned to help Lacy, but she was already standing. They both walked to the back of the truck and looked down. They were a few feet off the ground. Baldy waved for them to get out. Logan jumped and had to bite the inside of his cheek to stop from yelping. Baldy yelled at Lacy to move faster.

"She's in a dress and heels," Logan snarled. "She needs help."

Baldy just snorted and aimed his gun at the middle of Logan's chest.

"It's fine," Lacy said as she moved toward the edge of the truck.

Logan opened his mouth to argue but Lacy had already jumped off the back of the truck and landed on her toes. She stumbled a bit but quickly regained her balance.

He smiled at her. "Well, damn. That was impressive."

"Get moving." Baldy gestured with his gun for them to move around the side of the truck.

Logan took in his surroundings. There were boats everywhere, pleasure crafts of varying sizes, many of them being repaired in dry dock. It had to be some sort of marina. To the left, beyond the boats, was darkness and a body of water. A bay maybe? Hard to tell.

He glanced around for something that he might use as a weapon, but there was nothing close enough.

Baldy pushed Logan forward and motioned for Lacy to follow. They walked through the boat yard and turned left, heading to the docks. Logan kept an eye on Lacy, making sure she wasn't about to freak out. Outwardly, she appeared calm, but he had no doubt her heart was pounding in her chest. His certainly was.

They were marched to the end of one of the docks and ordered to board a yacht. It was a high-end pleasure craft. Not as big as the one the party had been on, but it was over a hundred feet by Logan's estimate. Something like this would cost big bucks, even if it was a rental.

Lacy stumbled as she boarded. Logan wanted to reach back and steady her but it was difficult with his hands tied in front of him. Lacy fell onto her knees. He was leaning over trying to help her up when Baldy hit him in the kidneys again. Grunting, he went down beside Lacy. The look she gave him... He wanted to tell her it would be OK, but he had no clue if that was true, and he was having trouble getting his breath. He just gave her what had to be the fakest smile ever.

"On your feet. Both of you." Baldy was at their backs, poking him with the barrel of his gun. After they regained their feet, they were led inside the ship to the salon, carpeted with a thick, cushy cream-colored carpet. The whole room was done in shades of cream and brown. The furniture was made of a wood that gleamed in the soft lighting.

"Welcome to my home away from home." Scar was standing behind a bar, pouring fifty-year-old Scotch into a glass with ice in it. He had taken off his suit jacket and rolled up his sleeves. He appeared like a well-mannered host entertaining guests, not a violent, crazed kidnapper. He gestured to Logan, as if to ask if he wanted one.

"Sure. A drink might go down nicely right about now."

Scar laughed. "I like a man with a sense of humor." He grinned, reached back and grabbed another glass, put ice in it, and poured in a couple of ounces. At a glance from his boss, Baldy brought it over to Logan.

"What am I, chopped liver?" Lacy piped up.

Scar grinned again. "Forgive my manners." He went through the drink ritual, and soon Lacy was holding her own glass.

Scar picked up his drink in a toast. "To new friendships. May they be profitable." He took a swig of the liquor. Neither Logan nor Lacy moved. "What? You both wanted a drink, and now you won't drink it?" His eyes narrowed. "I hate it when people are rude and disrespectful." He glanced at Baldy, who immediately took a step toward Logan.

"The toast didn't really move me," Lacy said. "How about we just drink to our health? Seems a bit more apropos." She took a large gulp of her drink. Logan took a sip of his as well. It was a very smooth Scotch. He was a bit surprised that Lacy hadn't choked considering the size of that swig.

Scar apparently felt the same because there was a look of admiration on his face as he nodded and said, "Ms. Carmichael, you do not disappoint. I had heard you were like your mother. Now I see it is true."

Lacy swallowed hard before saying, "Thank you. I take that as a great compliment." Her face tightened, and Logan wondered what that was all about. Who was her mother and what did she have to do with this whole thing?

"It's too bad I never had the chance to meet her. From everything I've heard, I think I would've been a great fan. She is still discussed fondly in certain circles." Scar walked out from behind the bar and crossed the room to stand in front of Lacy. "It is also sad we had to meet under such circumstances." He ran a finger down her cheek.

Anger burned a hole in Logan's gut. He wanted to reach out and strangle the man, but Lacy was outwardly calm.

"And what circumstances are those?" she asked. "You have neglected to let us in on what this little game is all about." She studied Scar without flinching and took another sip of her scotch.

"It is not a game, I assure you." He stepped back and went to sit down on the cream-colored leather couch under the main window of the salon.

The yacht's engines rumbled to life. Damn. They were definitely pulling away from the dock. He and Lacy rocked a bit on their feet as the engines kicked into a higher gear and the boat surged forward.

"Ms. Carmichael"—Scar paused, his eyes narrowing—"I can see why you changed your name. Hazel is such an old-fashioned name. And, of course, being a Fontaine would have marked you for sure. Every policeman in Europe would have had you on some list. Hazel Fontaine, the only daughter of Armand Fontaine."

Logan's stomach clenched as if Baldy had hit him again. Armand Fontaine. *Son of a bitch.*

Turning to face Logan, he asked, "Did you know her real identity, Mr. Callahan? Did she tell you?" He studied Logan as he waited for his answer.

Logan tried to remain impassive, but he knew his shock at hearing Fontaine's name had registered on his face.

Scar continued, "No. I think she did not. Well, no matter. This is Hazel Fontaine, heiress to one of the greatest arms dealing empires in the world. Her mother would be so proud that Hazel is following in her footsteps. It was her mother that started the empire."

She'd said her father was an arms dealer, but he'd pictured a guy with a pickup and a few crates of guns. Armand Fontaine dealt serious arms, like tanks and helicopter-level arms, through back channels. And he sold to the governments of many corrupt countries all around the world. He was the black-market king of military-grade weaponry. Logan closed his eyes and swore a blue streak in his head.

He had come down here to cross Lacy off the list of suspects involved in trying to steal Drake's prototype. Sun, fun, and relaxation with a bit of work on the side. Instead, he'd been kidnapped with the daughter of one of the largest arms dealers in the world. *Well, fuck.*

From the moment he'd seen Lacy on the yacht in that hot green dress, he'd known he was in trouble. He'd just thought it would be a different kind. It hadn't occurred to him the next few hours would hold murder, an ambush, and a double kidnapping. She must live one hell of a life.

Armand Fontaine. Logan flicked through his memory quickly, trying to dig up what he knew of the man. He had once worked a JAG case that had ties to the arms dealer. A couple of low-level clerks stole some RPGs and were selling them on the black market, if he remembered right. One of them had turned up dead. Fontaine's name had come up on the survivor's list of people who might have wanted him out of the way, so Logan had done some research on the man. It turned out that Fontaine was so major league these guys weren't even a pimple on his ass.

Logan glanced at Lacy. Scar had just confirmed what he had heard. Giselle Fontaine, Lacy's mother, had been the brains behind the business before she was killed almost twenty-five years ago. Lacy must have been a baby, no more than two or three.

Armand had been a big-deal importer/exporter, but Giselle was the one who'd started the arms dealing side of their business. Armand had taken over and devoted all his energy toward expansion—after, of course, he'd avenged himself on his wife's killers.

There was rumor that he kept their heads in a couple of boxes in his safe and took them out once in a while to deter others from getting the same idea. Quite the family tree. And here he was mixed up in the middle of it.

"So, Mr....?" Logan paused, hoping Scar would fill in the gap. "Speaking of rude, you have neglected to tell us your name."

Scar smiled. "My name is not important at this moment but soon you will know."

Russian? Ukrainian? Scar's strong accent definitely sounded like he was from that side of the world, but it was hard to tell. He must have been good looking once, but the scar was pretty intense. Logan didn't even want to speculate what had caused it. "Well, whatever. What do you want?"

"What do I want? Good question. I want what everyone wants. I want a world where children grow up blissfully igno-rant of war and are free to pursue their dreams. I want to live in the kind of place where my wife, and family will be safe in our home. I want to grow old on land that is mine, ruled by people, *my* people, who understand the values I hold dear, and have our best interests at heart."

"Wonderful," Logan said with sarcasm. "What does that have to do with us?"

Scar smiled. "With you? Nothing. You are just extra baggage that I am willing to dispose of at any time. Ms. Carmichael, however, is going to help me get what I want."

"If my father refused to sell to you, I doubt kidnapping me is going to help your cause. He tends to frown on that sort of thing." She smiled tightly and took another sip of her drink. "You would have better luck if you let me speak to him about your cause. This"—she paused as if searching for the right word—"behavior is not going to earn you any favors."

"That's where you are wrong." Scar got up off the couch. "This behavior is going to get me exactly what I want." He strolled forward and caressed Lacy's cheek again. She'd apparently had enough because she threw the dregs of her drink in his face. *About damn time*, but he immediately regretted the thought when Scar slapped Lacy hard across the face. Logan lunged forward, but Scar's minion punched him in the kidneys from behind, and he dropped to his knees.

Lacy's head had snapped back. When she lowered it, she swiped the back of her hand across the trickle of blood coming from the corner of her mouth. All while staring at Scar with hatred in her eyes.

Logan wanted desperately to smash the guy's face into the floor. He struggled to his feet again, but Hairy was now in front of him and the gun was pointed at Logan's chest.

"Alexey, take them down to the engine room," Scar ground out as he strode from the room without a backward look. Baldy was Alexey. Definitely Russian, or former Eastern

Bloc anyway. Alexey strode forward, forcing them out of the room.

Logan followed Lacy as Hairy took the lead. Baldy brought up the re, his gun pointed at Logan. No way to do anything but follow along.

Hairy led them down a hallway before coming to a stop in front of a doorway. He opened it, and Alexey pushed them in, following closely behind. He shoved them over to the wall and zip-tied their already-shackled hands around a protruding pipe. The bastard had cuffed them above a joint halfway up the wall, so they couldn't sit down. After making sure they were secure, both guards left. The click of the lock engaging was audible over the racket in the room.

"Are you all right?" Logan asked, "How's your lip?"

"It's fine. I've had better days, but I'm surviving. You?"

"Yeah." Logan took a look at their surroundings. Engine room. Loud, smelly, and dark. The only light emanated from the exit sign and some of the equipment. He sighed. What was with the dark, smelly spaces? His stomach lurched, and he glanced at Lacy. She was leaning against the wall with her eyes closed.

"Hey, weren't you in the Navy?" she murmured. She still had her eyes closed. "You must be familiar with this type of thing."

"Oh, yeah. I was kidnapped and beaten all the time in the Navy," he responded.

Her eyes snapped open, and she glared at him. "I meant you must be familiar with boats. I'm totally open to any ideas you have. I have to say I'm fresh out."

"Uh huh. I was in the JAG Corps, which basically means I spent my time in a courtroom, not aboard ships. Other than a few operations with my brothers, this is all pretty much new to me, too."

"Great." She sighed heavily. "I thought all you Navy guys

were supposed to be superheroes or something. You run a security company. Isn't there training for this sort of thing?"

"Well, sorry to disappoint, but I'm human. And the security company was a home security company until recently. We don't train people on boating safety or how to escape a kidnapping, but I'll be sure to add both to the list of services we offer when I get back."

"Wonderful," she snarked.

The throbbing of the engines was giving Logan a massive headache. He had no clue what Scar was planning, but it would be better if they weren't around to find out. Which meant they had to get the ties off. "You still have that plastic?"

Lacy nodded.

"Now might be the time to dig it out. Maybe we can use it to cut off the ties."

She tried to get the plastic, but no matter how she moved, the pipe kept getting in her way. There wasn't enough slack for her to move her hands.

"I can't get it." She swore as she tried again. The ties were biting into the skin on her wrists.

"Relax. Don't hurt yourself." Logan moved closer. "Where is it?"

She made a face and sighed loudly. "It's in my bra."

He tried his absolute best to keep his face neutral. "Uh, I think I can get it. My hands are at a better angle."

Lacy's glare told him he hadn't been totally successful at stifling his grin. She probably wasn't too keen on having his hands in her bra either, but hey, desperate times. At least there was an upside to this whole debacle.

Lacy leaned toward him as he moved forward. "It's on the left side."

"Oh. Um, can you turn a bit to give me better access?" He thought he heard her curse, but she did it anyway.

When he moved his fingers to the inside of her dress, she sucked in a breath. He glanced down at her. "Sorry, my fingers are a bit cold." She just nodded and bit her lip.

He tried to keep himself under control, but his dick had other ideas. Her breast was soft, round, and firm. From the earlier experience, he knew it would perfectly fill his palm. *Concentrate, Logan.*

He slipped his fingers deeper into her bra, grazing her nipple. When it puckered, she shifted away slightly. He had to stifle a groan. He was so hard he was rubbing uncomfortably on the zipper of his dress pants.

He reached a bit farther and felt the edge of the plastic, but she moved away again. This time his hand came out of her bra.

"Wait! I didn't get it. You have to stay still so I can grab it without cutting you, OK?"

He could see her clamp her jaws together. Was she really angry? It wasn't like they had a choice.

"Fine," she muttered.

He moved his fingers slowly along the inside of her bra, trying to keep his breath steady, but the feel of her warm, silky skin brought all kinds of unwanted thoughts into his head. Her nipple was puckered and rigid, and it wasn't anger that had her grinding her teeth. *Well, she wasn't the only one who was hard.* He swallowed and tried to focus on the job at hand. Finally, he got a grip on the jagged edge.

"Got it. Now, I am going to bring it out as slowly as possible. I don't want to cut you." His voice came out far huskier then he wanted.

Her eyes narrowed again. "You're enjoying this way too much."

He tried to feign innocence, but she pointedly looked down at his crotch. Busted. He grinned at her. "I can't help it. Natural reaction to having my hand on your breast."

She rolled her eyes. "Get on with it."

It took him a minute. He almost dropped it twice, but it finally emerged from her clothing. "Yes!" He was triumphant.

Lacy stepped back quickly. If he didn't know better, he would have said his touch repelled her. Logan watched her, but her face gave nothing away, and why would it? She was a woman who'd spent her life keeping dangerous secrets. He'd do well to remember that.

CHAPTER FOUR

L acy breathed a sigh of relief. It had been difficult to
stand that close to Logan, especially since she knew he
felt the attraction, too. Hard to miss that. She smirked at the
thought, but the smile quickly slipped away. She could still
smell his maleness, feel his hand damn near cupping her
breast. Heat was radiating up from her core and she was
slightly damp, not that she'd ever admit that to him.

This hypersensitivity to Logan had to stop. She had to get
herself under control. It was a distraction—one she could not
afford at the moment.

Her father would have to know by now that she'd been
kidnapped. There were people on his payroll all over the
islands. Surely, Omar, his head of security, was already planning some sort of rescue. But she couldn't wait to be rescued,
not if the opportunity to escape presented itself.

She winced a little as the blood-soaked lace of her bra
stuck to her cut. *Better not mention it to Logan.* He might feel
badly about cutting her with the plastic and want to check it
out. If she was salivating over him now, showing him her
boob would only make things worse.

She felt the weight of his gaze on her.

"Are you OK?" His eyes showed concern.

She cleared her throat. "Yes. Fine. How is it coming?" She glanced at his wrists but couldn't make out the ties in the dim lighting. "I think it would be wise if we're not in this room when they come looking for us."

Regardless of whatever her father's people might have planned, being a sitting duck was not a good thing by any definition. Was her father a sitting duck? She hoped Omar had doubled or tripled her father's security detail. He wasn't getting any younger—and he was a sick man.

The phone call she had received a few months ago when her father announced he had diabetes had rocked her world. Diabetes wasn't the worst thing in the world, but they were having trouble controlling it. At a low moment, he'd confessed he wasn't feeling the best.

Panic had gripped her and she'd wanted to rush to his side, but he'd insisted they wait for the visit that was already planned. Guilt washed over her. Though impatient to see him, she had ultimately agreed—after all, she wasn't quite sure how he'd take what she had to tell him...

She was still pissed at him for putting her off when she first arrived on the island. He wouldn't even let her come to the house. Maybe he knew something was up. But then, why didn't he say something? She'd given up trying to figure out her father a long time ago, but now she wished she'd insisted on seeing him right away. Tears blurred her vision and she rapidly blinked them away.

She'd been groomed to follow in her mother's footsteps and take over the business. After all, her mother was the great Giselle Fontaine; whip smart, business savvy, and wild, a star of the "underworld." But Lacy just wasn't interested, never had been. She'd only gone along with the plan to please her father. It was hard being an only child, especially since her mother, the great love of her father's life, was deceased. She was all her father had. And he was all she had as well.

She had gone to law school, as requested, and then joined a big firm in New York City. She was moving up the ranks quickly, but her heart wasn't in it.

None of her life felt like it was her own. Even her visits to her father were shrouded in mystery and lies, and she was sick of the whole thing. If—*when*—she got out of this predicament, she was going to tell her father the time had come for her to stand on her own two feet. She was going to forge her own path, and now that he was sick, she was determined to get him out of the family business as well.

Logan grunted and snapped his wrists apart. "Now you." She held out her wrists to him, praying he wouldn't feel her pulse pounding. It would destroy the cool and collected impression she was trying to make. He held them gently in one hand. "Hold still. I'll do my best not to cut you, but I make no promises."

"Don't worry about it. Just get me free so we can get out of here." She bit the inside of her lip, trying to keep calm despite the panic bubble rising in her chest, but before she knew it, the bubble burst, and she was shaking with laughter. Part of her brain knew how ridiculous it was to laugh, but she couldn't help it. Nervous laughter had always been her response to stress.

Logan cursed as he made a small cut on her wrist. He glanced up at her, but whatever he was going to say died on his lips. The sound of her laughter echoed around the engine room.

"Are you all right?" he asked with real concern in his voice. She could tell he was calculating what the hell he was going to do with this insane woman. He started sawing away furiously at the zip ties. It made her laugh all the more. She couldn't breathe she was laughing so hard, and tears were streaming down her cheeks.

She was finally getting herself under control when she felt the tie around her hands give. Logan watched her warily. The laughter started to build again, but suddenly there was a bang on the door to the engine room. It drove all the laughter from her chest. Frozen in place, she stared at Logan.

He put his finger to his lips and moved her away from the door, back behind one of the engines. They stood there silently, pressed together in the dark for several long minutes. It was the worst possible time, but her whole body suddenly felt alive with sensation. She wanted desperately to kiss him, stroke him. Who was she kidding? She wanted to have him here, *now*, on the engine room floor. She needed space, or it wasn't going to be pretty.

Logan finally moved out from behind the engine. She was simultaneously thankful and disappointed. "I think it's all clear. Our best bet might be to jump over the side and swim for it. Can you handle that?"

She could read between the lines well enough to tell he was asking if she was going to lose it again. "I'm fine now. I just needed to let off a bit of stress."

His facial expression clearly said he didn't believe her. Men. If women laughed in a moment of crisis, it was weakness. If men did it, they were laughing in the face of danger.

She sighed loudly. Schooling her features, she summoned her best lawyer voice and said, "I concur with your opinion. There are too many men onboard for us to take the ship, and it's not big enough to hide in for any great length of time. There are seven hundred islands in the Bahamas, only a few of which are uninhabited. Depending on which direction they took, we have a fair chance of being able to swim to one and seek help."

Logan nodded. "The water will be warmish, but it's still

very easy to get hypothermia. We won't have that long before we're in trouble. I'm assuming you can swim, but this isn't just a romp in a heated pool. Are you up for it?"

She could tell he was fighting some kind of internal battle. He ran his hands over his face. Finally, he appeared to come to a decision. "It might be better if I swim for help and you hide on the boat. It'll buy you some time because they'll search for me. And I can bring the authorities back with me," he stated in a firm voice.

She tried not to roll her eyes, but it was hard. "I don't think so. If you end up drowning, I'll have no way of knowing."

Logan's eyebrows shot up.

"I would rather take my chances in the water. I'm well aware of the water conditions and the hypothermia risk. I'm a good swimmer. Six years on the boarding school swim team." She set her jaw and glared at him. "Are we ready to go?"

He was obviously still unsure, but he shrugged his shoulders. Probably thinking, *It's her funeral.* Well, that was true either way, wasn't it? Nothing good could come of staying here. A small bubble of semi-hysterical laughter started up again, but she firmly stifled it. She could do this.

Logan walked over to the door they'd been pushed through and tested it. It was obviously locked.

"We need to go this way," Lacy said, pointing to a door at the opposite end of the room. When he turned and narrowed his eyes at her, she said with a shrug, "My father has a yacht like this."

"Of course, he does," Logan ground out.

Lacy ignored him and said, "This door should lead to a storage area for jet skis and the like. They're launched from there off the back of the yacht."

He shook his head and mumbled under his breath as he made his way to the door.

"Good thinking, Lacy," she muttered to herself under the roar of the engines. *Men suck*, she reminded herself. Sure, Logan was six feet plus of delicious sexiness, but facts were facts. She walked up behind him as he turned the handle, and to her great surprise, the door opened on the first try. Thankfully, no one was on the other side was waiting for them.

Logan stepped through the door with Lacy on his heels. The area was dark, but there was no back wall. The stern of the ship was open to the night sky. The opening was slanted with the deck sticking out further than the roof line. There were two jet skis gleaming in the ambient light. They were resting in the middle of the deck, but there was a small crane to pick them up and put them off the back of the yacht. *Escape*. Looking at them brought a burst of euphoria and then a wave of dread. "We can't take them, can we?" Lacy said in hushed tones. The sound of the engines wasn't as loud out here, and she didn't want to be overheard.

Logan shook his head. "The moment we tried to launch one, all kinds of bells and whistles would go off on the bridge. Besides, I'm not even sure the winch would work while we're traveling at this speed," Logan whispered back.

She nodded and walked to the side of the jet skis, toward the stern of the yacht, careful to stay underneath the slight overhang. If she went too far, she could be seen from overhead. They were right above water level, which was good, but they were also above the propellers. Not so good.

He came up beside her. "We're going to have to jump for it. Hitting the water at this speed is very dangerous. If you enter at the wrong angle…" He didn't finish the thought. He didn't have to. She had spent enough years swimming to know how dangerous water could be. Hitting water could be just like hitting cement if you didn't do it right.

"Well, staying here isn't really an option, so"—she shrugged—"let's go for it."

He nodded. "Agreed." He moved a bit closer to the edge of the boat and took a good look at their surroundings. There was a small platform off to one side for swimming that was at water level. It would be best if they jumped off that, but then they would be totally exposed to anyone above them.

"I don't think we have a choice," she said, guessing at his thoughts. "We have to use the platform. Better angle and less chance of being sucked under."

"I agree. I'm going to check it out. Stay back in case they spot me and start shooting."

"Great." She rolled her eyes. If they spotted him and started shooting, they were both done for. "How about we avoid that, hmm? Employ some of those stealth skills they must have taught you in the Navy. Even JAG lawyers must have to go through some sort of training."

He glared at her and shook his head. Then, turning around, he flattened himself against the wall and moved out slightly. He took it one small step at a time, always looking up in case there was a guard outside. Lacy held her breath.

Finally, after an eternity, he reached the end of the wall. He glanced around the corner and then disappeared from view. She instinctively moved forward to follow him before stopping herself. No need for both of them to take that risk. It would only up their chances of getting caught. She drummed her fingers on her leg as she waited for him to appear.

Just when she was starting to get anxious, he popped back into view. It was so sudden she damn near screamed. He edged toward her, moving quickly and quietly. "The good news is that there are islands close by. I could see some lights at the ends of docks and on decks."

She started to smile, but then his tension registered. "What's the bad news?" She leaned back against the wall to physically brace herself for it.

"There's a guard directly above us. If we go for the platform, he'll see us for sure. If we go off the side, chances are excellent he'll still see us. As a matter of fact, I can't figure out a way to get off this yacht without being seen." He dropped back to lean against the wall. "What we need is a distraction or cover of some sort."

She nodded in agreement. She could practically see his mind working through the problem as he glanced around the room they were in. Besides the winch and the two wave runners, there was nothing much in there. And if they did anything with the equipment, he was right—it would just bring people down on them.

It was so dark it was hard to see anything. There was no starlight. She guessed their speed was about 20 knots, roughly 23 mph, but she had no idea what direction they were going. The running lights were on but their glow barely cut into the darkness.

She froze suddenly and then moved around Logan. It was *too* dark. Where was the moon? Edging toward the end of the wall, she studied the sky. It was inky black. Not a star. Cloudy. She could feel the moisture in the air. She whipped around and banged squarely into Logan's chest.

He held her arms to steady her before pulling her back to their shelter. "What is it?" His hands were still on her arms, sending electrical currents across her skin, and his spicy scent surrounded her again.

"Gah." She swallowed and then tried again. "Rain."

"What?"

Pulling herself together, she stepped away from him. "Rain. It's going to rain. Listen."

He paused and then shook his head. "What am I listening for? All I hear are the engines."

"Listen harder." She was silent for a few seconds. "There. Did you hear it?"

Logan cocked his head. A few seconds later, a slow smile spread across his face as he nodded. "Thunder."

"Yup. We just have to wait for the storm to come closer. It'll give us the cover we need."

Sighing, he studied her for a second, then said, "It's a good thought, but we have no idea if we are moving away from or toward the storm. I don't think we have a whole lot of time here before they come check on us."

"Yes, I know that. I also realize the boat's taking us away from those islands, but what choice do we have? You said it yourself—if we go now, we will be seen."

"There's a chance they won't see us. It's slim but still there."

"Let's give it ten minutes. If we don't catch up to the storm by then, we'll go for it anyway. I think we have ten minutes before they check on us, and besides, I know it feels like we're going fast, but we'll still be within reach of some islands in ten minutes."

He gave her a long look and then he slowly nodded his head. "Ten minutes."

"Great. Um, do you have a watch?

"No. I don't wear one but, don't worry, I'll know when ten minutes are up."

She opened her mouth to argue with him—how was that even possible?—but then closed it again. She always used her phone, which of course she didn't have, but did it really matter if they waited for eight or twelve minutes? Probably not. Their plan was a crapshoot anyway, and they both knew it.

She leaned back against the wall and did something she hadn't done in years. She prayed. She prayed hard. For rain. To get off the yacht safely. To see her father again. To be done with this mess. Seeing Logan watching, she said with great regret, "I'm sorry.. I had no idea all this would happen. I—"

"Then why are you sorry? You didn't plan it. It's not your fault. It's just bad timing or bad luck. God knows, I've had plenty of both lately." He rubbed his face with his hands. Then, turning sideways, he leaned on the wall next to her and gave her a small smile. "We aren't done for yet, so don't give up."

"I'm not. I just wanted you to know." When her eyes met his, her core started to tingle.

His gaze then flicked to her lips, and she licked them in an automatic response. He took a step closer, head tilted just so. Her breath caught in her throat. As her hands found their way to his chest, her heart hammered under her ribs. His lips lowered until they were suspended a fraction of an inch from hers.

Then it happened. The flash and crash made her jump and fall into his chest. He steadied her as he glanced back toward the end of the yacht.

She followed his gaze. A slow smile spread across his face. The storm. Rain was already slapping onto the surface of the waves. And not just any rain. This was a bona fide downpour. They both peered off the end of the yacht, watching the wall of water descend. The lightening flashed, and the thunder gave an answering growl. The wind kicked up the waves up and rocked the yacht. They were in the thick of the storm now. She grinned and gave him a high five.

They made their way carefully toward the end of the

yacht. The sway of the boat was getting stronger. Logan scanned the upper deck and then gave her the all-clear sign. No guard. She wanted to break into a happy dance.

"Take off your shoes and anything extra that could weigh you down." Logan gave Lacy the once over, his eyes lingering in all the right places. "Um..."

Lacy glanced down at her dress. It was somewhat looking the worse for wear, but there was no way she was taking it off. She didn't want to be running around in only her black lace bra and matching thong. She kicked off her shoes. "There. That's enough."

"Ok. Are you sure?" Logan asked, a sexy grin spread across his face.

Lacy rolled her eyes. "Positive, thanks."

"Can't blame a guy for trying." He winked. "Look, once we're in the water, I'm going to take a second to do a couple of quick calculations to figure out the current, and then we'll head out for the island."

"Ah, sure." She wasn't sure about his skills, but she didn't have any other choice. She didn't want to be swimming for hours if she didn't have to be.

The sound of the engines changed a bit, making them both freeze in place. The yacht was slowing down. It was now or never. Logan peered back at her, and she nodded. After nodding back, he raced to the platform at the end of the yacht and dove into the water. She waited a beat. If someone had told her some day she would purposely jump into the ocean during an electrical storm, she would have called them crazy, but there weren't a lot of options.

Saying another short prayer, she leaped into the water and swam down and away as fast and hard as she could, making sure she was well clear of the propellers. Her lungs felt like they were going to burst. She finally changed direction and aimed for the surface, using strong kicks. With one last stroke, she broke the surface in a rush. She gulped fresh air and then immediately sunk back down into the waves. She needed to stay low. She didn't want the guards to notice her.

All her effort was for naught. The boat was too far away for them to see her through the storm. She took in huge gulps of air, which was made difficult by the downpour. She was almost giddy with relief. But her euphoria was brief—the darkness and rain weighed down on her, reminding her she was alone in the middle of an ocean during a thunderstorm with only a vague sense of where land might be.

"Logan?" she called out tentatively. No response. Putting a little more force into her voice, she called out again, "Logan?" Nothing. The waves were getting smaller, but the rain made it hard to see any distance around her. The longer she scanned the surface of the water, the more terror built in her heart. "Loogaaan!" she yelled.

"Shhh!" said a voice at her ear. "They can still hear you. Sound travels on water." She whirled around and threw her arms around his neck. "Ahh," he gurgled as they both went underwater. She let him go, and they surfaced again.

"Sorry," she mumbled. "I—I just thought something had happened to you. I was having visions of you drowning. "

"I'm fine. Now…" he said, looking around. She followed his gaze. It was really hard to see through the rain, but she could make out a few far-off lights. He pointed behind her. "I think we want to head in that direction. There should be an island over there with those lights on it." He was silent for a second, so she assumed he was doing his calculations. "It's maybe a mile or so. Think you can swim that far?"

"Seriously? Not only can I swim it, but I can do it faster than you." With that, she took off in the direction he had pointed. He swore and chased after her.

She knew she should save her energy and take it slow and

easy, but her adrenaline was flowing. She let herself burn through a bit more of it before she settled into a smooth and steady pace.

Every once in a while, she'd glimpse Logan, slightly behind her and on her right. He was keeping up without any apparent effort, which pissed her off, but she figured saving her energy was better than showing off. They could have a long night of swimming ahead of them, and although she hated to admit it, she was already starting to feel the cold. The rain that had been a blessing when they jumped off the ship was now a curse. Her muscles were getting stiff.

A short time later, she felt a tug on her ankle. Logan swam up beside her. "By my calculations, we should have been very close by now. Do you see any lights?" he asked. The rain had slacked to a light drizzle.

He appeared tired, and his breathing wasn't as regular as hers. She took a small bit of satisfaction in that, though of course she shouldn't—they both needed all the strength they could muster to get through this. She peered around again, but everything around them looked a flat, solid black. Even so, she was pretty sure they had been heading in the right direction. He had corrected the course a couple times by tapping her and pointing. She didn't think they'd strayed too far.

"It should be here," she mumbled through stiffening lips. She was getting cold. She peered out into the inky blackness, fighting for calm. She could see worry building on Logan's face—a look she knew was mirrored on her own.

Suddenly, she laughed. At Logan's pointed look, she sputtered in response, "No, I'm not losing it this time. Look." She pointed off to their right and slightly behind them. The clouds broke at exactly that moment, revealing what she had just realized. They had swum right past the island. The night was so dark the landmass had blended into the water line. A few lights flickered through the trees, but they could only be seen when the wind blew. There were no lights on this side of the island.

He smiled in relief and started swimming toward the island. Eager to be on dry land, she followed suit. Maybe there would be people and a nice warm house with a wonderfully hot shower and food. The thought of warmth spurred her on, and she easily overtook him to reach the shore first.

CHAPTER FIVE

L ogan stumbled when he finally put his feet beneath him and stood. He was dead tired. Unlike his brothers, he spent most of his time in his office, not in the gym. His limited workouts paled in comparison to the save-your-life sprint swimming he'd just done. Seeing that Lacy was about to flop down on the sand, he grabbed her hips and urged her forward.

"What?" she said, sounding indignant. He shushed her and kept her moving to the tree line.

Once in the cover of the trees, he turned her around to face him. "We have no idea who, if anyone, is on this island. The lights could mean people, or it could be one of those small islands they use to take tourists to for the day. Why don't we just take it slowly? No need to announce we're here until we have a better read on the situation. I don't know about you, but I've had enough surprises for one day."

He looked down at her, his hands still on her hips. She opened her mouth to argue, and the slight motion was enough to draw his gaze to her lips. They were so tempting.

He felt a sudden urge to kiss them, to trace them with his tongue.

She was an assignment he reminded himself. He needed to stay focused on the task at hand, namely staying alive, but he lost his ability to think straight whenever he touched her. That thought was enough to make him push her away slightly and drop his hands. "Let's go check out the island."

He stepped around her and walked into the woods. She stumbled, but he reached back and caught her by the arm. Grunting some unintelligible response, she leaned on a tree for a second and caught her breath.

"You're cold."

She nodded, her teeth chattering.

"Let's see what we can find. The last thing we need is for you to get hypothermia," he stated as he started forward again.

As they walked along the tree line, he realized it didn't go very far. He stopped at the edge, taking in the view that had appeared in front of him as soon as the trees cleared out. There was a huge built-in pool reflecting the little bit of light that had emerged in the sky after the rain stopped.

He could see the hulking shadow of what had to be a ten-thousand-square-foot house. There were a few lights on, but they weren't super bright. Solar, probably. The house was amazing and very expensive from what he could determine. It also appeared no one was home.

"What do you think?" she asked, her teeth still chattering.

He scouted around some more. "I think it's empty, but someone could still be in there and there could be a security system."

"W-w-well that would be our first piece of luck today, so I'm not going to hold my breath. If someone's there, they can c-c-call for help."

He still didn't move. He was worried about her, but he was also worried about the kidnappers.

"W-what's the big deal if the security system goes off? It's not like ADT is going to send out a squad car."

"It's not the security company I'm worried about. If the system goes off, there are bound to be a lot of lights and a lot of noise. Assuming our captors have realized we've escaped, they are probably doubling back this way looking for us. If we engage the security system, it'll be like a blinking sign that we're here."

She swallowed. "Shit."

"Precisely." He turned and looked at her. She was shivering more noticeably now. He sighed as he brushed his wet hair off his forehead. "Stay here. I'll go check it out. I'll be as quick as I can. Hopefully we can stay inside tonight..." He didn't finish his thought out loud. If he didn't get her warm, and *soon*, she was definitely going to get sick.

He stuck to the shadows and circled the perimeter of the house. He didn't see any signs that led him to believe anyone was there. Around the backside, there was a smaller outbuilding that, from looking in the windows, he surmised was the caretaker's cottage. That it was empty could either be good or bad.

He was unsure of what he was hoping for at this point. If there were people, maybe they could get help, but those people could also be dangerous. There were a lot of interesting folks in the Bahamas, which was one of the biggest tax havens in the world. It paid to be careful. If only he had remembered that earlier in the day.

Which brought his mind back to Lacy. He hated to admit it, but she'd impressed the hell out of him tonight. She'd kept her cool during the kidnapping, had the where-withal to pick up the plastic piece after being shot at, and handled getting off the yacht beautifully. Other than that one moment of hysterical laughter—which she'd been entitled to, he decided—she had been nothing short of amazing.

He gave his head a shake. "Focus," he whispered aloud to himself. "That woman is going to be the death of you." He started on his second run of the perimeter. This time he checked the windows to see if he could pick up a weakness in the alarm system.

When he looked through one of the kitchen windows by the back door, he saw an alarm control panel, red light on, meaning all the bottom floor windows were probably alarmed. But a small window had been left open a couple of inches on the second story. A bathroom, probably. There was nothing directly below the window for him to climb, but it wasn't too far in from the corner. If he used the drain pipe to the second story, then balanced on the corner of the balcony on the front of the house, he could reach it.

He made his way up the drainpipe and then swung over and balanced with one foot on the balcony rail. He reached over and grabbed the edge of the window frame. There was a screen in the frame, but it was spring-loaded.

He took the jagged plastic piece from his pocket, jammed it into the screen, and popped it out. After dropping the screen behind him on the balcony, he returned the plastic piece to his pocket and reached for the window ledge again. He worked his fingers underneath the small opening and then pushed the window all the way up.

He leaned against the house and took a breather. The night had taken a lot out of him, and this next bit would be tricky. Not so hard on a normal day, but today had been anything but. He glanced down. Two stories. Not enough to kill him, but chances were good he would break something.

The breeze hit him, and he shivered. Lacy must be really cold by now. That thought was what spurred him on. Pushing off from the balcony, he grabbed onto the window ledge and hoisted himself through, landing on the bathroom floor. He lay there for a second, saying a silent prayer of thanks, then got up and grabbed a towel off the rack. After quickly drying off, he started a sweep of the house.

The mansion was even bigger inside than it had appeared from the outside. The bedroom he walked through was huge It had to be the master. He came out on an open walkway that overlooked what he assumed was what real estate people liked to call a great room, aka, huge family room. There was a massive curved staircase that led to the lower floor. The other end of the walkway turned into an enclosed hall that he guessed had more bedrooms.

He walked over the stairs and started down. The stairway followed a wall down and curved at the bottom. The front door was about twenty feet away. The great room was to his right. It had a wall of glass going all the way to the ceiling. The view during the day would be amazing.

It was dark so he couldn't really see the furnishings but what he could see definitely seemed high end. He moved forward a few steps and determined that the formal dining area was off to his left on the far side of the door. The kitchen was on his right. There was a hallway behind him that ran parallel to the one upstairs.

Logan stood still for a second. No one was in the house. He knew it in his bones. It had that empty feel. It was time to get Lacy in and get her warmed up.

He walked over to the kitchen area. He entered through a large doorway and realized it had a pass through to the great room.

He couldn't help but notice all the high-end finishes in the kitchen. Even in the dark, he knew they hadn't missed a trick. He gave a silent whistle. It was the type of kitchen he aspired to own one day.

He hadn't told his family and had kept it from most of

his friends, but Logan Callahan was a secret Food Channel junkie. He loved to watch all the shows. He often spent his weekends experimenting with new recipes. Some day he wanted his own amazing kitchen to create in.

Sighing, he walked over to the alarm panel. It was a good system, but nothing too crazy. Thank God, his father had made him work in the family business every summer, starting when he was fifteen. His brothers had also worked for the company for a spell when they were younger, but he knew alarms best. By the time his brothers had come on board, a couple of years after him, the company was bigger, and his brothers had worked more in the office than in the field.

After finagling the wiring for a moment, the light flashed green.

Praying that the whole system was down, not just the panel, he opened the door to the deck. Nothing happened. Grinning, he walked out onto the deck and waved in the direction where he'd left Lacy. After a few seconds, he saw movement. Letting out a pent-up breath, he turned and went back into the kitchen.

"Logan?" she called softly from just inside the door to the kitchen. He emerged from the pantry with a flashlight in one hand and some cans in the other. "What are you doing?" she asked, puzzled.

"Making dinner"—he paused—"or an early breakfast, I guess." He checked her out in the beam of the flashlight. Her body convulsed with shivers, and her lips were turning blue. Not good. "Go upstairs to the master bath and take a shower. I already checked—there's hot water. See if you can find some dry clothes to wear. I'll make something to eat. I don't know about you, but I'm about to pass out from hunger." He walked toward her. "Here." He held out a flashlight. "They had extra flashlights in the pantry, and it's better if we don't turn on the lights."

She nodded and started out of the kitchen. His best guess was that she was too tired and cold to do much more than nod.

Twenty minutes later, with the Moroccan chicken simmering on the stove, he started a search of the house. He had been surprised by the well-stocked pantry. Not only had he found all of the spices he needed, but there'd also been a few veggies, fresh herbs, eggs, and some milk in the fridge. Not to mention wrapped and labeled protein in the freezer. The refrigerator situation suggested the owners would only be gone for a short period. He wasn't sure if that was a good thing or a bad thing.

He walked through the great room and went down the hallway, searching room after room for a phone or a computer, anything they could use to contact the outside world. So far, zilch. He strode into the last room off the hall-way, which turned out to be an office. He walked over to the desk, but no dice. There was no phone, and while there was a Mac laptop charger, there was no laptop. The owners had probably taken it with them but forgot the cable.

He went back to the kitchen to check on dinner. The savory smell set his stomach to rumbling. He added a bit more lemon and threw a bunch of cilantro on top and then headed to the master suite in search of Lacy. He hadn't liked how pale she'd been before her shower. What the hell would he do if she got sick?

He walked through the ginormous master and heard water running. He called her name loudly several times, but there was no response. He started to worry she might have passed out. Just in case, he chanced a peek into the bathroom and stopped short. She had angled the flashlight up so it bounced off the ceiling and lit the whole bathroom. She stood naked under the spray.

She was breathtaking. Her eyes were closed, and she was

standing there with her head raised to the showerhead, letting the spray run over her body, not moving at all. Her breasts were full and high. Her ass looked firm and rounded like a peach. The muscles in her legs, which marked her as an athlete, made them all the shapelier. His gaze roamed over her, his fingers aching to do the same.

When she moved to push the hair out of her eyes, it broke his reverie. He quickly ducked out of the bathroom. No need for her to think he was some sort of stalker. He tried to call her name, but discovered his throat was totally dry. He must have been standing in there with his mouth gaping open. Great. What an idiot! Good thing she hadn't seen him like that. He swallowed and tried again.

The third time he called her, she turned off the water and answered. He announced that the food was ready. "How are you feeling?"

"Better. Warmer. I'm tired of being wet, though. Just give me a minute to dry off. I'll be right down."

"No rush." He started out of the room.

"Logan?"

"Yeah?"

"I found some clothes if you want to change. Check the far closet. I think there are probably some in your size." He could hear her moving around in the bathroom and found himself picturing her naked again. Damn.

"Uh, yeah. Thanks. I think I'll eat first and then shower. I can change later." He rushed to leave the room. He needed to get his head back in the game. There were still kidnappers out there. Fantasizing about Lacy nonstop was seriously going to limit his ability to function.

When she entered the kitchen twenty minutes later, all of Logan's hard-won control went out the window. She'd found an oversized plaid shirt that covered some sort of white tank top. She'd rolled up the legs on a pair of soft-looking sweats.

Instead of looking silly, she looked divine. Her hair was curling about her shoulders, and her freshly scrubbed face had color in it. She seemed innocent and young, an effect that was emphasized by the oversized clothes and the dim beams the flashlight provided. Logan's heart gave a big thump in his chest.

"I know, I know, I look ridiculous, but I didn't have a lot to choose from." She walked across the kitchen self-consciously.

He just smiled. "You look cute."

"Cute is not usually a word I strive for, but I'll take it." She sat down at the breakfast bar as he bustled around plating their food. "Looks like there aren't any phones or computers in the upstairs bedrooms. Did you have any luck?"

He shook his head.

"Wow. Nice kitchen. I'd love to have a setup like this. My apartment has a tiny galley kitchen. A set up like this would be heavenly." She ran her hands along the granite countertop. "Nice job with the flashlight." Logan had placed it in the center of the table in the eat-in area of the kitchen. It pointed straight up at the chandelier above, making the light refract all over the room.

"You like to cook?" he asked as he placed a plate in front of her.

"Yes, when I get the chance, which doesn't happen often. When you live by yourself...well, you know. Cooking for one is not much fun."

He opened drawers until he found the one with the cutlery. He knew exactly what she meant. He tended to cook for friends or cook big meals and freeze the leftovers. His friends in New York loved his dinner parties, but he'd never invited his family. They had no idea about his secret passion.

He was two people in some ways. The Logan his family

knew and the Logan he had become. He was on the verge of sharing his new lifestyle when his father had announced he had cancer. Life was a whirlwind after that and with his dad's treatments and him and his brothers stepping in to temporarily help run the company, it just hadn't seemed important.

And then came the day when they'd all decided to make the change permanent. Although his dad wanted it, Logan hadn't been so keen. Gage had been, and so had Mitch, surprisingly. Mitch had always been the playboy of the group, but he seemed to want to settle in and make something of the business. He didn't give a reason why and, God knew, Mitch wasn't going to discuss it with him. They never really saw eye to eye on much of anything.

"This looks fantastic. Where did you get the food? Was the fridge stocked? Do you think people will be back tonight?"

Lacy's questions broke him out of his reverie. "The fridge isn't fully stocked, but it does have the necessities. I found some chicken in the freezer, and they had some boxed couscous in the pantry. I'm not sure when they'll be back, but it looks like they aren't planning on being gone for long. On the bright side, at least we get to eat well. I don't know about you, but I'm starving. Dig in."

"Smells fabulous." She grabbed her fork and was already digging in when he sat down beside her. "Mmm. Oh my God, this is amazing! And I'm not just saying that because I'm starving," she mumbled as she chewed.

He was inordinately pleased. He loved it when someone enjoyed his cooking. "Glad you like it." He started eating and had to admit it was pretty good. In record time, she hopped up from her chair and walked over to the stove. "Is there any more?"

He laughed. "Hungry, huh?"

She grinned. "Swimming always makes me famished!"

"Help yourself."

Lacy refilled her plate. She came back and sat down beside Logan again. "This tastes fantastic, and you were exhausted when you made it. You must like to cook." She put another forkful into her mouth and moaned as she chewed.

"I do like to cook. I find it relaxing and fun. It's the one time I get to be creative." Slightly embarrassed, he stared at his plate. He hoped his face was hidden by some of the shadows in the room. He hadn't meant to say anything. It had just slipped out.

"Your brothers must love it when you cook."

"Uh, they don't know. None of my family knows that I like to cook." He must be more exhausted than he'd thought. Admitting his secret to anyone wasn't Logan's style, but admitting it to the person he was supposed to be investigating, well he must have lost his mind out there in the water. . Except…she made him feel totally relaxed about it.

She glanced at him as she chewed. "I get that." She paused and took a sip of water from the glass he had poured earlier. "Want to know my secret?"

He raised an eyebrow. "Shoot."

"I want to be a party/wedding planner."

Now it was his turn to be surprised.

She shrugged. "Sure, it would be a waste of my law degree, I guess, but I'm really good at logistics, and I like order. Not to mention parties. I'd be excellent at it."

"I don't doubt it." He smiled. He could totally picture her ordering everyone about as she ran parties with military precision, which is probably where she learned her organizational skills, from her father's arms business.

"Would you ever go into it?" she asked as she scooped up the last bite of food from her plate. "Cooking as a profession, I mean."

"I, uh, would like to own my own restaurant."

His shoulders tensed as he said it, in the expectation she would laugh, but instead she asked, "What kind of restaurant?" She seemed genuinely interested.

"There's this place on the same street as our office. Not sure if you noticed it when you and Alex were holed up there with us. It's an old pub that's sort of falling apart. It has a prime location, though, and it could be really great if someone put the work in." As he warmed to the topic, his shoulders relaxed. "I'd like to overhaul it to be a place for people to hang out and relax while eating a great-tasting meal. I like things like this dish, Moroccan Chicken, not too complicated but flavorful. I want to have traditional pub food like fish and chips and burgers, but also interesting salads and seafood dishes."

CHAPTER SIX

T he joy bloomed on his face as he spoke about his dream. There was no sign of the bossy, condescending Logan she'd observed when he'd been on the opposite side of the boardroom table. No sign of Lucifer, the take-charge lawyer who made her hot despite herself. Against *this* Logan, she had no defense.

"You should totally do it," she said. "If this meal is any indication, your food is amazing. With food like this and a prime location, your place would be a hit from day one."

"What about you? Would you ever start your own wedding planning company?" he asked as his blue eyes sparkled at her in the dim light.

Swallowing, she pretended to inspect her plate. "I'd love to have my own party planning business in the city. There are so many cool venues, and I have lots of ideas on how to utilize them better." She paused. "Anyway, that's my dream."

"Sounds like a good one to me and very doable."

She sighed. "We'll see."

"Why wouldn't it be?" he asked quietly.

"Well, on top of all this mess, my father has diabetes. The

doctors are having a hard time getting it under control. His condition is serious."

There, she'd said it out loud. She hadn't even mentioned it to her best friend, Alex, yet. but here she was talking to Logan about it. Somehow, it felt natural to share with him—maybe because he had done the same with her. Once again, she found herself questioning her earlier impression of him. Maybe he wasn't as domineering as she'd thought.

"I'm sorry, Lacy. That's tough." He reached out and touched her arm. "It's not easy to have a sick parent." She saw sadness flicker across his face.

"Oh God, Logan, I'm sorry. I forgot about your mom. And your Dad."

He smiled a sad little smile. "Don't worry about it. I can't believe it's been over four years since she passed. It's taken all of us a long time to recover, especially my dad. And he's doing well, too. The doctors say he should be fine. I just meant that I know firsthand how hard it can be, so if you ever want to talk about it, I'm here."

She nodded. There was a lump building in her throat.

"You know, I used to cook for my mom when she was sick. I would visit and bring her soups and things. I'd tell everyone the food was from a restaurant in the city, but she knew better. It was our secret."

He paused, then said, "Your father will be fine, Lace. With all the medicines out there today, they'll figure it out. Diabetes can be managed. Just hang in there." He rubbed her back, and to her embarrassment, she could feel tears threatening behind her eyes. She searched the kitchen for a distraction. She was afraid if she started crying, she wouldn't stop.

Something caught her eye. "Ohhh," she squealed and leapt clear of her chair to dart across the kitchen. He watched as she grabbed a mug and hit a button. The smell of fresh coffee filled the kitchen in seconds.

"Nothing like a built-in coffee maker," she cooed while surreptitiously wiping her eyes. "What I wouldn't give to have one of these babies. Can you imagine getting up in the morning and having coffee almost instantly? Without having to prep it the night before? This machine is worth its weight in gold." She stroked the outside of it. "I would marry someone for this machine."

"I take it you like coffee." He put his plate in the sink and joined her by the machine.

"Yessss. It runs in my veins," she purred. "Not having coffee for the last umpteen hours has been its own form of torture." She smiled at him. "Want some?"

He stilled.

"Coffee," she blurted out. "Want some coffee?" she croaked. She hadn't meant it as an invitation, but the look he had given her made her toes curl.

He'd cleared his throat before speaking, but his voice still came out husky. "No, I'm good."

Taking a sip, she tried to remember why sex with Logan would be a rotten idea. Maybe they could date. Except for the fact that it was all her fault they were running from kidnappers. Besides, there was her father to think about. She had to get him out of the Bahamas and out of his current line of work, and then there was his health to get sorted. No, it was better to put the whole idea of Logan Callahan on hold. But it was so hard when he was leaning in close...

She wrinkled her nose, suddenly aware of a horrible odor. "No offense, but you smell. You should take that shower now."

He jolted back as if she'd slapped him. "Yeah. No problem," he said. "Glad you're feeling better and you're no longer hungry or anything." The words dripped with sarcasm. She tried to think of some response or apology—the words had just popped out—but before she could speak, he shook his head and left the kitchen.

Lacy smacked the countertop. Her coffee, which had tasted so good a minute ago, soured in her stomach. She poured the rest down the sink and started doing the dishes. Least she could do was clean up. He'd gone to all this trouble for her...and she'd just insulted him. What he had gone through today because of her, well, there were no words to cover it. "I'm sorry" wasn't remotely good enough. She owed Logan Callahan in a big way.

Sighing, she finished the dishes, grabbed her flashlight, and then wandered around the house. The large, sprawling family room had a deck that boasted a breathtaking view of the sea. The glass doors could be pushed to the sides so there was no wall separating the house from the stunning panorama. The whole house was that way, full of grandeur, and yet it was cozy, too. Somebody really loved this place. Two somebodies, if the clothing in the closets was any indication. Two male somebodies.

She picked up a picture from the desk in the study. Two smiling men stared back at her. They seemed very much in love in the picture, so much so she couldn't help but smile back.

Glancing at the clock, she noticed it was 3:30 a.m. Fatigue hit her in a sudden wave, threatening to draw her under. Calling Logan's name, she pulled herself up the stairs and entered the bedroom. The water was still running, so she sat down on the huge master bed. A gas fireplace directly across from the oversize bed, promised further warmth, so she found the remote before crawling back onto the mattress. Moments later, huge flames lit up the fireplace with a whoosh, making the room instantly cheerier. She lay back on the bed, waiting to apologize to Logan, but promptly fell sound asleep.

A LOUD CRASH woke her out of sound sleep. Sitting bolt upright, she whipped her head around wildly, trying to figure out where the hell she was and what the sound had been. The sound happened again. Thunder. With the next boom, everything came back to her—Markus, the car accident, the kidnapping, the boat, swimming to the island. She took a deep breath and flopped back down on the bed.

"You OK?" a voice beside her asked calmly.

"Ahhh!" She jumped and twisted at the same time, landing with her feet on the floor, facing Logan. "Oh, for the love of Pete! You scared the hell out of me. Why didn't you tell me you were there?" She ran her fingers through her hair as she tried to calm her breathing.

"I was trying not to startle you. You were disoriented." He was grinning as he pushed himself up on the pillows.

"Well, you failed. I think I just had a heart attack."

His grin was even wider as he watched her. She glared at him. Of course, he looked fabulous. All sleep-tossed hair and a dark shadow on his jaw. Her heartrate skyrocketed when she took in the sight of his bare chest and abs. Dear God, the man was shredded. Just looking at him made her nipples hard.

"What time is it anyway?" she asked in a breathy voice as she turned away. Closing her eyes and biting her lip, she chastised herself for having such a physical reaction to him. No way was he going to miss that. Men never did.

"Not sure. The storm cut the power off. Probably late morning, early afternoon." His voice was soft. She turned to look at him. Big mistake. He was watching her. His eyes darkened when he'd caught sight of her nipples through her white tank top. She tried to pull the plaid shirt across her chest to cover them, but it was too late. His expression said he knew exactly what she'd been thinking.

The room lit up suddenly, followed by a thunder crash.

"Umm, I could use some coffee. How about you?" She had to get away from Logan before she made an even bigger fool of herself.

"There's no power, so your wonderful machine won't work." His eyes danced over her, taking in every single thing. Damn. Her hair was probably a rat's nest and her face was no doubt puffy with sleep. Why wasn't she like one of those girls in the movies who woke up looking hot and made up every morning? Maybe a shower would make her feel better.

"Right. Well, I'm going to grab a hot shower and then see if there's any instant coffee." She headed into the bathroom.

"There won't be any hot water." His voice rumbled out of his chest. She stood stock still in the bathroom, her face flaming red in embarrassment. He even sounded sexy in the morning. *Damn. Damn. Damn.*

"Right. I'll just grab a quick cold one." She needed one. She shut the bathroom door, went to the shower stall, and turned on the spray. "Need to get rid of the cobwebs before we plan our next step," she said loudly as she stripped off her clothes.

"I wouldn't do that…" he said, his voice muffled by the closed door.

She hopped in the shower and closed the heavy glass door behind her. She had to bite down hard on her cheek to keep from screaming. Cold was not the word. Ice. The water felt like little icicles stabbing into her skin. Well, at least it was working. Her mind was no longer on Logan. Instead it was on how much of an ass she was. Damn, indeed.

Within seconds, she was out of the shower and toweling off. Trying desperately to keep her teeth from chattering, she wrapped the towel as tightly as possible around her body. In her haste, she had forgotten to get some fresh clothing out of the closet.

She walked quickly past Logan, who was still sprawled in the bed, and into one of the walk-in closets. She had determined last night that the clothing in this closet was smaller than that in the next one. It was all men's, but at least it was something.

Taking a deep breath, she closed the door behind her. There was a bit of light streaming in from the small window at the back of the closet. She started rummaging through the clothes, promising herself and the home owners she would replace the clothing. She picked a white T-shirt off the shelf, followed by the only sweater she could find. It was a maroon, lightweight wool V-neck. She hissed when she pulled it on. The cut on her chest stung a bit. The icicle shower must have knocked off some of the scab that had formed, but hopefully it wouldn't bleed.

She had washed her underwear last night and hung it to dry in the bathroom, but it was still damp. She searched for something to wear on the bottom. She opened drawer after drawer before finally finding underwear. She wasn't going to wear a strange man's underwear, but maybe there was a new, unopened pack. After rummaging farther, she came to the conclusion that it was all used.

About to give up, she opened another drawer. Jackpot!

It was some sort of junk or discarded gift drawer. It had all kinds of interesting things in it, including a pair of boxer shorts still in the plastic. Unfortunately, when she opened them, the shorts had the words *Kiss me* written in a strategic location. Well, beggars couldn't be choosers. She pulled on the shorts and tried to forget was written across her vagina. Chances were extremely good that no one would see it anyway.

She found another pair of sweats, navy this time, and

rolled up the bottoms after she pulled them on. There was a full-length mirror in the closet, so she stood in front of it and adjusted the clothing. Her hair was curling and standing out from her head, so she pulled it back into a tight bun tucking the ends under the bun to hold it in place. With one last glance in the mirror, she decided this was as good as she was going to get and opened the door and reentered the bedroom.

Logan was sitting up against the pillows. "Are you getting up soon?" she asked. "We need to plan how we're going to get back to Nassau. Maybe we could do another search of the house now that it's light out. There must be some kind of phone here somewhere." She smoothed her hair back. "Maybe the caretaker's cottage has something we could use."

He had been watching her wordlessly. Finally, he said, "I actually checked it last night after you fell asleep. No phone or computer. It looks like the cottage has been empty longer than the house. Very little in it. A few sticks of furniture and some old sheets. That's about it."

"Great. Any ideas how we're going to contact the outside world or get back to Nassau?"

"In case you missed it, it's storming pretty badly out there. I don't think we can go anywhere in this weather, but there's a boathouse I want to check out once the rain stops. I was just too tired last night."

She frowned, but she couldn't deny he had a point. They couldn't do much in this weather.

"Be thankful," he said. "No one is out in this weather, which means the owners probably won't be back today, and Scar and the gang won't be looking too hard either. This wind has to make the waves high and visibility low. We should be good here as long as the storm lasts."

"Well, I guess you have a point." She stared at him,

chewing on her bottom lip. The blankets had fallen to his waist, and she couldn't drag her eyes away from his chest.

"Like what you see?" His voice was deep.

"What?" Her gaze met his, and a blush crept up her cheeks. His grin widened. "I was looking at your side," she fibbed. "Are you all right?"

He turned slightly to look at his ribs. The sight of the vicious black bruises where Alexey and Hairy's blows had landed, sucked all the air out of Lacy's lungs. Her eyes filled with tears when they met his.

Blinking rapidly, she tried to keep her composure. "I am so sorry," she whispered and then cleared her throat and tried again. "I am so very sorry." It came out in a strong, clear voice this time. "I know that doesn't make up for anything, but I want you to know if I could have found a way out of this for you, I would have. It's horrifying enough to be in this mess, but knowing that you were hurt because of it…" She smoothed a hand over her hair again and then wrapped her arms around her middle. "My family owes you a great debt."

Not taking his eyes off her, he got out of bed and started moving toward her. Her heart started beating faster—was he going to hug her? Kiss her?—but instead he nodded once before doing an about-face and disappearing into the bathroom. As she watched him walk away, she couldn't help but notice his butt in the black boxer briefs he wore. She'd been so excited at the thought he might touch her. Now she felt as if he'd kicked her in the stomach.

He hated her. He must, and who could blame him? After everything he'd been through, she was surprised he could stand to share the same space as her. When a tear rolled down her cheek, she swiftly brushed it away.

The least she could do was go down and get some food going. There had to be a way to make coffee as well. If there was ever a moment when she needed coffee, this was it. She headed for the kitchen, vowing to herself she would find a way to make it up to Logan. Even if it killed her.

HE STOOD over the sink in the bathroom and closed his eyes. His ribs and kidneys were painful, but the look on Lacy's face had hurt him more. He'd wanted to hold her and tell her he would be fine. Maybe he should have, but if he had walked over to put his arms around her, there would have been no going back. She had looked so small, so vulnerable, so in need of protection that he'd wanted to wrap himself around her and never let go.

He had to toughen up, focus on the job at hand. He was here because he was following Lacy. She could be part of a much larger crime ring that had killed people. He needed to remember she had emailed someone about Drake's new facial recognition/aging software prototype. He was in this mess because he needed to find out the truth. That was it. That was the goal. He needed to forget whatever it was he was feeling toward Lacy and remember his duty to his brothers and their clients. The work had to come first.

He opened his eyes and studied his reflection in the candle-lit mirror. It all sounded reasonable, but it was all bullshit. "Who are you trying to kid?" he asked out loud. He walked over to the shower and turned on the spray. Maybe if he took a cold shower he could rid himself of this burning desire for Lacy Carmichael. Fat chance, but anything was better than looking himself in the eye. Coward.

The frigid spray bit into his shoulders and robbed his lungs of oxygen. He only had to stay in for a couple minutes for the shower to do its job. He still wanted Lacy, but he was back under control. He walked over to the far closet and poked around for some clothes to wear.

He found a black V-neck sweater that was his size and a pair of jeans. There wasn't any unused underwear, so he opted to go commando. At least he had clean clothes. His stomach growled as he made his way to the kitchen.

Things could be worse. They were holed up in a beautiful mansion that had water, a gas stove, and a pantry stocked with canned goods. Things could definitely be worse. Only hours before, they'd been tied up in the engine room of a psychopath's yacht.

He rounded the corner into the kitchen and stopped dead in his tracks. Lacy was biting her lip as she poured water into a French press. All the good the shower had done him was gone in an instant. She was so cute. He wanted to kiss that lip she was biting and maybe bite it himself. Cursing silently, he told himself to calm down. He took a breath and then said, "Need some help?" Damn. He hadn't wanted his voice to come out so rough. He swallowed.

"No, I've got it." She glanced in his direction. "You can check on brunch or lunch or whatever meal this is." She indicated the stove with her chin as she slowly depressed the plunger onto of the grounds.

He turned to the stove, mentally trying to get his mind and body under control. He was in pain. Going commando had a serious downside. He shifted to try and relieve some of the agony his zipper was causing.

He stirred the pan of corned beef hash and checked on the eggs Lacy had been frying. The heavenly smell was making his stomach rumble. Pronouncing it done, he turned off the flame and started sliding the food onto the plates she had laid out on the kitchen island. She'd also spooned some canned fruit into two bowls beside the stove, so he brought those over, too. When she finished making the coffee, she joined him at the island.

After a moment, the silence started getting to him. He

searched around for a safe topic. "How's work? I mean back in New York, not the work you do here for your Dad." *Good one Logan, real smooth.*

"It's, um, fine." She spared him a quick glance. "What secret project are you down here for?"

"Secret project?" he asked, his voice rising. *Did she know something?*

"You said on the yacht you were down here doing some work for your old law firm. That only makes sense if one of your old clients demanded you worked on a project. Lawyers hate to have to pay consultancy fees, so it must be something big."

"Ah, I see. Well, um, I can't really discuss it. Confidentiality and all that. He opened his mouth to explain further but took another bite of food instead. He hated lying to Lacy. Doing this kind of spy work was not his thing. For the millionth time, he cursed his brother Gage for making him do this.

"Look, I know I owe you big time," Lacy said. "I'm not sure I will ever be able to pay you back, but I'll do my best to make sure you get out of this in one piece. I promise."

He knew she was being serious, and he loved that about her. The fact that she was this anxious about keeping him safe made her even more appealing. The guilt about lying to her was a hard nut to swallow. His heart thumped in his chest, and he desperately wanted to kiss her. He nodded because he didn't trust his voice to respond.

They finished the meal in a silence that lingered as they cleared the plates and cleaned up the kitchen.

She ran a hand along her pulled-back hair. "I'm going to explore the house some more." She turned on her heel and left the kitchen.

He finished putting the dishes away and then wandered into the pantry. He found a box of pasta and a jar of sauce.

They'd have dinner if they had to stay. Leaving the kitchen, he decided to sweep the house for anything useful. He had no idea what that might entail but figured he would know it if he found it.

He went through the dining room and the great room. He checked out two bathrooms. It was hard to see because it was dark outside, but nothing in particular jumped out at him as helpful. If Gage were here, or Mitch, they would be much better at this. While he'd spent his time in the Navy in the JAG Corps, his brothers had both been Special Ops. Feeling useless, he sighed.

When he walked into the den, he found Lacy curled up in a chair behind the desk, cleaning a gun. Nonplussed, he stopped short. It had never occurred to him that she could handle a gun. Stupid. Her parents were arms dealers—*of course,* she could handle a gun. He shook himself mentally. He had to stop picturing her as an innocent young thing in need of help. Hell, she could be part of a corporate espionage ring. He had to remember that.

She kept proving how capable she was of looking after herself. Just because he wanted to protect her didn't mean she actually *needed* him. That idea bothered him to no end. It just wasn't something he was used to. He was the responsible one, the one who took care of everything and everyone. He didn't know what to do if he wasn't needed.

She smiled at him. "Hey, look what I found. I thought this might come in handy."

"I see." His voice was dry as dust. "You know your way around guns well enough."

"Arms dealing is the family business, remember?" She clicked the slide back into place.

"Yes. How could I have forgotten?" He sounded wooden, even to his own ears. "What was that like growing up? Must have made for interesting times."

She peered at him, eyes narrowed. "It did," she responded, her voice tight.

Anger burned in his eyes. He was suddenly very pissed off. He didn't want to be here. With her. It was too much. Too hard. He liked her a lot. He didn't want to play these spy games. He didn't want to know what her secrets were. He just wanted to go back to his office in the city and run the business. This sneaking around shit was not for him.

She put the gun down on the desk. "What are you angry about?"

"This isn't just about some maniac trying to blackmail your father. It doesn't make sense." It had been eating at him. He'd been mulling it over ever since they'd hit the island. Things just didn't add up. And seeing her with the gun had jettisoned him over the top. "There's more to it, isn't there? Hell, they didn't even bother to take a picture to show your dad they have you. You'd think that would be the first thing they did."

He glared at her. Many had wilted under his fixed stare in the court room, and he damned well wanted Lacy to feel his wrath. In the past twenty-four hours, he'd survived a car accident, several beatings, a kidnapping, and a mile-long swim. And she was just sitting here cleaning a gun like it was something she did every weekend. He'd had it.

She took a deep breath. Placing her hands in the middle of the desk, she pushed herself up to her full height, such as it was, and glared back at him. "I know as much as you do. We haven't been separated for more than a couple minutes this entire time. If they're not trying to force my father's hand, I have no idea what they want."

"Bullshit. You have a much better idea of what's going on than you're letting on. If they just wanted to blackmail your father, they would have called him as soon as they had you on that boat. I think it's time you started talking." He knew he should stop, but he couldn't help himself. "What's going on? What else are you involved in?" he demanded.

She ground her teeth. "I've told you, I don't know any more than you do. If they don't plan on blackmailing him, the only thing I can think of is…is…" She paused and drew a breath. "That they want to kill him." She was blinking rapidly, probably fighting tears. And just like that, all the anger left his body.

Logan leaned against the door jam. "What makes you think that?"

"Well, they kidnapped me but, like you said, they didn't take any pictures or have me talk to him, so ransom seems to be out. Why take me then? The only answer I can think of is to get to him. His security is tight. Really tight. If they wanted to force his hand on something, they would have sent him proof they had me. But"—she swallowed—"if they wanted to lure him out to kill him, then having me is their best bet."

"But wouldn't they have to send him proof that they had you?"

"My father has great resources on the island. He already knows they took me, I'm sure of it. You've heard the rumors about my father. He won't stand for someone hurting me. He'll go after them."

"But if your father knows they have you, then we're back to maybe it's a ransom thing and they just didn't have a chance to take your picture for proof of life before we escaped." They were going in circles. Logan had privately come to the conclusion there was just a lot more going on than they knew. Too many missing puzzle pieces for them to solve the problem. His anger had gotten the better of him earlier.

Lacy threw her arms in the air. "I don't know then. What do you want me to say? I don't have a clue what's going on!"

Lacy didn't know any more than he did and she was working herself up. There were tears in her eye. Logan couldn't help himself. He walked around the desk and opened his arms.

She didn't hesitate. She walked right into them.

CHAPTER SEVEN

His arms closed around her and crushed her in his embrace. She shuddered and took a deep breath. Cursing silently, he rested his butt on the desk and drew her away so he could see her expression. "I'm sorry. I shouldn't have pushed."

Seeing her tear-stained face, he ran a hand through his hair. "Fuck. I...just lost it a bit, I guess. This whole thing has been a bit unexpected." He was talking about her. The kidnapping and everything that had followed had certainly been unexpected, but not nearly as much as his reaction to her. He knew he was attracted to her physically, but he had never realized how much he liked her as a person. She was as smart as she was sexy.

She wiped her face. "Not your fault. I know I got involved in this accidentally, and like I said, I owe you big time for sticking with me this far." She stared him squarely in the eye. "As soon as we get back to Nassau, you should head home. I can deal with the rest on my own."

He froze. The thought of leaving her to deal with her own problems hadn't even occurred to him. "No," he ground out. "I am not leaving you by yourself until this whole thing has been sorted." Not to mention he hadn't figured out if she was involved with the Drake thing or not.

He still had her in the circle of his arms and legs. He fought the urge to tighten his hold. This visceral need to protect her surprised him, but it was undeniable.

"I appreciate you feel obligated to help me, but"—she squared her shoulders—"despite what it may look like, I can take care of myself."

He was still stuck on her previous pronouncement. "Obligated? I don't feel *obligated*." He ran his hands through his hair again and took a breath. He wasn't sure what he was feeling, but it certainly wasn't obligation. "I'm not leaving you alone with those guys on the loose."

"You don't think I can take care of myself?" She arched an eyebrow at him.

"No. Ah, I mean yes, but not by yourself."

She gave him a look like he was crazy. "That doesn't even make sense. Need I remind you I was the one who had the sharp plastic piece we used to cut off the zip ties? I knew which door to open on the ship, and I would have managed to break into this house if you weren't here. So, all in all, I think I can do perfectly well on my own." She was obviously angry now. Her glare warned him to tread easy.

How had this gone so wrong? Normally he excelled at getting people to do what he wanted, but with Lacy, he was at a loss.

"I am not disputing those facts," he said, "although I could. I am just telling you I would feel uncomfortable leaving you on your own until this mess is sorted out."

"Well, get comfortable. I'm going my own way as soon as we hit Nassau. I don't need to worry about looking after you. Go home or stay, I don't care, but you can't stay with me."

She turned to move away, but he snapped his legs and arms shut, effectively trapping her.

"What the hell, Logan?"

He reached up and cupped the back of her head, turning her so they were eye to eye. "I'm not leaving you on your own, so you can just forget it right now."

Her gaze snapped fire at him. She started to protest, but he didn't give her a chance. He swiftly claimed her mouth with his own. When she winced and went still in his arms, he instantly pulled back. "Your lip. I'm sorry," he groaned. "I forgot."

But before he could release her, she brought her lips up to meet his again. He tasted her sweet mouth, and their tongues danced. He slid his hands down over her back until he cupped her ass and brought her closer. Her fingers wove through his hair as she deepened the kiss and leaned into him. He groaned in response and ground his hips against hers. The zipper was painful against his rock-hard dick, but he didn't want to stop. He wanted to taste all of her.

Moving from her lips to her neck, he kissed the hollow where it met her shoulder. She moaned and shivered in response, running her hands down his back and tugging at his shirt. And when he kissed the hollow behind her ear, she moaned again and plunged her fingers back into his hair.

She pulled his mouth back to hers, and their tongues met in a frantic battle. The heat between them was unbearable now. He tugged down her sweats, desperate to touch her skin. Her sweats hit the floor, and he held her slightly away from him so he could help her remove her shirt.

He stopped suddenly and blinked at what he saw. Did her underwear have writing on it?

SHE SNAPPED back into consciousness and glanced at Logan before looking down to see what he was staring at. A flush crept up her cheeks as she followed his gaze. The fucking underwear.

"Did you think I needed directions?" Logan's laughter echoed deep in his chest.

Her eyes narrowed. "I didn't have much of a choice in clothing," she ground out between clenched teeth. He glanced at her, and the laughter in his eyes died at the look on her face.

"Hey, I was only teasing." He tried to bring her in for a kiss, but she backed up and almost fell over. When he reached out to steady her, she twisted out of his reach and pulled up her sweats. Humiliation made her cheeks flush. *Asshole.*

The crash shook the house. Both of them froze for an instant, and then he grabbed the gun off the desk and made for the door. She followed close behind. They worked their way down the hallway toward the great room. Once there, she tried to move to the opposite wall, but he held her in place. As much as she hated it, she couldn't lead. She had to follow the guy with the gun. She should have grabbed it off the desk first. God only knew if Logan could actually shoot.

She watched him do a quick check around the corner. Apparently, the room was empty because he shook his head. They moved quickly through the great room and then into the kitchen, making sure it was empty. They returned to the great room and headed up the stairwell.

As they neared the top, she could hear something. It took her a moment to place what it was. Dripping water. They exchanged a puzzled look and then went down the hallway toward the sound. Logan peered around the corner into one of the spare bedrooms and then stopped short.

Lacy peeked around his shoulder. A felled tree had punctured the outside wall, right where it used to meet the roofline. The storm must have knocked it over. "Well, that's a problem." She started forward into the room, but he grabbed her hand and hauled her back.

"Yes, but it's not our problem. Just leave everything the way it is. We have no idea if the roof will continue to hold or what other damage might have happened." Still holding her arm, he pulled her out of the room.

"We need to get out of here and back to the mainland ASAP." He tucked the gun into his waistband. "I'm gonna go take a quick look outside, case the rest of the island. Stay downstairs but keep away from this side of the house." He leveled one final glance at her before hurrying down the stairs, a man on a mission.

She bit her lip as she watched him go. She wanted to argue with him but, honestly, she wasn't in the mood to get soaking wet. She just hated being told what to do. She went back downstairs and threw herself on the sofa in the great room.

Her cheeks turned hot as she thought about what they had almost done. What had she been thinking? Well, she hadn't been thinking; she'd been feeling. And his touch had felt damn good too, but what would have happened if she hadn't had a…wardrobe issue? They would have, what? Had sex on a stranger's desk? Their couch?

"Oh, God," she groaned as she pulled a throw pillow over her face. Humiliation aside, it was probably a good thing they hadn't had sex. It was much better this way.

Except that not fulfilling her deepest desire didn't feel better this way. She could still feel his lips on her skin and taste him in her mouth. Her lady parts were all tingly. She literally ached for him.

No. She had to get her shit together and stay away from Logan. Having sex with him would be a big mistake. He definitely had to go as soon as they got out of here. *If* they got out of here.

She stared out the window. The rain hadn't let up yet. It was only very the beginning of hurricane season, but if this storm was any indication, it was going to be a harsh one. She'd been looking forward to coming down to the sunshine when she was in New York. Spring had been unseasonable cool and had the temps only warmed up in the last couple weeks. She and her father were going to spend some quality father/daughter time. She immediately swallowed the lump building in her throat.

Ignoring what Logan said—who was he to give her orders, anyway?—she walked back into the master bedroom and lay down on the bed. She pulled the blankets over her and watched the fire. Good thing they'd left it on last night. She yawned. Yesterday had taken a toll. She rubbed the slight ache in her shoulder. It had been ages since she'd swam so much and she was feeling it. She needed to relax and figure out what to do next.

WAKING WITH A START, she found she had tangled herself in the blankets. She had been having a nightmare about being chased off her father's yacht. She sat up and tried to clear her head. After taking a few deep breaths, she noticed it was finally quiet outside. The storm must have passed. Sure enough, the sky outside the window was blue. Great. Now, to get off this island. She bounced off the bed, squaring her shoulders once again, and went off in search of Logan.

She met him at the top of the stairs.

"I was just coming to get you." His face gave nothing away, and it hit her that she was not the only lawyer in the house.

She turned away, trying to hide the flush that was creeping up her neck. "I see the rain has stopped. We should try to find a way off the island."

"I was thinking the same thing, but I think we should eat first. We can't leave until dark anyway."

"Works for me. I am a bit hungry. What time is it?" Which was a total understatement. Her stomach hadn't stopped growling since she'd woken up.

"It's probably around sixish. I found some pasta and sauce earlier."

"I think we should open a bottle of wine. I don't know about you, but I could use a glass." *If not three*, she added silently.

Logan frowned. "I'm not sure wine is a great idea."

"Maybe not for you, but I think it's the best idea I've had all day." Lacy went around him and down the stairs.

"Fine. I'll start dinner," he said and followed her down the stairs.

She nodded and headed toward the den where she'd noticed a wine rack during her exploration of the house. As she bent down to choose a wine, she noticed something tucked behind the rack. She couldn't tell what it was because there were too many bottles of wine blocking her view. She reached back and pulled it out. "Yes! Finally something we can use." She grabbed a bottle of wine with her find and headed to the kitchen.

When Logan emerged from the pantry, she was standing at the island, playing with a battery-operated shortwave radio. She continued to fiddle with the radio.

"Not here. Go check the next one." The voice came through loud and clear. "Yay!" She clapped and smiled up at him. "Now we can find out what's up with the weather." She noticed he had gone still and was puzzled. "Wha—"

"Shh." He listened intently again. There were some other

voices, but it was hard to make out what they were saying. He walked over to the window and scanned the back yard..

"We have to go," he announced and then turned to look at her.

"Why? I thought we were going to have food and drink." She smiled and held up a wine glass. "And then leave when it's dark."

"No. We have to find a way off now. That voice was Scar's. I would know it anywhere. They're searching for us, island by island. We need to go now."

Her heart started pounding. She stared at the bottle wine and then put the glass down with a thunk. "Shit. Do you think there's another way off the island besides swimming?"

"There's a boathouse. I skipped it when I was scouting earlier. Figured I would check it out after the storm ended." He grimaced, then started walking toward the door.

"Well, there's no time like the present. Grab the gun and anything else that might be useful and come back here. Once you're done, stay in the kitchen. I'll check things out and come back for you. Keep a look out. It's still daylight. It won't be dark for another couple of hours." He frowned. "If I find a boat, we might have to risk it and leave immediately." He fiddled with the alarm panel and then headed out the door.

She went through every room, but in the end, the only thing worth taking was the gun and a supply of drinking water. She went to the cupboard. She studied the dry goods, trying to decide if she should pack some. What would she pack it in? Canned goods would be heavy and hard to carry. Still, it would be better than starving.

She found a couple of plastic bags and two to-go coffee mugs. She threw some cans of food into the bags and filled the to-go cups with water. Then she searched the entire kitchen for a can opener. She couldn't find anything but an electric one. She grabbed a sharp knife from the drawer and decided that would have to do. She wrapped it in paper towel and put it in the bag with the cans.

She started pacing the length of the room. The waiting was endless. The sky had gotten marginally darker but it was still easy to see. The radio crackled to life every once in a while, but the words were unclear. Hysteria was bubbling right underneath the surface, so she kept taking deep breaths, trying to keep it down. Then it hit her—their clothes! They could hide them, but the best way of ensuring they weren't found was to wear them.

She ran back up to the closet and changed back into her old dress and underwear. The gown had shrunk dramatically because of the salt water. Now the bottom of it barely skimmed the tops of her thighs. Great. Still, it was better to leave them guessing. She put the clothes she'd been wearing in a pile on a shelf, hoping the owners would realize they needed to be washed. Then she gathered Logan's clothes and dashed back into the kitchen.

Her brain kept flicking between what Scar and his cohorts were doing and where the hell Logan had gone. Movement off to the left caught her eye. She watched, letting her eyes adjust to the growing shadows. A few seconds passed before she saw it again. Suddenly, Logan appeared on the end of the porch. All the air left her lungs. He had scared the hell out of her, but there was no need to admit that to him.

He opened the door carefully and walked in. The kitchen wasn't facing the setting sun, so it was hard to see his features clearly, but she had the distinct feeling he did not have good news.

"I cased the whole island this time. It's smaller then I had hoped. Just the house, the caretaker's cottage, and the boat house. No other buildings. There aren't any boats, but there are paddle boards and a tandem sea kayak."

"Great. Any good news?"

He did a double take. "Why are you wearing that?"

"I thought it would be better if we didn't leave our clothes behind. That way they won't know for sure we were here." His eyes darkened as they ran up and down over her dress. Unbidden heat uncurled in her belly and spread like wildfire across her whole body. She swallowed hard.

"Ah, I think you should change, too." She handed him his clothes. He nodded but stayed silent.

"Any sign of the yacht or Scar?"

He ran his hand through his hair. "I think they're close. I caught a glimpse of a yacht on the other side of the island. It disappeared behind another island, but if it's them, they'll be here before too long."

He grabbed her by the shoulders and looked directly into her eyes. It was getting harder and harder to see his features in the encroaching dusk, but she could feel his eyes boring into hers. "Are you up for this? Paddling off the island?" He stared hard. "If not, we can try and hide out here or make some sort of a stand…"

"There's no way we could hide. And we don't have enough weapons, ammo, or people to hold them off. No, we have to go," she stated flatly. He nodded once and then pulled her in for a bone-crushing hug. Just as quickly, he let her go.

"Grab a flashlight and the rest of the supplies." He glanced around the kitchen. "We'll leave right after I change and return these clothes to the bedroom."

"Maybe we'll get lucky and they'll focus on the other islands. We could use some luck right now."

He smiled down at her and dropped a quick kiss on her nose. "Yeah, we could." He left the kitchen to change.

It took forever, and she was practically dancing by the time he got back. "What took you so long?"

"I cleaned out the bedroom and put all of the towels back." He made a face.

"I know, I feel bad about it, too. The couple who lives here are going to come home and use dirty towels and clothes. Still they have bigger things to worry about like a tree through their roof so there's that. Maybe they'll wash all of their clothes anyway just in case a creature or bugs got in." She shuddered. "That would definitely creep me out." She grabbed the bags of supplies off the counter.

"Come on, that's the least of our worries." He ushered her out the door and reset the alarm.

"Why are you resetting the alarm?" she whispered.

"If they come this way, they probably won't bother to hack it. They'll just set it off. Sound carries far at night. It will give us an idea of how far behind us they are." With that, he closed the door, took the travel mugs from her, and moved toward the boathouse. He stopped and listened a couple of times, but if he heard anything, he didn't tell her. She didn't hear anything, so she took that to be a good sign.

He let them into the boat house, closed the door after them, and turned on the flashlight. It was a New England style boathouse, built right over the water. There was room for a couple of boats in the middle and a walkway all around.

Logan pointed with the flashlight. "There's the kayak. Help me get it down."

She set down the bags of supplies then went to the other end and grabbed the small craft off the wall. It wasn't heavy since it was one of the cheap plastic ones, which was kind of surprising since everything else in the house was so upscale. They lowered it into the water.

"Figures it had to be bright orange. Why couldn't it have been black or navy or something?" she mumbled. There was a jet ski parked in the water next to where they put the kayak. "We should take that."

He shook his head. "Not sure where the keys are. I couldn't find them earlier, and I have no idea how much gas is in it. Even if I did manage to hotwire it, it also makes noise. They would definitely check it out and find us. If they were just using the yacht, we might be able to out run or out maneuver them, but they have jet skis and a speedboat. We can't outrun *those*.

"The best thing we can do is travel silently. If we manage to do that, we should be able to make it." He raised the flashlight to the wall.

There was a map of the Bahamas with their island clearly marked. It also showed Nassau. They were about twenty miles from their destination. That was a lot of paddling. She frowned.

"I also found this." He held up a compass.

"You know how to use one of those things?"

He sighed loudly. "Look, I might not be a SEAL, but I was in the Navy. I can use the compass." His voice was tight.

Apparently, she'd insulted him. She knew she should probably apologize. After all, he'd calculated for tide and current during their swim. "Sorry," she mumbled.

He helped her into the kayak. It was one of those orange plastic ones where she could sit in the hull so she had space around her. Logan handed her the bags, which she tucked in by her legs, and then he handed her one of the oars. He got in behind her with the other. With a couple of smooth strokes, they were out of the boathouse and on their way. He held the flashlight low in his seat before turning it off.

"OK," he whispered. Then he turned the kayak and started paddling.

They paddled along in silence—the only sound was their oars slicing through the water. The water had been a little rough when they started, but it started to smooth out. The sky was clear, which made her nervous. The sun had dipped below the horizon and it was finally getting truly dark. She glanced up at the half moon in the sky. At least it wasn't full.

Logan's navigation was benefiting from it, however. He hadn't bothered to check the compass again. She knew because he hadn't turned on the flashlight they'd brought. She could only assume he either knew where he was going or was navigating by the stars, which didn't seem too damn likely, but she was too afraid to ask.

As they continued paddling into the still night, the silence pressed down on her. They passed the occasional island but no one seemed to be on them. She tried to think about happy things but the ache of her shoulders and her palms from all the paddling was making it difficult. She had blisters already.

Her ears strained for every sound. Panic bubbled up in her chest. Desperate to stop it, she blurted out, "Why didn't you tell your family you want to be a chef?" It was a deeply personal question, but for some reason it was the first thing that had popped into her head. Besides, she really wanted to know the answer.

Silence hung between them for a good minute, long enough for the panic to swell again. She was literally praying she could keep it together when he finally spoke, startling her.

"When we were kids, my brothers and I would talk about what we wanted to be when we grew up. Gage wanted to be a professional surfer, and Mitch wanted to do any extreme sport, didn't matter which one. I would say I wanted to be a lawyer and win big cases, because even then I knew I couldn't hold a candle to them when it came to sports. I just didn't share their love for it.

When I was sixteen, I went to work for my father for the summer. He made me start as a gofer for the guys installing the alarm systems, but by the end of the summer, I had learned how to install the systems myself. My dad was impressed, I guess. He told me I was more like him than my brothers were. And he admitted he was glad one of us was following in his footsteps. Over the next few summers, as my brothers kept doing their sports and bringing home their trophies, he took me under his wing and taught me how to thrive in business."

He stopped speaking again, and she couldn't hear his oar hitting the water anymore. She wanted desperately to turn back and look at him but thought it might break the spell.

"It took a long time for me to realize that, although I was good, maybe even great at working in corporate America, I just didn't have any passion for it. My brothers have always had passion for their work. I never did.

"It started out small—I used to watch a lot of Food Network when I wanted to wind down from law school, and then work later. There were a few things I tried out on my own. It was something fun to do, and I always loved watching my mom cook when I was a kid. Before long, I was coming up with my own recipes, and I started holding dinner parties for my friends. I'd find myself thinking of ways to tweak recipes at work.

"When Dad announced he was retiring and my brothers wanted to take over the company, I went along with it, thinking that maybe if it was my own company, it would be different. I would be passionate about it." He stopped speaking again, and his oar splashed through the water.

"Anyway, it just didn't work out that way. I like working with my brothers, more than I even thought I would, but it still doesn't excite me the way cooking does. I guess all this is a very long-winded way of saying I haven't told them because I don't want to let them down.

"Neither one of my brothers has the right skillset to take over the company just yet. They need more time and experience. And if I tell them I want to quit, it'll put them in a tight spot. I promised my mother I'd look after them, and my dad deserves to retire without worrying about the future of the business, especially now. Maybe one day I'll have my own restaurant, but not right now, so why bother talking about it?"

Her heart constricted in her chest. "I know exactly how you feel," she said, the words bursting out of her. She turned back to glance at him. "Family expectations can be hard to manage." His intense gaze made her feel exposed so she turned back around. This wasn't something she could talk about while looking at him.

"My mother died when I was just a baby, and all my life, I heard how wonderful she was. She was like a star, lighting up any room. Her laughter was infectious. She was beautiful, bold, smart, and an amazing businesswoman. She built an empire through sheer willpower and guts. And the descriptions go on and on, each one more flattering than the last."

She sighed. This next part was harder to get out; she'd never shared it with anyone, not even her best friend, Alex, but it had been weighing on her more lately.

"I grew up hating her instead of loving her," she said in a whisper. "Everyone would look at me as if searching for a spark of her. It was awful. I was always being compared to her in some way, and I never, ever measured up."

Lost in thought, she jumped a little when Logan squeezed her shoulder. Warmth radiated from the point of contact.

She took a deep breath and continued. "Anyway, like you, I worked very hard to excel at school since I knew my mother had dropped out in her teens. I pushed to complete my degree early, and then I pushed myself to climb the ranks in a big law firm. I wanted everyone's approval. And I had it.

The people in my father's circle would tell me how smart I was, just like my mother." She sighed again.

"I'm burnt out, I guess. I don't want to do it anymore. It doesn't make me happy. Like you said, I'm good at it, but I don't like it. Hell, I hate it, to be frank." The sound of his strong, steady rowing made her feel calmer.

"I guess I always knew my greatest skill was logistics. In boarding school, I was always the one on all the planning committees. I loved organizing parties. I still do, but how do I tell my father that I want to be a party planner? How can the daughter of the great Giselle Fontaine want to plan weddings and bar mitzvahs for a living? It's just not done."

She slumped a bit in her seat, and he squeezed her shoulder again—a silent show of support that sent strength through her.

Suddenly, the silence was broken by the sound of a house alarm. It wasn't as loud as she'd thought it would be, but she whipped around and stared into the dark. She wished she could see.

"We're fine." His voice, little more than a whisper, came to her on the breeze. "It's not as close as you think. We've been paddling for about three hours."

"Really? We've been paddling that long?"

"Yes. About that."

"How much farther do we have to go?" She waited for a response, but none came.

Finally, he said, "Don't think about it. Just paddle. We're a long way off yet."

She tried to settle back into position and get her rhythm back but it was hard. Her arms and hands were in serious pain, not to mention her butt was completely numb. She wondered if Logan was as miserable. She was trying to be Zen, but she had her ears perked just in case.

Sure enough, a short time later she heard the distant

sound of a speedboat revving and then taking off. Her heart pounded in her chest. She wanted to turn and look at Logan again, but what was the point? She couldn't see him anyway. She felt him touch her back, and she stopped rowing. They sat in silence for a second, trying to gauge if the boat was coming toward them or going away.

"It's moving away." His voice floated over her shoulder again. She nodded and assumed he could see it because he immediately started rowing again. Both of them picked up a bit of speed with their oars, finding a slightly faster rhythm.

Another hour passed, and she was lost in thought when a slight buzzing sound broke through her reverie. It took her a moment to place it. The speedboat engine, and it was definitely getting closer this time. She whirled around to look at Logan. He had stopped rowing as well.

Like before, she couldn't see him well, but suddenly his body jerked at bit. She whipped around the other way and strained her eyes to see. There. Off to the right, the boat was flying toward them. It wouldn't be long before they were seen.

Logan gave her the signal they had discussed previously, and the two of them flipped the kayak. It was harder than it seemed to flip, so it took a couple of tries, but finally the cool water rushed over her head. She slipped out of the kayak and stuck her head where her butt had been moments before. There was a small air pocket there so she could breath. She had no clue how long the air bubble would last, but that was the least of her worries at the moment.

She tried not to panic as she clutched her oar with one hand and forced the length downward to line up with her body. She wrapped one leg around the paddle to hold it in place and held on to the kayak with the other. Cursing silently, she shook her head. She had forgotten about the gun and the food, which was probably on the bottom at this point, who knew how many feet below them.

"Logan," she whispered. Hearing nothing, she tried again. "Logan."

"Here." He came up under the kayak right beside her. After maneuvering the two oars between them, he held on to her and them tightly.

"I dropped the gun and the food into the water," she whispered. He just shook his head as they heard the speedboat draw closer. She prayed the boat would continue on to the next island, but no such luck. The sound of the engine being throttled down met her ears. She bit her lip.

"It's OK," he whispered right in her ear. She appreciated the thought, but they both knew it wasn't true. This ruse would only work if the guys in the boat stayed far away. The Caribbean waters were crystal clear, even at night. If Scar's men had a strong flashlight they would be seen. The water level was starting to rise. They both had to bend their heads back to keep their mouths above the waterline.

She held her breath as the boat came closer still. She could hear voices now.

"What is it?" The interior of bright orange kayak lit up like a Christmas tree. She could see the light glowing through the cheap plastic. The air left her lungs completely. His arm tightened around her.

"Kayak."

"See any oars?" The light danced away and then came back. Then it danced away again. She didn't recognize the voices but that didn't mean much. Scar probably had a bunch of men working for him. Her father certainly did.

"No. What do you think? Should we go turn it over?"

"Nah. It probably got loose in the storm. If it was theirs and they ditched it, there would be oars." The flashlight took one more dance around the kayak before the boat's engine moved off idle. The boat came very close to the kayak, the sound of its motor deafening, but it continued on its way.

She finally managed to take a deep breath. "Do you think it's safe?" she whispered into the darkness a minute later.

"Don't know," he whispered back. "Stay here and I'll check." He let go of her and disappeared under the surface of the water. A minute later he was back. "Coast is clear."

"Thank God!" She relaxed and immediately let go of the oar. She lunged through the water after it and managed to grab it again. Surfacing, she sputtered a bit and looked around for Logan.

The inky darkness made it hard to find him, but she caught sight of his outline and uttered a soft prayer of thanks. It took them a couple of tries to get the kayak righted and crawl in. By the time they managed, she was absolutely exhausted. She found it hard to get into a rhythm this time. She was tired, cold, stiff, and the kayak had water in it, making it really uncomfortable to sit in. This night could not end soon enough.

CHAPTER EIGHT

"Lacy." She could hear her name being called, but it was far away. "Lacy." There it was again. She could hear waves lapping on something. She felt damp. Water. Strange dream. She felt a nudge and jerked awake.

"Wha…? What? Where?" She looked around frantically. Then it all snapped into place. "Sorry," she groaned as she turned to face Logan. "I guess I fell asleep," she said sheepishly. "I'm just so tired." She wished she could see his face. He must be just as tired as she was. She suddenly remembered his bruised ribs. Rowing had to be miserable for him. "Your ribs. I am so sorry."

"Don't worry about it." He shrugged. "But I need you to help now. We're caught in a current, and I need help pushing through it." She turned back around and started paddling again. Every muscle in her body ached, and she bit her lip so she wouldn't groan out loud, but she managed to find a rhythm.

It was almost dawn by the looks of things. The sky was getting lighter, and soon the sun would be up. She was thirsty. She could only imagine Logan felt the same way. What an idiot she'd been to let go of those travel cups.

"Lacy." His voice broke through her concentration.

"I'm paddling. I really am." The sound of a chuckle reached her ears. She had whirled around with the intent to tell him off when she saw he was pointing at something. In the distance an island rose out of the sea. She swore. "Is it real? Not a mirage?"

"It's real." The dry voice came over her shoulder again. "And it shouldn't take more than a couple of hours for us to reach it." A couple of hours of paddling. She had been all set to cheer and do the happy dance, but the prospect of another couple hours of paddling sucked the joy right out of her.

Reading her thoughts, he said, "Think about how good a shower, food, and sleep will feel when we get there. You can do it. Just keep paddling." She started rowing again, but now all she could hear in her head was Dory from *Finding Nemo* saying, "Just keep swimming," over and over again. Great. At this rate, she was going to go insane by the time they reached land.

As the sun rose and she hummed Dory's song, they crept closer and closer to shore. "Are we just going to paddle right up to the beach? Look at us." She glanced down at herself. "I'm wearing what used to be a green cocktail dress in a material that apparently wasn't intended for salt water." The dress had shrunk so much it was a second skin around her chest and ribs. It was so short now it barely covered her ass. "And you—" She whirled around to look at him. "You look…"

Damn, if he still didn't look fine. His complexion, which had been slightly pale when she'd first seen him on the yacht, no doubt from hours spent indoors, was bronzing up nicely. His previously white shirt was all wrinkly and somewhat off white, but it still hugged his chest and made him look delectable. She licked her lips. She had no doubt his wrinkled dress pants would outline his butt in the best way.

He cocked an eyebrow. "You were saying?"

"Suffice it to say, we look pretty rough." The difference was that rough looked damn fine on him. She turned back. "What if people ask questions?" she called over her shoulder.

"No one will ask questions. Don't you recognize what's ahead?" She looked around, this time taking in the whole area, not just the beach.

"Is that Sand Dollar Quay Resort?"

"Yes! We've been paddling south all night. I was aiming for this. I haven't lost my navigation skills." There was a note of triumph in his voice.

"Ah, that's great but, ah…were you aiming for here, specifically?" This was one of the nicest resorts in all the Caribbean. And expensive. Very expensive. They had no money on them.

She thought about her father. The rules were quite clear, and they had been set up by her father's security people years ago. If disaster struck, she was to be at a specific place at a specific time by herself. No calling for help. No deviations from the plan.

She bit her lip. She should just be happy they'd finally reached land. And she was, most definitely. Sand Dollar Quay was amazing, but she didn't have the energy to walk anywhere. Town was several miles away on the other side of the bridge, and the hotel they were registered at was on the far side of the island.

Logan didn't answer her question about the resort, and she didn't want to appear ungrateful, so she held her tongue. Even so, she immediately started brainstorming ways to get to town that didn't involve walking or money or—*shudder* —kayaking.

They paddled the last few strokes and rode the

momentum up onto the beach. It took her several tries to get out of the kayak. Her legs were so stiff she wasn't sure she could walk.

Logan gave her a hand out of the kayak and walked her out of the surf and onto the beach. People were watching them. And why not? Two people in disheveled evening attire crawling out of a kayak in the middle of the morning was quite the sight.

She tried to act like this was normal, but it was hard. She kept tugging down the hem of her dress to keep it from rising any higher. He grabbed hold of her arm and kept her moving.

"Where are we going?"

"You'll see." They walked past the vacationers on the beach, many of whom were still openly watching them, and continued past the people by the pool. The wait staff all paused to watch as well. She could feel the flush creep up her cheeks.

They followed a path around and right up to the entry to the hotel. "You don't plan on going in, do you? They'll call the cops, and I can't have the cops involved." She was starting to panic, but he wouldn't let go of her arm. "Logan," she tried again.

"Trust me." He kept a firm hold on her arm as he moseyed right up to the check-in desk. The hotel was decorated in marble with fresh flowers on the tables and large comfortable sofas and chairs scattered about for guests to relax in. It was all so normal, which made the situation feel even more bizarre.

"Hi Cecil. How are you?" Lacy whipped her head around to stare at Logan. Cecil? Logan knew this guy?

"Mr. Callahan! How good it is to see you! I didn't know you were coming to town." Cecil appeared to surreptitiously take in Logan and Lacy's attire.

Lacy was trying to create a plausible story in her head that might explain their appearance, but it was unnecessary. Cecil just focused on the computer screen and dashed off a few quick keystrokes. Looking puzzled, he said, "There must be a mistake. We have no record of your visit."

"It was a last-minute thing, Cecil." He put his arm around her and brought her in close. "You know how these things go." And he winked. He winked! She seethed silently.

Cecil glanced at them and then nodded. She could only imagine what he must be thinking. Though she'd never felt more embarrassed, she smiled and tried to look convincing.

"No problem, Mr. Callahan. Your suite is always ready to receive you. I'll just have one of the bellmen bring up your luggage."

"We don't have any."

Cecil, after the barest of pauses, nodded. "Of course, Mr. Callahan. Could I have the boutique send some clothing up for you both?"

"That would be wonderful, Cecil, but could you give us some time to settle in before sending up the clothing?"

"Of course, Mr. Callahan. Why don't you call when you are ready?" Cecil came out from behind the counter, and they all started walking toward the elevators.

"Thank you so much for your help, Cecil. I knew we would be well taken care of in your capable hands."

Cecil held the elevator doors open for them and then handed Logan a key. "Of course, Mr. Callahan. Wonderful to have you back with us." His gaze flicked over her again. "Enjoy your stay." He stepped back, and the doors closed.

"Unbelievable." She turned to look at him. "Care to explain all of that?"

He just gave a concise shake of his head, and they spent the rest of the ride listening to elevator music. The doors opened, and she followed him down the hall to a set of double doors. He used the key to unlock the door and pushed it open for her.

She stepped into one of the most luxurious hotel suites she had ever seen, and that was saying something. The marble floors gleamed. The floor-to-ceiling windows offered an almost one hundred and eighty degree view of the ocean. The furniture was as sumptuous as the space. She ran her hand along the back of a sofa that was as soft as silk. There was even a fully stocked bar at one end.

"I've died and gone to heaven."

He laughed and immediately handed her a bottle of cool water. She had never tasted anything so good. "Here." He handed her a thick book. "It's the menu. We'll order room service before showering."

Her eyes danced over the menu choices while her mouth watered. She made several selections. "I know my eyes are bigger than my stomach, but I'm willing to give it my best shot." He grinned and made the call to room service, adding several choices of his own to the order.

"Seriously, though, I didn't think Callahan Security would keep this kind of suite."

"We don't. It belongs to my old firm in New York."

She frowned until she remembered their conversation on the yacht. "Right. You said you were down here to do some work for them. Why didn't you stay here in the first place?"

"Ah, I wanted to relax in my own space, away from prying eyes. Being here always makes me feel like I am under a bit of a microscope. Anyway, I'll make a call and let them know I'm here."

She didn't want to be, but she had to admit she was impressed. She knew money. Understood money. But her father's power was based on what he could get people. Logan's power was totally based on his intelligence and personal accomplishments. She wondered if he was aware of how sexy that was? Probably. She sighed.

"Where is the shower? I am in desperate need."

"There's a bedroom on either end. Take your pick. They're dual master suites, so both have attached baths."

Before she could stop herself, she blurted out, "Do you stay here often?" She could picture him here with all sorts of women and parties.

His lips twitched at the corners. "Sometimes."

She should have known better than to ask. She turned away and took the bedroom on the left. Just like the central room, it boasted floor-to-ceiling windows with incredible views. The bathroom was glorious to behold, all marble with a huge tub and a separate shower stall that could accommodate half a dozen people.

She opened what appeared to be a linen closet and pulled out a towel and one of the bathrobes that was hanging there. After turning on the shower, she stripped off her ruined green dress and stepped under the hot spray, letting out a moan of absolute pleasure.

Forty-five minutes later, all pink-cheeked and smelling like citrus, she emerged from the bedroom. She immediately took a deep breath. The food smelled fantastic. Her mouth watering, she tucked her oversize robe close around her and shuffled into the central room where all the room service trays had been laid out on the dining table.

"You look—" Logan paused—"refreshed." She turned to find him sitting on the sofa. The clothing had obviously arrived because he was wearing a pair of jeans and a blue button-down shirt that made his eyes look even bluer, if that was possible. She swallowed as she remembered his kisses. Heat trailed up her cheeks.

She put a hand up to smooth her hair and then swore silently. She had pinned her hair directly on top of her head after getting out of the shower and had forgotten to take it down. She probably looked like some kind of Muppet. "Are you laughing at me?" she asked.

"No." His eyes sparkled.

"You are obviously lying, but I'm so hungry I don't care." She plopped down on one of the seats by the dining table and started lifting covers. He sat down opposite her and helped her get the serving dishes sorted. He then handed her an empty plate so she could fill it with whatever she wanted. He followed suit after pouring her more water and some champagne.

"What's the champagne for?" she asked as she swirled the liquid in the glass.

"After what we've been through, I thought we could use a nice treat."

She took a sip. It was delicious. She loved a good champagne. "Thanks for this. It all looks so good." The mountain of food on the table was more than she could ask for. There was steak and seafood and everything in between. It was so overwhelming, she almost didn't know where to start. She slowly filled her plate with a little bit of everything.

"Bon appetite," Logan said, and then the rest of the meal was consumed in silence.

Stuffed to the gills, she declared she was finished, got up, waddled over to the sofa and crashed down on it. It felt like being enveloped in a warm hug. After that long, hot shower and their room service feast, she could feel her eyelids drooping.

"Go to bed."

She gawked at him. How could he not be as tired as she was? "Why aren't you exhausted?"

He smiled slightly. "I am, but I have a call or two to make. I'm going to crash after that." Did you want to call your father?"

She frowned. "Um, that's not really possible."

His eyebrows shot up. "What do you mean? Why not?"

Sighing, she stood up. "Look, my father can't talk openly on the phone at the best of times. In case you haven't noticed, this isn't the best of times. Technically, I'm not even late for work yet. I wanted to meet earlier last week, but he told me not to come before Monday. He was quite clear."

"So, who were you going to call when we were stuck on the island?" Logan asked.

"Um, well, I thought you would call someone for help."

Logan was staring at her like he couldn't quite believe what he was hearing. She bit her lip. How could she explain that there was no one for her to call? It sounded awful, like her father had left her in the lurch on purpose. She shrugged, but that's just the way it had to be.

"Anyway, there is a certain protocol that has been set up for this type of situation, and it very specifically does not involve calling my father."

He blinked slowly as he digested that news. His face then went blank, and he said, "I had them bring up some clothes for you to try on. He gestured to the opposite sofa. Why don't you take a nap and then find something that fits? We can plan our next step after that." He had turned to face the windows. She didn't blame him. Her life was very confusing to an outsider. Hell, it was confusing to her.

She watched him for a minute, drinking in every nuance she could. Though she had to follow protocol— and that certainly didn't include bringing an outsider into the mix— she had to admit the thought of parting from Logan made her feel a bit lonely. She liked him a lot. But at the moment, Logan Callahan was just another worry she didn't need.

CHAPTER NINE

H e turned and watched her go, willing himself to stay exactly where he was. He wanted to go after her. He wanted to shake her and tell her that the life she was leading was crazy. That she needed to distance herself from her father. Actually, he wanted to beat the hell out of her father. Who would endanger their kid like this? It was fucked up.

Then he wanted to spend the rest of the day making love to her. She was so damn cute in that huge robe with her hair piled on top of her head. He wanted to touch and taste every inch of her.

Enough. He had to get his head on straight if he was going to take care of business. And that meant keeping all his thoughts strictly above the belt.

He waited for her door to close before heading over to the desk. It would cost him, but it was worth it. She was so happy in her fluffy robe, eating twice her weight in food. It made him smile to remember the moan she'd made while biting into the chocolate lava cake he had ordered for dessert.

Damn. All his thoughts kept revolving back to Lacy. If only there was someone she could call, someone he could trust to keep her safe. *She grew up in this world,* he reminded himself. *She doesn't need you, remember?*

Sighing, he walked back to the table to grab a cup of coffee. Maybe it was time to check in with his brother.

He was exhausted, but he took a big gulp of coffee, sat down at the desk, and started dialing. First up was a call to his old boss to smooth the way for the hotel stay. He wasn't looking forward to this call. Carl Montgomery III was not a generous man. He would not be happy at all about Logan using the suite. He would want his pound of flesh for it for sure.

"Logan! This is an unexpected surprise. I couldn't believe it when Janet told me you were on the phone." Carl's voice boomed down the telephone line.

"Carl. How are you doing?"

"Excellent. What about you? How are *you* doing?"

Logan frowned at the phone. Carl's tone was off. It was too jovial. He was only like this with clients, or with his wife when he knew he screwed up somehow.

"I'm fine, Carl. Listen, I'm in the Bahamas, and I was wondering if I could borrow the suite for a few days?" Logan's gut clenched waiting for the yelling to start.

"Of course. Stay as long as you like," Carl said. "Please enjoy it. You always work too hard, Logan. You need to take more breaks."

Logan damn near dropped the phone. *Who was this man and what the fuck happened to his old boss?* "Ah, thanks, Carl. I, um, really appreciate it."

"No problem. Gotta run. Talk soon." *Click.*

Carl was gone. Now that was the Carl Logan knew and hated. Logan put down the receiver. Strange was the only word to describe that whole interaction. Logan took another sip of coffee and tried to figure out what just happened. *Nothing. Nada.* But no looking a gift horse in the mouth.

Picking up the phone again, he dialed. "Callahan," came the voice from the other end. His brother Gage.

"Hey, it's me."

"Logan, what's up? How's your semi-vacation going? Do you miss us yet?" He could hear a snort of laughter in the background.

"Mitch is with you. I can hear him laughing. When did he get back from Europe?"

"Just last night," Gage replied. "There's been some developments with Drake. Here, let me put you on speaker."

"Yo, how's the sun and surf?" Mitch called out.

Logan sat back in his chair. "Not as much fun as I anticipated."

"What's wrong, bro? Things not going your way with the ladies? Try relaxing. Maybe ditch the suit." Mitch sniggered.

Logan ignored his brother. "What's going on? What are the new developments?"

"Someone took a direct run at Drake. They tried to grab him." Gage's voice had gone serious.

Logan sat forward in his chair. "Did anyone get hurt?"

"No. We're all fine. It was a bit intense, but we got him out of there." Mitch gave a dry chuckle.

"Glad you're OK, Mitch." Logan realized just how much he meant it as he said it. After what he'd gone through over the last forty-eight hours, he had a brand-new appreciation for what his brothers did in the military and what they continued to do for Callahan Security.

There was a brief silence. "Um, thanks," Mitch said.

He and Mitch had never had a great relationship. He'd always thought Mitch was lazy and a goof-off but, now, he realized his brother deserved any downtime he got.

"What are you doing back in New York? I would have thought Drake would want you by his side twenty-four seven."

"He does, but after he talked with Gage and myself, he decided to send me back here with a copy of the prototype. He wants to make sure there's a spare copy just in case we need it."

"Makes sense," Logan said.

Gage piped up. "He's concerned that his programmer may be compromised in some way. She's near completion, but she's sent him some encrypted messages saying she thinks she's being followed. I'm going to have to go to her location and maybe do an extraction. We'll see how it plays out. Mitch is going to go back to Europe tonight. Don't worry. I'm leaving Dragan in charge. He should be able to handle things until you get back here."

Mitch spoke up, "Speaking of which, how are things on your end? Find anything out yet? When can you come home?"

Logan briefly entertained the idea of lying to his brothers about the mess he was in. They both had a lot on their plate. But he was nothing if not pragmatic. His brothers would both be better equipped to handle the situation than he, and keeping Lacy safe was the most important thing. "Ah, about that. There's more going on down here than we anticipated."

"What do you mean? Is Lacy Carmichael actually involved with the Drake mess?" Gage asked.

"Well, I haven't gotten that far." Logan sighed. "So, I ran into some trouble." He went on to explain the last two days' adventures to his brothers.

"Fuck, Logan, if I'd had any idea that this was even a possibility, I never would have sent you." Gage swore again.

"Yeah, I know. None of us had any idea she was Armand Fontaine's daughter." Logan took a sip of his now cold coffee.

Mitch asked, "Do you think he's behind the whole mess with Drake? It would make sense since he's a broker. Maybe he caught wind of its existence and now he wants a copy to sell. Or maybe Fontaine is trying to acquire it for a client?"

"It's a possibility," Gage agreed.

"I don't think so," Logan said. "I had to do some research on Fontaine back in my JAG days. I don't think he'd hire out to get the prototype. He'd use his own guys—ones he trusted. I know he's here on the island, or at least he was up until a couple of days ago. I'm pretty sure he's not in Europe at the moment. Presumably, he would have his best guys with him, especially with his daughter in danger. Although..." He thought about how Lacy had to follow some stupid protocol that said she wasn't allowed to contact her father. Maybe he didn't care all that much.

"What are you thinking?" Gage asked.

"I guess I'm thinking it's a possibility. I don't think Fontaine is involved with the Drake case, but I can't rule it out completely." He needed to talk to Lacy for that.

"How safe are you at this moment?" Mitch asked.

Logan glanced around the hotel suite and thought of Cecil downstairs. "About as safe as possible given the circumstances."

"What are you thinking, Mitch?" Gage asked.

"I'm thinking that the best thing we can do for the moment is have Logan sit tight. We need to get some stuff sorted here and get help sent his way, but with the kidnapping attempt and our other stuff, we're stretched thin. It may take a day or two. I'd advise him to get the hell out of there, but without cash or his passport, that's just not possible. If we send cash, it will take twenty-four to forty-eight hours before he can get it anyway."

Mitch continued, "Logan, I know this sucks, but you just have to stay put and keep your head down for the next day or so. We'll be there to get you, but we have to plan. If we waltz in there, and Fontaine is involved with Drake, then we could be setting off a chain reaction where the shit will hit the fan all over the globe."

Logan leaned back in the chair and swore silently. He didn't blame his brothers. What Mitch said made sense. He just didn't know how he was going to keep Lacy from leaving. He had to keep her safe and had to find out the truth.

"Logan are you there? You OK?"

Gage's voice snapped him out of his thoughts. "Yeah, it's fine. We can stay here a while. I'll do my best to find out the truth about Lacy and her father. But guys, don't take too long."

"We won't. Promise." Gage said and rang off.

Logan's gut churned. The coffee had turned sour. He wanted to grab Lacy and take the next plane home, but his money and passport were at his original hotel, and there was no way he was going there. By now, Scar had to know where he and Lacy had been staying. It was surely being staked out by someone, probably Hairy.

He took a deep breath and rolled his shoulders. He was in over his head, but he decided then and there, if they got out of this mess alive, he was going to open his own restaurant and Lacy was going to do her party planning business. Life was short, and spending it doing things other than following his dream seemed really stupid at the moment.

He got up off the couch, then walked into his bedroom, making sure to leave the door open so he'd hear Lacy when she got up. They needed to talk. He peeled off his clothes and crawled into bed in his boxers.

His mother's voice echoed in his head as he closed his eyes. *You have to watch out for your brothers.*

No, mom, they have to watch out for me, he thought as he drifted off to sleep.

HE WOKE WITH A START, roused by the sound of a door closing. He leaped out of bed and made a mad dash for the living room. He had told himself Lacy wouldn't try to sneak out without saying good bye, but he wasn't so sure. Rounding the corner, he skidded to a stop when he saw her standing there with a waiter. They both looked at him in shock. The waiter was obviously used to seeing strange things since he recovered quickly and gave him a nod. It took Lacy a moment longer. She handed something to the waiter and showed him out.

"Is everything alright??" When she gave him a once-over, her cheeks turned a becoming shade of pink. He was standing there in his black boxer briefs.

He scratched his neck and then shrugged. "Yeah. I heard the door and I guess I was worried. And half asleep. Not a great combination. Now that I'm up, is that coffee I smell?" He walked toward the table where a pot and two cups were laid out.

"Um, yeah." Her voice was slightly husky to his ears. When he smiled at her, her cheeks turned pink again.

"Your ribs look a bit better and you don't seem to be in as much pain," she said as she walked over to the table and sat.

"It's amazing what good food, sleep, and some ibuprofen can do." He filled both of their cups and handed hers over. His fingers brushed hers, making him aware of her closeness and his lack of clothing. He took a gulp of coffee and choked on it.

"Hot?" she asked innocently.

"A little." He sprawled on the couch. "So, how did you sleep?"

"Like the dead." She smiled, but it faded quickly. "That probably isn't the best analogy right now."

He admired her ass as she rose, and with her coffee cup in hand meandered toward the window. She peered out at the water. The pair of khaki shorts she was wearing fit her perfectly, making her ass look high and round, and his fingers ached to touch. He had to get his brain going in another direction. "What's your plan?" he asked.

She turned around and eyed him speculatively. She smoothed down her hair, an unconscious gesture he now recognized as her attempt to maintain some sort of control. She walked toward him. The white, sleeveless, collared tank she had on stretched across her chest. He had a hard time keeping his gaze on her face. She was so damn sexy.

"I'm going to go into town in a bit," she said. She hesitated for a moment and then said, "Like I said before, there's a certain procedure I have to follow in emergency situations. It was put in place by my father's security team. I have to be at a certain location at a certain time. Then his people will come get me." She took another sip of coffee.

"Not to be harsh, but how do you know your father is still...?"

"Alive?" She completed his thought. "I don't know for sure. I won't know until later. There's a signal that will be given if my father is dead."

He watched her closely, but her face was an expressionless mask. He knew she was expecting him to fight with her about going alone. It's what he wanted to do, but he'd decided he wasn't going to get anywhere doing that. If he agreed to let her go, he could follow her, make sure she made it to safety. The idea of letting her go anywhere alone had his insides tied in knots. He had an overwhelming desire to hold her close. Keep her safe while he could. Hell, he just needed to touch her.

He got up off the couch, moved over to her, took the coffee cup from her hand and put it on the table. "Wha—" His mouth was on hers before she could finish the thought.

She was all fire and ice. Passionate in the courtroom, yet

positively frigid toward him in person. Every time they'd met over different cases, and then with her friend, Alex, he'd admired her intelligence and sharp wit, but her shields had always been up. Nothing personal between them. No acknowledgement that he even existed as a man.

And then when he saw her on the yacht, she was so sexy in that green dress and so vulnerable when she was fighting with Markus. It had been his undoing. Now that he had her in his arms, he was going to enjoy every minute of it.

Her mouth tasted of coffee and strawberries, and more. It tasted like heaven. He'd been waiting so long for this moment. He'd always wanted to kiss her, but hadn't been aware of the deep, driving need she stirred in him. As their tongues danced, he knew he'd never be able to leave her on her own.

He deepened the kiss and pulled her hips to his. He was desperate to feel every inch of her pressed against him. As if she was his drug and he was an addict, he drank in every bit of her.

She wrapped her arms around his neck as he left a trail of kisses across her jaw and down her neck. He found that soft hollow right behind her ear and bit gently. She whispered his name while she fisted his hair. It was enough to push him over the edge. A wave of fierce possession washed over him as he claimed her mouth again in a fiery kiss.

Undoing the buttons on her shirt with one hand, he continued to cup her ass with the other. He didn't want any space between them. When he got to her bra, he pushed the strap down and dipped his head to suck her nipple.

She moaned when his tongue swirled around the hard bud. She stroked her hands from his hair down his chest, then wandered on to his boxer briefs. When she touched the waistband, he took a quick breath. He was throbbing with need.

He bent his head to suck her other nipple and then stopped dead. He gazed into her now open eyes. "Did I do this?" There was a cut on her breast. It wasn't long, but it appeared deep and very sore.

"Ah, the plastic cut me a bit. It's fine now."

He swore.

"Really, Logan, it's fine." She touched his cheek and then sunk her fingers into his hair again and brought his mouth back to hers. He tried to be gentle, but she wouldn't let him. Her mouth was demanding. Her hands ran down his back, pulling him closer.

When she finally touched him through the fabric of his underwear, he groaned. He couldn't help it. He wanted her touch badly, but he knew if she started, he wouldn't have the power to stop her. And he had so many things he wanted to do to her first.

"You need to wait," he said in between kisses and then grabbed her hands.

"But I want to touch you," she said as she strained against his grip.

He dropped her hands and swept her up into his arms. He carried her into his bedroom and laid her softly on the bed. He positioned himself over her and slowly lowered himself. As he kissed her he pushed her top off. After she helped him unhook her bra, he dropped her clothes on the floor.

She was so incredibly beautiful. He lowered his mouth to one nipple and then the other. Slowly, he left a trail of kisses down her stomach to her shorts. After he undid the button, she lifted her hips to help get them off. His breath caught at the sight of the tiny scrap of fabric that served as her underwear. He got harder still, if that was possible, as he ran his fingers across the lace.

When he reached the middle, he let his fingers dip lower.

"Logan," she said, her voice breathy. The sound of his name on her lips drove him into a positively primal state. He curled his fingers around the lace and tugged. It gave very quickly, and he dropped it to the floor.

He sucked her nipple and then moved lower. He hovered his mouth over her. He blew a cool breeze and she whispered his name again, straining her hips to reach him. He dropped a kiss on her core.

"Oh, my God, Logan." Her fingers fisted in his hair as he slid his hands under her hips to bring her to his mouth. He used his tongue to tease and suckle her, taking her to the brink before stopping again.

"Say my name," he demanded, his voice gravel. He'd never felt such a savage need to possess a woman before. She was his.

"Logan," she breathed. "Logan," she said it again. "Logan, please don't stop!" Her words came out as a moan. He smiled as he brought her to the brink once more, his tongue dancing over her sweet spot. He drove his fingers inside her in a steady rhythm, faster and faster until she crashed over the edge, yelling his name as she arched beneath him. He felt incredibly powerful and insanely possessive of her. It didn't make sense, but he was beyond caring. She was amazing and incredible, and she was his.

LACY COULD SCARCELY BREATHE. She'd wanted Logan Callahan since the first moment she'd seen him in the courtroom. One look from him, and she was a quivering wreck. She'd done her damnedest to hide it, but she was sure he'd guessed when she and her best friend had been hiding out at Callahan Security because of the whole Drake fiasco. Being so close to him in the engine room of the ship had driven her to the very edge. She'd wanted to rip his clothes off then.

Now, touching him didn't seem real. His caress was better than she had ever imagined, and she'd imagined a lot. His body was hard and unyielding, and she loved it.

She reached up and ran her hands down over his chest again and then around to his back. She brought his mouth down to hers and claimed it with a harshness she didn't know she possessed. This man drove her to want things in a way she had never thought possible, and she wanted him. Inside her. Now.

Their gazes locked as she reached down to rub him through his black boxer briefs. He swore as her hand stroked him. He was hard as rock. Power surged through her. He was hard for her. She stuck her fingers inside the waist band as he bent down to kiss her neck. She started pushing them off. He lifted his hips and helped her pull them down.

"Wait," he said as he shifted his weight and reached for the bedside table drawer. He reached in and brought out a condom.

Her eyes narrowed. She hadn't thought about condoms, but obviously he had. "Pretty confident, were you?"

He shifted back so he was resting on his side. "No. A box came with the clothes and the toiletries." Taking in her expression he said, "I swear, I didn't plan this. If you want to stop, we stop."

She gazed into his eyes and then pushed off the bed with her left hand while she held him with her right. She had him flipped on his back with her on top. "No chance in hell are we stopping now."

She kissed him hard, her tongue stroking his. She broke off the kiss. "I want to feel you inside me," she purred. His eyes darkened, and he reached for her, but she batted his hands away. "Now it's my turn."

She rained kisses down his jaw and ran her hands across his chest. She sucked on his nipple and then blew on it. She did the same with the other nipple. He groaned. She loved that she had the power to drive him crazy with her touch. It was intoxicating.

She shifted her weight until she was straddling his hips. She slowly rubbed her core across his cock. He flexed against her. His hands reached for her, but she shook her head. "Not yet." She pushed his hands down onto the bed. "I'll let you know when you can touch me."

She grabbed the condom from where it had fallen on the comforter. After ripping the package open with her teeth, she pulled the condom out and threw the package on the floor. Their eyes met as she took Logan's cock in her hand and slowly rolled the condom down. His blue eyes turned indigo.

Her core was hot and wet again. She raised her hips and moved over his cock. She lowered herself down onto him. First, she just let the tip enter her. Teasing him, she pulled back. He swore.

Smiling, she started lowering herself again. This time, she took in more of him. She wanted to tease him longer, but she couldn't handle it. She needed him now.

He reached out and grabbed her hips. She didn't deny him this time. Instead, she rode him, picking up the pace. The feel of him inside her, filling her up, was exquisite.

Her breath puffed out in small, sharp gasps. She was going to come. She said his name and urged him on, her hips rushing to meet his rhythm, her fingernails raking across his chest as he pounded into her. Nothing had ever felt this good, this right. She was teetering on the brink and had to bite her lip to keep from screaming.

He thrust deep inside her, and she crashed over the edge, euphoria filling her every cell. Logan followed her, and her body kept squeezing him as wave after wave washed over her.

She fell on top of his chest, sweaty and out of breath. Neither could move. What they shared was nothing like her experiences with other men. She wanted to feel this good all the time. Bliss settled around her as she clung to Logan. She closed her mind to all the thoughts that were trying to push their way in. She'd just had the best sex of her life. Reality was going to have to wait a bit longer.

CHAPTER TEN

As he stood in the shower, he wondered once again how the hell he had gotten here. His plan had been to come down to the islands for a few days and keep an eye on Lacy. See if she was a corporate spy.

He'd blown it so badly his brothers were going to have his ass. Sleeping with the target was not something a good operative did. Not that he was an operative. Still, even he knew it was a huge mistake. One that he would make again and again at every opportunity. He had it bad for Lacy Carmichael, and he wasn't about to give up the chance to be with her again.

He grabbed the soap and started washing his chest. How was he going to find out if she was involved in the Drake mess now? It wasn't like he could ask her. He could well imagine how that would go. He'd seen her blow up before, and it wasn't pretty. The lawyer who had set her off was mince-meat by the end of her tirade.

Just thinking about her brought a smile to his lips. He loved the way her skin felt, the way she responded to him, and the way she moaned his name. She had gotten under his skin with her beautiful green eyes and her cute smile, her amazing ass and her wickedly smart brain. She was great under pressure, a quick thinker, and a dreamer—just like he was beneath it all. Yes, Lacy Carmichael was the whole package. And now he had to find out if she was part of a deadly conspiracy. Shit. There had to be a way to do it without losing her trust.

As he got out of the shower, he caught sight of his bruises in the mirror. What the hell was he thinking? He had let his dick rule his brain. *She's an assignment, remember, jack ass?* He had been kidnapped, beaten, and was currently being hunted because of her. He'd forgotten all about Scar and the gang. She'd truly addled his brain. *One problem at a time*, he told himself as he toweled off.

Yawning, he padded into the bedroom and eyed the bed. Those few hours of sleep he had gotten earlier just hadn't stretched far enough. He was tempted to crawl into it now, but there was no way he could let Lacy go anywhere by herself.

As soon as he was ready, he went and poured himself some coffee. Ten minutes later, Lacy entered the living room showered and dressed to go out. He had been sitting on the couch, but he got up and poured her a cup of coffee. She took it with a grateful look.

"Would you like a lift into town?" he asked politely.

Startled, she lifted her eyebrows.

He explained. "I had my brother wire me money. It's waiting for me in town. I thought you might like a lift since I'm going that way anyway." He mentally crossed his fingers that it wouldn't click with her that it took longer than a day to get money wired. He hated lying to her, but it wasn't like he could confess he was going to follow her. It was the only excuse he could come up with for going into town.

Lacy eyed him suspiciously. "Uh, sure. A lift would be

great. But once we're there, we have to go our separate ways," she said in a tone that suggested she was ready for a fight on the matter. "I have to take this meeting solo."

"Of course. I have things to do as well. I am concerned about leaving you by yourself, though." Understatement of the century. It was killing him to let her go anywhere without him being immediately beside her, protecting her. He'd promised his brothers he would find out if she was involved in the Drake mess, but she'd never let him go with her, so following her was his only option.

Mitch didn't say it, but Logan was pretty sure that it had been a close call in Europe. His brothers were important to him, more than he'd ever realized. He hated lying to Lacy about anything but if Lacy knew anything about the Drake situation, he needed to know. No matter how much he cared about her.

Stop right there. Don't even think it. He ground his teeth. But it was too late. He knew he cared for Lacy. He'd fallen for her long before this little adventure. His stomach knotted with a hard twist. This trip was pushing his protective streak into overdrive.

Surprise flitted across her face before she managed to school her features. "My father's security team will be meeting me. I'll be fine." Doubt shadowed her eyes but was quickly replaced with determination.

Damn. She wasn't sure about her own safety. He had to turn away from her. He couldn't say what he had to and look at her. She'd know he was lying. He cleared his throat. "OK. I'm sure your father's security team can protect you far better than I can. I wouldn't want to get in the way."

"I totally agree. I feel bad about leaving you like this, but if your brother wired you money, you can get on a plane and get out of here. I'll feel much better once you're out of danger. I feel horrible about getting you caught up in all of this."

He glanced back at her, and the sorrow on her face told him it was true.

Though he knew he needed to find out if she was embroiled in the attempted theft of the prototype, her guilt about his involvement in her kidnapping was gutting him. It was like sharp knives to his conscience.

"No need to feel bad. It all worked out." He managed to choke out the words. "Let me just get my shoes on, and we can leave."

He walked back into his bedroom. As soon as he was out of sight, he steadied himself with a hand on the wall. His whole body was wracked with tension, and his every instinct was screaming at him to stay with her. To ask her the truth and confess to following her. But it wouldn't go well. He had no way to know if she would tell him the truth, and it was damned obvious she was amazingly good at keeping secrets.

He swallowed hard and moved forward. After grabbing his shoes from beside the bed, he turned and went back into the living room. He was feeling shittier by the minute, but he had to play it like it was all good. How did his brothers do it?

She just stood there, eyes slightly narrowed. She smoothed her hair, which was already pulled back in a tight bun. The gesture was her tell. She was nervous.

He wanted to grab her and hold her close, keep her safe, but he just bent to tie his shoes. He glanced at his watch. It was one of the gifts from his mother. He was beyond relieved that it still worked. "We need to get a move on if we're going. The bank will close shortly."

"Of course." Her voice was a bit stilted, but she moved toward the door without pausing. He grabbed the room key and joined her. He opened the door, ushering her through.

She smelled of citrus again. How could he possibly want her this much after having had her less than an hour ago?

Since he had called down for a car, one was waiting for them as soon as they hit the drive of the hotel. He held the door open for Lacy before walking around to the other side. His heart started to pound as the car pulled away. He could feel himself becoming hyper-aware of his surroundings, and anxiety built in his chest, constricting his lungs. Great. Now he was going to have issues taking cabs. Nothing like a little PTSD to make life more interesting. *Shit*.

Glancing over at her, he could tell she was feeling the same way. "It's OK." He wanted to reach over and grab her hand but stopped himself. He had to keep his distance. She was his Achilles' heel, and if he wasn't careful, she would destroy him.

"You didn't check out when we left. Are you going back?" Lacy asked.

"Ah, yes." He wasn't expecting her to ask questions about his plans. "I, er, can't fly out until I get a new passport. Left mine in the safe of the original hotel. I am sure Scar has that staked out," he said in a quiet voice.

"Right. I had forgotten about that."

Logan directed the driver to let them out in front of the bank, and they were deposited at the curb in record time. "So," he said, turning to face her, "this is my stop."

She looked over at him. "I can't apologize enough for everything you've been through. I won't forget everything you've done for me." Her eyes were very serious. It made his heart clench in his chest.

He couldn't help himself. Swallowing hard, he grabbed her hand. "It wasn't all bad." He smiled as he brought her hand up and brushed his lips over her knuckles. "As a matter of fact, I'll remember some of it quite fondly."

Her cheeks turned a delicate shade of pink and her

tongue swept in a lazy circle around her lips. His gaze followed the movement. Cursing silently, he swooped in and claimed her mouth roughly before stepping away. "See you around," he called over his shoulder as he disappeared into the bank.

Taking a few steps inside, he immediately plastered himself against the wall and watched her. It had damn near killed him to walk away from her so casually. He had almost ruined it with the kiss, but he'd managed it. Taking a couple deep breaths, he watched her square her shoulders and walk away.

CHAPTER ELEVEN

Don't cry. Don't cry. Don't cry. Lacy repeated the mantra as she walked away from the bank. She wasn't sure what had just happened. She felt summarily dismissed. Not that she wanted Logan with her. It was far better, safer, for him to head home. So why did she feel like crying?

Exhaustion. She was exhausted and stressed out, and it was playing tricks on her emotions. Once this was all sorted out, she would be able to put this situation in perspective. Sighing, she smoothed her hair back in its bun and headed toward the first marker.

Long ago, when she was just a teen on one of her boarding school vacations in Nassau, her father had created this plan. It was a plan between the two of them. If something happened to him—if he died—the flag at a particular corner store would fly at half-mast.

She'd asked if he'd cooked up the idea with his security team, but he'd said no. They'd created the pick-up plan if she was in trouble, but they knew nothing about the flag.

She guessed that whoever owned the store was a friend or had some sort of inside knowledge, otherwise how would they know to lower the flag? She'd asked him about that as well, but he'd brushed her off. Told her it wasn't important, but she could trust in the flag.

So whenever she was worried about him but unable to contact him directly, she could come and check. She couldn't go in and ask questions—no one inside would know the answers—but always trust the flag.

Walking toward that corner store now, it all sounded so ridiculous, so make-believe, but what choice did she have? She approached from the side of the store, but the flag was out front. She wouldn't know until she rounded the corner.

About ten steps from the corner, her courage waned. What if it was half-mast? She took a deep breath. She would deal with it. She would deal with whatever came, just like her father had taught her.

She turned the corner and slapped a palm on the gritty bricks of the building, her breath coming easier for the first time since she'd left Logan at the bank. The flag was limping along in the slight breeze at full-mast. Saying a silent but fervent prayer of thanks, she walked past the store. A huge weight lifted off her shoulders, making her steps light and springy.

The way she'd felt while walking toward the store, not knowing whether the flag would be up or down... Life was too damn short for this kind of cloak and dagger stuff. She wanted her dad around for her wedding.

Whoa. She wasn't sure where that thought had come from, but she liked the idea of setting roots, having a family. She had a flash of what it would be like to share a place with Logan back in New York. She'd have her event planning business; he'd have his restaurant. Maybe they could even work together on events.

Don't go crazy, she warned herself. Still, there was a bit more pep in her step as she made her way toward the port where the cruise ships were docked. She was looking for her father's head of security—specifically, at the tables on the cruise ship docks where the ladies did hair braiding. Omar would come twice a day at 8 a.m. and 5 p.m. until she made contact. Glancing at the time displayed on one of the store fronts she was passing, she realized she had better get a move on if she wanted to make the 5 p.m. pick up.

A short while later, she mixed in with the cruise crowd and wandered in the direction of the tables. She scanned the crowd but didn't see Omar. She decided to stick with the crowds. She didn't want to stand out just in case Scar or his people were looking for her in the vicinity. She wandered in and out of the little shops, keeping an eye on the tables, but Omar wasn't there.

Something caught her eye. A little chef's hat magnet. It was perfect for Logan. A little something to remind him of his dream that no one else would notice. She noted which stand it was so she could come back later.

There was a group of ladies standing just outside of a shop, having a cool drink. Lacy wandered over and stood a few feet away, as if she'd just come out of the shop, too. One of the ladies noticed her and smiled. She took this as a good sign and started chatting with the group.

She asked them about the cruise and if they were enjoying it. She kept a careful eye on the crowd, but there was no sign of Scar or his gang, and no one was taking any undue interest in her.

The crowd of ladies started to move, and she moved with them. As they approached the tables, she broke away. She was tired, and since no one was interested in her, she decided sitting wouldn't hurt.

Suddenly, a hand grabbed her and hauled her back. She opened her mouth to scream, but a familiar voice said, "I don't think you want to do that."

She whipped her head around.

"Just keep pretending to be part of the crowd. Sitting still makes you too vulnerable and easy to spot."

"Logan, what are you doing here?" she ground out.

"Keeping an eye on you."

She was furious and relieved and happy and sad, all at the same time. "I thought we had an agreement."

"We did, but I decided you were wrong."

Anger won out. She wanted to reach out and strangle him right then and there. "I can take care of myself." She wrenched her arm away from his grip.

"Possibly, but I wasn't willing to take the risk. Also, I'm guessing your father wouldn't be too pleased with me if I left you to your own devices without making sure you're safe. I have no desire to get on his bad side. Now, why don't you fill me in on your plan? You said you were meeting someone here?"

They were approaching the ship, so they would lose the crowd soon. Lacy pushed Logan toward a bench and yanked him down on it. She held his arm tightly forcing him to stay put. She was so angry she could scream. He was acting like a domineering asshole. Maybe she had been right about him all along. Fixing him with a deadly stare, she was about to tell him off when she noticed movement out of the corner of her eye. Omar. He had come to take her to her father, and the whole thing was moot.

Logan was free to go.

Ignoring the sinking feeling in her stomach, she got up from the bench and said, "Look, I appreciate what you're trying to do, but you can go now. My ride is here. I'm safe." She headed back in the direction of the tables where Omar was waiting.

Logan easily caught up with her and slid an arm around her waist, the contact sending a jolt of electricity right down to her center, which immediately tightened. Damn him. She cursed a blue streak in her head as he made her slow down and blend in with the crowd.

"Since everything's going according to plan, why don't you tell me what's supposed to happen?" He tightened the arm that was around her and kept his head on a swivel, his eyes dancing over the crowd. It angered her how it made her feel safer, stronger.

"The guy at the beginning of the pier dressed in jeans and a white shirt. The one with the buzz cut. That's Omar, my father's head of security. He's here to pick me up."

"I see." The muscles jumped in his jaw. He guided her over to one of the stands. "Why don't we just stay here and watch for a couple of minutes? He'll be there for a while."

She wanted to argue, but she was exhausted. She just didn't have any energy to waste on arguing with him. "Fine, I'll stand here and pretend to look at hats and sunglasses for a bit, but it's really not necessary."

He plunked a hat on her head. "I think it is." He smiled at her and then shifted around her so he had a better view.

For twenty minutes, they stayed immersed in the crowd, carefully tucked out of Omar's line of sight. No obvious problems jumped out at her and, apparently, Logan didn't see anything either since he didn't mention it.

The crowds started to thin, meaning that their presence was about to get a whole lot more obvious. "Logan, it's time for me to go. I really do appreciate you coming back to check on me." She hesitated. "Maybe we could grab dinner or something back in the city." When he didn't respond, she continued in a rush. "I totally owe you, so it'll be on me."

"Uh-huh." He wasn't paying attention to anything she was saying.

She narrowed her eyes at him. "I'm going now." She turned on her heel and started to stalk off, but he whirled her around and kissed her. She wanted to resist, but it was too damn good. Finally tearing her lips away, she managed a strangled, "What are you doing?"

"Hiding you." He grabbed her arm and started marching her away from the tables.

"Wait! What do you mean 'hiding' me? I don't need to hide. Omar is right there!" She pointed in the general direction of the tables.

He grabbed her hand and pulled it to his mouth, kissing her knuckles. All the while his teeth were clenched. "Don't point or do anything to draw attention this way," he said. "Just follow my lead and walk quickly."

"But—"

"You can argue with me later. Right now, you need to listen!"

He all but dragged her through the thinning crowd until they reached the line of shops abutting the pier. He practically threw her through the open door of the first one. It was a knick-knack shop full of shells and T-shirts, touristy stuff. Logan pulled Lacy to the window.

The only other customers were an elderly couple inside, and she could hear them arguing about the color and size of a T-shirt for their grandson.

The old man was shaking his head. "He is not going to wear the purple one, Gladys."

Lacy continued to scan the street in front of the shop, mindlessly paying attention to the argument behind her, but wildly aware of Logan's tense body standing so close to her.

"Why not? What's wrong with purple?" The woman lowered the shirt she held to glare at the old gentleman across from her. "I think he would look good in purple."

"Possibly, but since it has a picture of a big stuffed bear with a pink bow around its neck and the words *I can't bear it* on the front, I think he'll pass." The lady quickly turned the

T-shirt around and then returned it to the pile. "Humph. Maybe you're right."

The old man rolled his eyes. "Do you think so?" he mumbled.

"What do you see?" Logan demanded, drawing her attention away from the quarreling couple.

"I am getting pretty damn tired of you manhandling me. So just stop it right now! You are *not* the boss of me." She started toward the door, but Logan dragged her back once more. Her voice was loud enough that the elderly couple had stopped bickering and openly stared at them. Logan gave them a friendly smile and then turned her to face the window again.

"Wha—?" She shot him a dirty look and then peered out the window with exaggerated patience. "Omar's talking to some guy—" She leaned forward and squinted. "What the hell?"

She rubbed her eyes and stared again. It couldn't be. Her heart started slamming in her chest, and all the air hissed out of her lungs. Scar. Scar was standing there talking to Omar. They were in it together. They'd planned it. Markus, the boat, the kidnapping. One of the people her father trusted most in the world was working against him.

"I—I, I can't believe it. I simply can't believe it. Omar and Scar. My father... I—I just can't."

"Calm down," he said. "We need to get out of here so we can figure things out."

She nodded, her breaths still coming in gasps.

He scouted the area. The crowd had dissipated enough they might be noticed if they left the store. He glanced back at the clerk. The store was empty now, too. They couldn't stay here much longer.

"Do you have a back way out of here?" Logan asked the clerk.

The clerk pointed toward the doorway on her left. "Go straight down the hall. The door opens to an alleyway."

"Thanks." Logan said. "You're a life saver."

The clerk nodded as if she did this sort of thing every day. Of course, maybe she did. The Bahamas was a strange place. Logan grabbed her hand and started down the hallway. His hands were hot while hers were cold—colder than they should be considering they were in the tropics. She knew she was in shock, but she was removed from it. The whole world was covered in a thick fog.

"STAY HERE FOR A SEC." Logan went back along the hallway to the front of the store, hoping to borrow the clerk's phone, but Alexey was standing outside with his back to the store window. Logan recognized him immediately. "Shit." He went back down the hallway, grabbed Lacy's hand, and hurried to the back door. He opened it slowly and checked the area. "It's clear. Let's go. We have to find a way to call the hotel, so we can get a ride back."

"Why can't we catch a cab?" She was still somewhat pale, but color was slowly returning to her cheeks. Her hand was getting warmer. He took that as a good sign.

"No money. It won't arrive until tomorrow."

"So you lied to me earlier."

"I—" He hesitated. "Look, now is not the time to explain."

"Fine, but I want the truth soon, Logan."

He looked at her and nodded. She deserved the truth, even if he wasn't sure what the whole truth was at the moment.

He sighed. They were right back where they'd started. He had no clue what to do other than go back to the hotel.

There was no way he was leaving her unprotected again until this mess was sorted. She meant too much to him. That sat heavy in his gut. Daughter of an arms dealer. Possible thief. Did she try and steal the prototype? Was she the one who was behind the attempted kidnapping of Drake that Mitch just mentioned? He had no clue. And he wasn't sure he cared because he was falling for her. He now understood the shit his brother must have gone through before deciding to make a go of it with his thief, or whatever Alex called herself.

He glanced at Lacy. If she had followed her father's plan, she would have met with Omar, and he would have handed her off to Scar. And then she would have been— He stopped himself from going any further down that line of thinking. He just couldn't take it. His hands were shaking as it was.

They reached the end of the alley and turned right, heading away from the water. There were a few people scattered about on the street, but no one he recognized from Scar's crew. They walked quickly, sticking to the growing shadows. The sun was setting, and soon it would be dark. Good in one way, but bad in another.

"Excuse me," he heard Lacy say as he felt her hand slip from his. Turning around, he saw she was addressing a nice-looking middle-aged lady. "May I borrow your cell phone for a minute? Ours was stolen down by the docks and we need to call our hotel." The lady just clutched her bag more tightly, her face twisted in on itself as if she was eating a lemon. "My husband will give you his watch to hold if that will make you feel better. We really just need to get back to our hotel. They stole our wallets too, so we can't catch a cab."

"Well, I guess it would be fine. So sad what the world is coming to." *If you only knew the half of it*, he added silently. The lady shook her head as she handed over her cell. He reached for it and googled the hotel number while Lacy made small talk. Within a minute, he was chatting with a desk clerk, who assured him that a car would be there to pick them up. They arranged a meeting place, and he hung up. As he handed the phone back to the lady, he gave his thanks and Lacy did the same. The older woman was still lamenting the sorry state of the world when they walked away.

"How long?"

"Twenty minutes, give or take. I told them to pick us up a few streets away from the dock. It should be safe enough." There was no point in telling her they were sitting ducks—nowhere in Nassau was safe enough. She undoubtedly knew. A shiver wracked her body, in spite of the heat. He wrapped an arm around her and pulled her close. "We'll get back to the resort and figure out the next step." He said a silent prayer that it would be true.

They started heading toward the bank. When they turned the corner, she made a small squeaking sound. He saw Alexey walking down the sidewalk in their direction. "Shit." He pulled her back around the corner and started speed-walking the way they had come. He turned down the first alley they came to and started to run.

"Do you think he saw us?" she puffed.

"No, but we need to keep moving." They turned left down another passageway and then made right. They came to the mouth of the backstreet and plastered themselves against the wall. He stuck his head out and did a quick search of the street. He saw no one familiar, but he waited a few more seconds anyway.

"I think we're close to the bank. There's another path right behind it. We're going to hide there until the car arrives, OK? I asked them to meet us at the bank, so we have to keep an eye out for the car."

She nodded. "Fine."

"Walk quickly but don't run. We're just tourists with somewhere to be." She nodded again. He grabbed her hand

and they set off down the street together. He kept his head on a tight swivel, looking for any familiar faces, but they appeared to be in the clear. When they arrived at the alley behind the bank a few minutes later, the car wasn't there yet.

She said, "Now what do we do?"

"We wait. It shouldn't be too long. Keep your eyes open for Scar and his friends, just in case."

She ran her hand over her hair and then rubbed her arms. "I still can't believe it. Omar…" Her voice faded out, and she was pale.

He wanted to distract her, but he couldn't come up with anything. She'd been betrayed by someone she trusted. There was nothing he could do about that. Guilt hit him once again. He was doing the same thing to her. At least it felt like that to him. Who knew if she really trusted him? If she was involved in trying to steal the prototype, then telling her he was on to her was like painting a target on his brother's back. He was responsible for Drake's safety. Mitch would be in the line of fire. He just couldn't do that to his brother.

He was so lost in thought, he almost missed the resort car driving by. He waved his arm, and the driver pulled to the curb slightly down the street. When the driver unlocked the vehicle, Logan opened the back door and helped Lacy in. He immediately followed. "Back to the resort, please." The driver just nodded and pulled away from the curb.

As if in silent agreement, they held hands but hunched down in the seat as the car rounded the corner. The windows were darkened, but there was no need to take chances. This afternoon had been too close of a call.

CHAPTER TWELVE

L acy said nothing for the entire ten-minute ride back to the hotel.

Omar had been around for as long as she could remember. He was family. She just couldn't fathom his betrayal. She froze. What if Omar had known about the whole flag thing? Was her father really alive? Or was Omar trying to lull her into a false sense of security? She could barely breathe through the fear clutching at her chest.

After exiting the car, they headed directly up to the room. "Are you OK?" Logan was watching her, concern etched on his face.

"I…I'm just not sure." She sat down heavily on the sofa. "It's so hard for me to imagine that Omar would turn on my father. He's spent Christmases and vacations with us for as long as I can remember. My father never treated him like an employee." She looked at Logan. "Why would he turn on my dad?"

"I don't know." He ran his hand through his hair and walked over to look out at the ocean. "Who knows? Power and money do strange things to people." He turned back to face her and leaned against the window. "I've seen grown men do tremendously stupid things to get an office with two windows instead of one. They go absolutely bat-shit crazy if a corner office is involved." He shook his head. "I knew a guy who had an affair with a VP to get a promotion. Cost him his wife and kids. But he got the corner office and a lot more money. I asked him if it was worth it. You know what he said?"

She shook her head.

"Yes." Logan shrugged. "Power and money mean more to some people than anything else on earth."

She watched him walk toward her. She patted the cushion next to her, and he sat. Turning to him, she said, "I owe you my life. Again." He started to protest, but she put a hand on his chest and stopped him. "No. It's true. If you hadn't followed me, I would have gone with Omar, and I'd probably be dead now. I was being stubborn and stupid, and you saved my ass."

He grinned. "I won't be allowed back at work if something happens to you. Your best friend would take out a hit on me, if not kill me herself."

She choked out a laugh and then leaned back on the sofa. So much for her girl power. Normally she did a damn good job of taking care of herself, but this situation was as far from normal as it got. Things were upside down and backward.

She glanced at Logan. And she'd had good sex—amazing sex—with a guy she bickered with non-stop. The stars were out of whack, or Mercury was in retrograde, or the poles were reversing, or whatever. Things were just not right in the world. Who knew what would happen next. Maybe, Ernie and Bert would announce they'd been secret lovers for years. Actually, that would make sense. They were so totally in love. They should come clean to help generations of kids feel understood.

"What are you thinking about?"

"*Sesame Street.*"

He shot her a worried look and took her hand. "Go have a shower or a bath. I'll order some dinner, and we can figure out what to do next."

She hesitated. "I—" she began.

"You can thank me later." His eyes sparkled, and he winked.

She grinned back at him as she stood. Maybe he was right. A bath might make her feel more human. Plus, her lady parts were tingling at the mere thought of having sex with Logan again. She had to go find her dignity and her willpower somewhere.

HE WATCHED her go and let out a long breath. He'd been tense since he walked away from her at the bank. He still didn't know what the hell he was going to do, but he'd followed his gut, and that was something he wouldn't regret.

He crashed down on the couch, laying his head back on the pillows. It was all just too much. Usually, he had his shit together, but this was totally out of control. Even though he was worried about the Drake situation, he felt one hundred percent better knowing that Lacy was safe. It sickened him to think how close she had come to falling into Scar's hands. She could have been killed.

Swallowing hard, he got up off the couch, went to the bar, and poured himself a stiff Scotch. As the heat from the drink spread down his throat and into his stomach, he felt marginally better. His hands had stopped shaking, and the knot in his gut was slowly loosening. *Lacy is safe.* He kept repeating that to himself.

An hour and two Scotches later, Logan was sprawled on

the couch watching TV when Lacy came back into the living room. She was wearing the fluffy robe and slippers again.

Flopping down across from him, she said, "I see it like this," she immediately started in. "Scar wants my father dead because he wants to take over his business. He wants me dead because everyone knows my father is trying to groom me to take over when he retires. If he just kills my father, I would be a threat to him. So, he takes me to get to my father and then plans to kill us both."

Logan handed her a glass of red wine from the coffee table. He'd poured it for her a while ago figuring she'd want a drink once she got out of her bath.

"The problem with this whole scenario is that if Omar is working for Scar, he really doesn't need me to get to my father. The fact that he doesn't just run out and kill Dad makes me think there is more going on here. What do you think?"

"I keep coming back to that point as well. We're missing something. Remember how Scar talked about his family when we were on the yacht? He said something about how he wanted a world where his wife and family were safe, and his children could grow up not knowing of war. Do you think it's possible that something happened to his family, and he holds you and your father responsible?"

She mulled it over in her big fluffy robe with her hair up. His groin stirred. He was willing to bet she wasn't wearing anything under that robe. He'd almost lost her. A fierce desire to protect her tore through his whole body. But, and it was a big but, she seemed too vulnerable at the moment. She'd just been hit with what he would bet was the biggest betrayal of her life. He wasn't going to take advantage of that. He cared too deeply for her.

She shrugged. "I guess it's possible. It does make sense."

SHE SHIFTED IN HER SEAT. "I tried to call my father," she announced. "I know it might have put us in more danger, but I had to try. What if he doesn't know about Omar?" She braced herself for the yelling that was bound to come. She had known before she picked up the phone that calling her father's compound was stupid.

If Omar or Scar found out somehow, they could easily trace the call, and then their safe haven would be ruined. What if they had cloned her father's phone? She hadn't thought before trying the call. She was more screwed up than she realized.

Logan blinked hard, the muscle in his jaw ticking like a clock. He opened his mouth and closed it again. Finally, he said, "Well, that changes things."

"What do you mean?" she asked, still expecting him to yell at any moment.

"I think our time here is more limited than I would like but"—he shrugged—"it was limited anyway. We can't stay in one spot forever."

"So what do we do now?"

Logan stood up from the couch and moved over to stand in front of her chair. He reached down and pulled her to her feet.

She licked her lips in anticipation. Logan's eyes followed her tongue, sending a little zip of electricity through her. He wound his hand through her hair and was leaning in to kiss her when a knock sounded at the door. He stopped, his lips mere centimeters from hers.

"Now," he growled, "we eat dinner." He let her go and walked around her to answer the door. She stumbled a bit at his sudden departure and reached up to smooth down her hair. Her hand shook, but she wasn't sure if it was from anticipation of being with Logan or because the knock had scared her. She hated to admit it even to herself, but finding out about Omar had shaken her to her core. She was terrified he was going to come through the door at any moment. It made her feel weak, and she hated feeling anything but in control.

Logan let the waiter into the living area and followed him to the table. The waiter whipped out a tablecloth with a flourish and had the table fully set and ready to go in no time. Logan signed the bill and ushered the man out.

She sat down at the table. "What did you order?" She started to lift the lids off the plates.

"Surf and turf. After the day you've had, I thought you could use some serious sustenance." Instead of handing her one of the meals, he took an extra plate and filled it with a bit of everything. Once it was full, he offered it to her. "I want you to eat all of it."

"What am I, two? You don't have to tell me to eat my vegetables," she snarled at him.

He cocked an eyebrow at her.

"Sorry," she sighed. She didn't want to say it out loud but honestly what the hell were they doing having a date *now*? As if being chased by killers wasn't enough, she'd just made a phone call that could lead to them being discovered. They should be…doing what? There was nothing to do but wait at this moment in time. She sighed again. "I guess I'm still a bit on edge."

"Understandable," he replied.

She took the plate and picked up her fork. Silence reigned while they ate. She was so lost in thought that it took her a while to log the fact that Logan had stopped eating.

"Are you finished already?" she asked. His plate was empty, but she still had food on hers. "Wait." She looked back and forth between the two plates. "Did you give me extra?"

"You were busy getting napkins so I made sure you wouldn't go hungry."

"Great. Now I've eaten enough for two people." She immediately put down her fork, suddenly feeling very full. "Why are you over-stuffing me?"

He ignored her question. "Dessert?"

"Are you serious? After everything I just inhaled?"

Logan grinned and winked. "I like a woman with a good appetite." Her stomach did flip-flops. He took the lid off the last plate and arranged it in the middle of the table. "Chocolate brownie with caramel sauce and butterscotch toffee."

The smell hit her nose, and she took a deep breath. "Well, maybe just a taste."

He smiled again and grabbed a fork. "I think I'll join you." He cut off a piece and popped it in his mouth. He moved it around a bit and nodded. "Pretty good."

She picked up her fork, but Logan got to her mouth first. He offered her a piece from his fork, watching her intently. She slowly put her mouth around it and slid it off the fork. She was teasing him, and judging by the expression on his face, he knew it. His eyes darkened as he watched her mouth. She was enjoying toying with him, building the anticipation. They were stuck and she couldn't think of a better way to pass the time. Besides, she needed to release some of the enormous amount of tension she was feeling, and she knew just how she wanted to do it.

Logan cleared his throat and got up abruptly, ending her fantasy. She sighed as she watched him go over to the bar area to pour them both some coffee. His ass looked amazing in his jeans. He'd picked a navy-blue polo shirt to go with them. Whoever had sent up the clothing had done a fabulous job. They picked colors that flattered Logan. She idly wondered if it was a woman and if she knew Logan personally. A flash of jealously made her heart rate speed up, but she quickly dismissed the thought.

The clothing sent up for her was also the correct size and in colors that she would have picked for herself. Cecil, she decided, had a very good eye and a keen sense of style.

"So…" His voice was rough. A small consolation for the lack of sex, but it brought a smile to her face.

He cleared his throat again. "We need to come up with a plan."

By the time he came back to the table, he was back in control. Damn. Too bad. She was having visions of all the things she wanted to do with him. Her imagination was a much happier place to dwell—it meant she could put all her worries and fears on the back burner for the moment.

"Lacy," Logan said, giving her a pointed look.

"Um, yeah." She sighed to herself. "You're right. A plan."

"How many of your father's people know who you are?" he asked, taking a sip of coffee.

"Maybe a half dozen. Dad always pares his staff down to the bare minimum when I'm coming. We usually meet and then take the yacht out so we can speak freely with less prying eyes."

His eyebrows went up. "I thought you staying at the Ocean Beach Resort."

"I was. He didn't want to meet until Monday. He told me not to come to the compound, so I chose Ocean Beach for the weekend. It was odd. He knew I was coming, but he blew me off as soon as I landed." She took a sip of coffee. "Do you think something happened or he suspected something and that's why he waved me off?"

"It's a distinct possibility," Logan agreed. "I think we also have to assume that Markus was working for Omar."

She put her coffee cup back on the table. "I hadn't

thought of that. Honestly, I had forgotten all about Markus. You think he came to the yacht to kidnap me?"

He nodded. "It would have been a lot easier and quieter if you would've gotten in the car with him willingly."

"But why kill Markus?"

Logan shrugged. "Maybe he changed his mind and decided he didn't want to turn against your father. Or, maybe he was killed because he failed to bring you in. I don't know. We won't know until we know the rest of what's going on."

"I refused to go with Markus because my father was very clear about when we'd meet this weekend." She lifted her cup but didn't take a sip. "He knew. My father knew something was up. I'm convinced of it now. I hadn't really stopped to think about it with everything that's gone on, but all the signs are there. He was trying to warn me off, buy himself time to handle it."

"Except he didn't handle it and you ended up in trouble," Logan reminded her.

She couldn't breathe. Her worry about Omar knowing about the flag signal was back, and it hit her like an elephant. "Do you think my father is still alive?" It was barely a whisper.

Logan leaned forward and grabbed her hand. "Yes. He's most definitely still alive. If he were dead, they wouldn't bother with you anymore. I think they want to use you as collateral to make your father do something. Without you, your father won't be forced into it. That's my theory, and it makes sense."

She nodded slowly. She hoped with every fiber of her being he was right. She didn't want to think her father could be dead. Her chest hurt at the mere possibility of losing him.

"Back to your father's staff. So, who are the people that know about you?"

"Well, the yacht captain. The chef. Reggie, who helps

with security. Omar, the head of security and Aziz, one of Omar's guys. Oh, and Petra, the housekeeper, or yacht keeper, I guess it would be. That's the usual crew. Just enough people to run the yacht. Like I said, everyone knows I exist, but my identity has been a secret for a long time. To the outside world, I'm just another one of Armand's lawyers.

"I didn't spend much time with my dad growing up, just holidays. I was at boarding school. Omar would come and get me, then hide me until I met with Daddy somewhere very private. Other times, I would be brought to some shop or museum, and Daddy would be there in some secret room. We would chat, catch up, have a snack, and then he would be gone again. Christmas was our special time, though. He would get me to pick a port city, and he would anchor the yacht there. We would spend a few days exploring and enjoying each other's company.

"Once I graduated from law school and passed the bar, I was offered a job at my firm. It was corporate law, but I liked criminal better, so I learned both. Don't get to do much criminal work, but I volunteer at a legal aid clinic a couple times a month to keep up my skills."

"You're what, twenty-six?" he asked.

"Twenty-eight."

"Still. That's a lot of experience in a limited amount of time."

She sighed loudly this time. It was the same question she always got. "Look, I fast-tracked everything. Did a four-year degree in three years. Took extra classes every semester. Did the same in law school. I graduated a semester early, and then I basically didn't sleep for a few years.

"Besides, look who's talking! What are you, thirty-two? You were the head of the legal team for your big Wall Street firm. Isn't that a bit unlikely?" She raised her chin and looked him in the eye.

He shrugged. "Looks like we're both overachievers." He poured more coffee and settled back in his chair. "Does anyone else know of your existence?"

"My existence? Yes. Do they know I'm Armand Fontaine's daughter? No." She shook her head.

"No one?"

"Well..." She paused. *How much do I tell him?* "I mean Alex knows, of course. There are a couple of friends of my father that know."

"I was thinking more locally. Is there anyone locally who might be able to help us? Your father isn't reachable, and I think we might need some help. My brothers should be here in the next couple of days. Not to put too fine a point on it, but we don't have a lot of time. We need to find another place to hide until help arrives and we can get off this island."

"I can't leave without my father. I can't leave him to those men." She was shaking her head.

"Lacy, we don't even know for sure what his situation is. I am sure he wouldn't want you to stay. It would be better to get you to safety and then figure things out."

He was using his *I'm trying to be reasonable but you're not helping* voice. She'd heard it many times when they were on opposite sides during a negotiation, and it pissed her off to no end. She shot out of her chair. "No! There is no way I am leaving this island without finding my dad. I won't abandon him!"

He stood up. "We may not have a choice."

"What do you mean by that?" she snapped.

He walked over to her and put his hands on her arms. "Lacy—" he started.

She took a step back, moving out of his reach, and narrowed her eyes at him.

"Think about it."

She could hear the frustration creeping into his voice.

"There's no doubt they knew you were staying at the Ocean Beach Resort originally that's why we can't go back there. There are only so many resorts other resorts in this island chain. Scar and Omar will be asking around on most of the islands. They will eventually stumble upon us. It's bound to happen."

"They think we died in the storm."

"Doubtful. Omar was waiting for you today. If they really thought you were dead, they wouldn't have bothered."

"So? They don't know for sure. There's no reason to think they'll find us here."

"Except we pulled up on the beach in a kayak, both of us dressed in wilted party clothes. We had no luggage and no cash and had to buy clothes from the hotel. Not exactly low key. The room might be listed under my old firm's name, but it won't take them much research to figure things out." He shook his head. "Realistically? We shouldn't even stay here tonight, but we have no cash and I don't want to spend a night on the streets unless we have no choice."

It was true, all of it. The weight of their situation pressed down on her. She turned and walked toward the windows and then, paranoid that people could see her, turned back. "There is one person." She hesitated. "I've always suspected he knows, but I don't have any proof. He might be able to help us." She paused and took a breath. "Peter Trenthom."

"The detective from the yacht?" he asked. She nodded.

"I thought you wanted to avoid him the other night. What makes you think he'll want to help?"

She shrugged. "Just a gut feeling, I guess. He would occasionally drop by to see my father while I was here in Nassau. My father would never vary from the story that I was one of his minions, but I always had a feeling that Trenthom knew it wasn't true."

"But I thought you said he was a local cop? Why would he drop in on your father?"

"He's *supposed* to be a cop. He would come to harass my father. Try to intimidate him or something. Let him know they were watching. The thing is, it was like both him and my dad would make a big production of his visits. He would pretend to inspect and threaten. My father would pretend to be upset and annoyed." She shrugged again. "I think—" She bit her lip. "I think the whole thing was a sham. That they were somehow working together." She scrutinized Logan. Did she share her thoughts? What choice did she have?

"I know it sounds crazy, but I think Trenthom is actually CIA, not a detective—or at least not *just* a detective. I'm pretty sure he's my dad's contact."

Shock registered on Logan's face and then confusion soon followed. His eyes narrowed. "Let me get this straight. You think your father works for the CIA?"

"No. Not works *for*, exactly. My father works *with* the CIA. Think about it. If you were the CIA, wouldn't you want close relations with one of the top arms dealers in the world? Not only would you always have access to untraceable equipment, but you could also influence which groups were sold what weaponry. Could make a big difference in the war on terror."

CHAPTER THIRTEEN

Logan sat heavily on the couch. His mind was racing. If Lacy was right, it opened up a whole new can of worms. "So, your father works *with* the CIA on certain things?"

She nodded.

"You think Trenthom knows you're Armand's daughter." He was sorting through things in his head. "Why? Why would Armand tell Trenthom that? Why were you trying to avoid him on the yacht?"

Lacy shook her head. "I don't know why my father would tell him. Maybe to protect me? Or maybe Trenthom found out somehow. He is CIA. I think.

"Before Markus was murdered, he was acting strangely. Then we argued. No matter who Trenthom actually works for, he would have to take me to the station eventually. Any time anything like that happens, there is always a risk of exposure. I'd rather the world didn't know my real identity just yet." She grimaced.

"So, Trenthom goes around pretending to be a local police detective, but you think he's really CIA. You think he might help us because if he's CIA and your father is working with him, he won't want to risk losing such an important asset. That's your theory," Logan said.

She shrugged and then nodded. As she paced back and forth in her fluffy robe in front of him, he cursed his brother once again. This was so not his jam. He did courtrooms and boardrooms. Guns and henchmen were way outside his comfort zone. And now he might get involved with the CIA. Oh and he still hadn't figured out if Lacy is a corporate spy. *Shit. How did things go so wrong?*

Why couldn't he have fallen for a kindergarten teacher or a librarian? Someone safe and normal, someone that the CIA wouldn't dream of being interested in? His brain froze for a second. Every time that thought came, it was a shock, but it was starting to come easier. His respect for his brother Mitch grew. Mitch had told him that he didn't get to pick who he fell for, but he'd been doubtful. Now he understood.

"You know where we can find Trenthom?" he asked.

She nodded. "I have a pretty good idea."

"Why don't you get dressed. I've got to go do a couple things downstairs and then we'll go see him. The sooner we get help, the better our chances."

"Alright," she said and headed into her bedroom.

The friggin' CIA. He hated the CIA. He ground his teeth as memory after memory assaulted his brain. He had tangled with the CIA back when he was with the JAG Corps, and he had gotten badly burned. So much so, in fact, those experiences were the reason he'd left the Navy. The CIA was only out for the CIA, and if they helped you, it was because it directly benefited them or it was incidental to what they needed. No way this guy would help them unless it benefited him personally, but what choice did they have?

A few minutes later, Logan headed down to the lobby.

"Cecil," he called softly from across the lobby. Cecil turned, saw him approaching, and smiled.

"Mr. Callahan, how are you?"

He leaned closer. "Cecil, I need a huge favor."

"Of course, Mr. Callahan. What can I do for you?" Cecil's face remained neutral.

"Cecil, I need money. I can't get any until tomorrow. I lost my wallet and ID." He gauged the reaction, but apparently, Cecil was used to this sort of request.

"I'm sorry to hear that, sir. Did you lose it on the property? Can I call security for you?"

"No. No, Cecil. What I need you to do is give me some money."

Now Cecil's face changed ever so slightly. Surprise flitted across and then disappeared. "Ah, well sir I, ah—"

"Let me explain. I want to buy something and charge it to the room, but I was hoping you could charge me for more than it costs and give me the extra money in cash. Not all of it, of course," he said, winking. "The charges will be paid, I promise."

Cecil's face closed up once more. "Sir, I, um, how much money are we talking about?"

"I need a few thousand dollars."

Cecil's eyebrows shot up.

"I know it's a big favor, Cecil, but it's very necessary."

Cecil swallowed, and after a moment's hesitation said, "Wait here a moment." He disappeared through a door into what was presumably a back room. A minute later he returned and nodded. "Come with me." There was a hint of a smile on Cecil's face.

Logan knew it was a go. He followed Cecil down the main walkway of the resort before they came to a stop in front of a jewelry store. Cecil said, "Wait here, please."

"Sure." Once again, he wondered where he'd gone so wrong

that a little light stealing from his former company presented no moral dilemma. It wasn't that he wouldn't make good on the money. What was more startling was to realize it didn't bother him in the slightest to do it. He was becoming more like his brothers every day, and he wasn't sure it was a good thing.

Cecil greeted a tall young woman dressed in a white blouse and navy skirt who stood behind the counter. He said a few things that made her smile, then leaned forward and whispered in her ear. She nodded once. He whispered some more. She nodded again, and then Cecil glanced back at Logan and motioned for him to come in.

When he walked through the door, Cecil said, "Pick out something nice for your lady friend." Buying Lacy something wasn't what he'd been thinking when he came downstairs, but the idea appealed to him greatly. He scanned the display case, discarding the things he didn't think Lacy would like or things that wouldn't do her justice.

After a few minutes, he found the perfect gift—a set of emerald earrings. Shaped like tear drops, they were designed to hang off the ear. Tiny diamonds surrounded the central stone, making the earrings sparkle in the light. The deep green color of the gem reminded him of Lacy's eyes.

He nodded to Cecil, and the young woman came over. Logan completed the purchase, and the sales girl went off to wrap the earrings. Logan thanked Cecil and gave him a rather large tip. Two minutes later, he walked away carrying a wad of cash and some very nice emerald earrings. Doubt crept into his mind. Maybe buying Lacy earrings wasn't such a great idea. He barely knew her, and she was a master at keeping secrets. Based on their current situation, it was hard to say if they were going to make it out alive, let alone manage to go on a real date. So what in God's name was he doing with these emerald earrings in his pocket?

He was walking toward the elevator when he spotted a couple men he recognized from the night he and Lacy were grabbed. With as much stealth as possible, he slipped behind the enormous flower display on a table near the wall. He peeked around a flower half the size of his head and watched as the men showed a piece of paper to the two women at the front desk. Both shook their heads.

"Shit," he mumbled. Two ladies walking by eyed him and gave him a wide berth. He circled back behind the table and tried to come up with a plan. The men were between him and the elevators, so he couldn't get in one without being seen. His gaze landed on the stairs. He could run down a level and grab one of the elevators there, but it would be just his luck if it stopped on this level and the men were waiting to get on.

He peeked around the tree again. They were talking to Cecil, who was shaking his head no, bless him. "Thank you, Cecil," he muttered. *Have to tip him more next time.* He watched as the men headed over to the concierge desk. Movement caught his eye. Cecil was staring straight at him, gesturing toward the sign for the stairwell. He felt his shoulders droop. The suite was on the twenty-first floor, but he really didn't have a choice. He made the dash to the stairwell and went inside. It was a long way up, but he didn't waste any time.

When he finally reached their floor, he took a few seconds to catch his breath. *More time at the gym,* he promised himself. *If* they got out of this. He opened the door a crack and, seeing no one, slid out into the hallway. He walked into the suite and stopped short. Lacy was standing there in jeans and a white tank top. She was wearing wedge sandals and her hair was curling around her shoulders. The recent time in the sun had really brought out the blond highlights in her chestnut hair and the freckles on her nose. She was gorgeous.

"Hey," she said. "Ready to go?"

"Um, yeah, about that. Scar's henchmen are in the building."

"Oh, my God. Now what?" She grabbed his sleeve. "We need to get out of here." She was already heading for the door, which he'd closed behind him, when the phone rang. He gestured for her to wait, then picked up the phone. "Yes?" he said in a neutral tone.

"Mr. Callahan, you have some unwanted visitors on their way up."

"Thanks, Cecil. I owe you one." He put down the phone and gazed absently at her. While he didn't want to take the stairs again after the endless run up, at least it would be easier to go down.

"What?" she asked.

"They're on their way up. Let's go for the stairs. I know where they are."

He moved across the room past her and checked through the peephole in the door. "The hallway is clear. Let's go." He opened the door and started toward the stairwell. When they were adjacent to the elevators, Logan heard a faint ding. The elevator had arrived at the floor below theirs. He grabbed Lacy's hand and started running. They hit the door to the stairwell at full speed and started down.

Lacy took the lead. *Definitely need more time at the gym*, Logan repeated to himself, trying to keep up with her. She moved quickly and efficiently. And while he was gasping for air, he couldn't help but admire her ass. A grin split his face. It was official, he was losing it.

It took forever, but they finally hit the lobby floor. Lacy's hand was on the knob to enter the lobby when he stopped her. There was another flight down. "Let's go," he huffed as he took her hand.

They headed down the last flight and came out into a sort of parking garage. It was half under the building. One wall was open to the night sky. The other three had a few doors scattered about but no windows. The hotel was built into a hill. That was helpful. Now they only had one direction they had to watch. Of course, they only had one way to exit as well. There were all kinds of vehicles parked. Cars, SUVs, even golf carts.

"Now what?" Lacy asked.

"Now we go over there," he said as he pointed to the open section of the garage, "and try to hail a cab."

CHAPTER FOURTEEN

"Do you think the coast is clear?"

"I'm guessing it is. The guys I saw were a two-man team, but it's possible more of Scar's men are lurking around. Let's just keep our eyes open," Logan said as he stood on the sidewalk.

She watched him search for a cab but come up empty. She hated standing outside on the sidewalk like this. She was exposed. Any minute Scar's men could find them, and then it would be all over. "Do you have any idea where we can find Trenthom?" Logan asked.

"So, being that it's Sunday, my guess is that Trenthom will be at his golf club, which is on the other side of the island, for family night."

"Trenthom's married?" Logan asked surprised. "I never thought of CIA agents as the marrying kind."

"Best cover ever. Who would think a nice, married detective with two kids would actually be a CIA operative?" She shrugged.

"I don't even know if 'operative' is the correct word. Maybe 'handler' would be a better term? Anyway, Sunday night is a de facto family night here, so there's a good chance he's at his club. I know which one he frequents because he and my dad used to bicker about it. Trenthom's club isn't a true country club, more of a family club with lots of stuff for the kids. A lot of locals belong to it. He and my father argue about who has better food. Anyway, he should be there tonight. If I'm wrong, they'll at least have his address on file.

"We'll figure it out," Logan said, "but first let's find a cab." He grabbed her hand and walked back toward the resort.

Lacy stopped. "Wait! Where are you going?" It had taken them forever to get out of the garage and off the property without being seen. Why was he heading back?

"We aren't having any luck here. We need to go back to the cab stand."

"But what about the guys that are after us? We spent all this time trying to get away from them. I don't want to go back and run into them." She pulled her hand from Logan's.

"We don't have much of a choice. We'll be careful. And if Scar's guys find us, we'll raise holy hell so everyone comes running."

It didn't sound like much of a plan to her, but she had to agree they weren't having any luck otherwise. "Fine, but be very careful."

Logan nodded and grabbed her hand again. They made their way through the paths around the property to the cab stand. They quickly hailed a cab and set out for the country club.

Logan hadn't explained his sudden source of money, but she'd decided to let it go for now. She tried to relax, but all the cab rides they'd taken lately had been fraught with danger.

He must have sensed her trepidation because he linked his fingers with hers and held her hand for the whole ride. It was silly how much comfort she took from that small gesture, but this was a moment she wanted to remember. God only knew what the next few days were going to bring.

They exited the cab and walked up the steps of the club house. Logan asked, "What's our play?"

She shrugged. "Play it by ear. See what happens."

"That's the plan? I thought you were organized."

She shrugged again, suddenly feeling exhausted. By now, Trenthom had no doubt heard that Markus had had a fight with a woman on the yacht. He was a very good detective by all accounts, and she would be surprised if he didn't know that woman was her. So, how hard could it be to find him if he was already looking for her? She walked across the lobby to the woman at the dining area podium. "Hi."

"Hello. How can I help you?" The woman had given them the once over, and her tone made it clear she knew they weren't members.

"We are here to see Detective Trenthom." She used her official court room tone, and it got the desired results. The woman behind the podium immediately reassessed them. She could tell the hostess had written them off as tourists who were looking for a place to dine, but her direct request had recast them as Trenthom's professional colleagues.

"Let me check." The woman ran her eyes down the page. "Yes, he's here. Would you like me to take you to him?"

"It would be better if you could just tell him we're here. We'll wait over there." She pointed to a couple of formal-looking Chesterfields sofas in the foyer.

"Of course." The woman nodded. "Who should I say is here?"

She paused for a second and glanced at Logan before returning her gaze to the waiting woman. "Tell him Hazel Fontaine is here to see him."

His jaw clenched. "Was that wise?" he asked as soon as

the woman was out of earshot. "What if Trenthom doesn't know you are Fontaine's daughter?"

"Honestly, I don't care. It was going to come out eventually. Might as well be today. Besides, now he'll come for sure and not just call some of his cronies to question me about Markus's murder. He'll listen to us and hear our story."

"It's a hell of a gamble." His eyes narrowed when she shrugged.

"I'm tired of running and hiding, Logan."

They stood in front of the Chesterfields for about three minutes before the woman and Trenthom came around the corner. He was wearing dress pants and a purple linen shirt. His dark eyes showed no surprise when he saw her. His only movement was running his hand over his bald head. So, he already knew. Now she was sure of it.

He walked over to them. "Mr. Callahan, Ms. Carmichael. Good to see you." He hadn't blinked an eye while saying her assumed name, and he knew Logan's name. She was starting to feel more confident in asking him for help. "Won't you step this way, please?" He led the way down a hallway and then opened a door on the left. After gesturing them both inside, he closed the door behind them.

It was a small conference room, a table and some chairs with one small window at the end. Trenthom gestured for them to sit, and once they were all seated—him on one side of the table, them on the other—he stared at them silently for a minute. "So, you're alive," he finally said. "We weren't sure. We found a cab all shot up. The driver is alive, by the way."

"Good to know." Logan's voice was cool.

Trenthom leaned back and studied both of them. "Why are you alive?"

"Good question," she responded. "Not really sure. When they shot up the cab, I thought they were going to kill us, but apparently they wanted us alive because they kidnapped us instead."

"I have a theory," Logan said quietly. She turned to look at him. He hadn't mentioned this theory to her. "I think there was some confusion about what they were supposed to do. When Scar arrived on the scene, he stopped the shooting. I don't think they were supposed to shoot so much. Just enough to make it look good. They got a bit carried away. Scar wanted her alive."

"Scar?" Trenthom cocked an eyebrow.

"The man that kidnapped us. We don't know his real name," she said. "He has a big scar on his face."

Logan, glancing at her, continued his thought. "They kept me alive so they could threaten me to control her."

Trenthom nodded. "What about Markus, Ms. Carmichael? I know the two of you argued on the yacht. How did he end up dead?"

"He wanted me to go with him. I told him I wasn't going to the house until Monday." She stopped and took a breath. "I think he was plan A. He'd flipped to Scar, and he was supposed to bring me to him. When that didn't work, they killed him. A show of force and cleaning up loose ends, all in one shot." *Oh, my God, did I really just make a pun?* "I didn't mean to be flippant."

Trenthom nodded. "Stress does interesting things to people. So, what now? Why are you here? If you were kidnapped, why not go to the station to report it?"

She took a deep breath. *This was it, the moment of truth.*

"You know why. You know who I really am." She took a deep breath. "I think you're my father's CIA contact. He told me that he works with someone from time to time. I'm pretty sure it's you." She stared at him, willing him to give her some indication that she was right. She could feel Logan tense beside her. If they were wrong, if Trenthom was just a local cop, or if he worked with Omar…well, she didn't want to think about it.

Trenthom shifted in his chair and studied them both. "Say you are correct. Say I am your father's contact."

She let out the breath she was holding.

"Why come see me?"

She leaned back in her chair. "They want my father dead, but obviously I'm part of their plan. Maybe they want to use me as leverage to make him do something first. I need your help to get word to him that his own people are plotting against him. I need your help to get him out safely."

"Why would I help you? If I am, as you say, his CIA contact, helping you would likely expose me."

She narrowed her eyes. "You have a relationship with my father that affects what happens all over the globe. As fabulous as I'm sure you are, that relationship is important. The CIA would be willing to sacrifice your cover if it means maintaining the ability to direct arms wherever you want them around the world."

Trenthom smiled. "You are very much like your father. Pragmatic. And yes, you are correct. The relationship between your father and my people is important, but of course I'm not willing to admit *which* people. I do like to think t I am a big part of that work, but you are also correct in assuming it would be continued without me." Trenthom got up and went to the end of the room. He retrieved bottles of water from a small mini fridge that she hadn't noticed. He offered one to each of them and they both accepted.

At his seat, he asked, "So, what do you know?"

"Not much," Logan replied. "We know that Scar and his guys want Lacy, presumably to use against her father. We don't know for sure that Armand is still alive, but it wouldn't make sense if he were dead."

"He is alive," Trenthom stated matter-of-factly.

She almost burst into tears, the relief was so acute.

Logan leaned over and squeezed her hand under the table. "We aren't sure if Scar is the top guy or if he works for someone else, but I'm inclined to think he is the top guy. And we are pretty sure that at the end of this, they'll kill both Lacy and her father."

Trenthom nodded. "I agree with you on that. There's no way they plan to keep them alive."

She inhaled sharply.

"So, you just want to get to your father and warn him of the plot?" Trenthom asked. "And you want my help in case it all goes south. Does that sum it up?"

She nodded. "I have to let him know he's in trouble if he isn't already aware. And now that I know some of the people from his inner circle have been compromised, I don't know how to do that without getting taken again, or worse. I need your help."

Trenthom studied them for a minute and then nodded once. "Scar, as you call him, is Viktor Voloshyn. He is a leader of a pro-Russian rebel group in the Ukraine. When it comes down to it, he's more of a warlord. Comes from the Debaltseve area." Trenthom took another sip of water and then continued, "Are you aware of the civil war that broke out in the Ukraine in 2014?"

"I am familiar with it," she said, nodding. "It's important to be aware of this type of thing, given my father's career choice."

Logan nodded as well. "Slightly."

"Good. Voloshyn and his people received backing from the Russians until the original Minsk Protocol was signed in September of 2014. Following the agreement, there were some more flare-ups, and the warlords took control of different pieces of land in and around Debaltseve, which meant everyone had to come back to the table to sign Minsk

II. After the signing of the document, the Russians ended their support—they could no longer actively supply guns and equipment to the insurgents.

"We don't know for sure, but our assumption is Voloshyn tried to buy from your father. I have no idea what happened after that. We weren't involved in this deal, although we would have loved to know about it. Your father is good at keeping secrets, even from me."

She reached for the bottle of water, hoping the water would help her swallow.

"So," Logan started, "do you think Voloshyn is after equipment?" He reached under the table and squeezed her hand again.

"No. There's got to be more to it, but we're not sure what. My people are digging around now to see if we can come up an explanation for what's going on, but our intel is spotty."

Lacy finally found her voice. "But why would any of my father's people support Voloshyn?"

Trenthom shrugged. "Money."

"What else?" she asked.

"We think Omar is helping because he plans to take over once your father is gone."

She opened her mouth to protest, but Trenthom cut her off. "Think about it. He knows the players and the ins and outs of the business. Your father's customers trust him. All he has to do was wait for the right time. Your father always has a skeleton crew around him when you come home for a visit. It's the perfect time for your father to get toppled. Then Omar can tell the world he warned your father of the dangers of short staffing, but he didn't listen, and the two of you paid the price."

At her swift intake of breath, he nodded. "Yes, you need to die, too. Otherwise you'll be a threat to his claim on the family business. He'll probably make sure to get hurt in the battle just to sell it. It's a dangerous world your father lives in. Omar can totally pull this off."

Logan shifted in his seat. His hand was still gripping Lacy's under the table. "And the CIA doesn't give a shit because they can work with whoever has the connections, right?"

Trenthom turned his palms up and nodded his head. "The CIA would prefer to keep your father in the position he occupies currently, but working with someone new is not out of the question."

"So what do we do?" she asked with trepidation. "Are you going to help us?"

"I like your father, and I don't like Voloshyn. I am not a huge fan of Omar at the moment either." He tapped the table with his fingers for a second. Then nodded again. "This is what we're going to do. There's a shack on a private beach. I'll take you two there. You should be safe enough. I'll make some calls, and when I get back, we can work out a plan."

"That sounds good, but it'll just be me," she insisted, giving Logan's hand a squeeze before releasing it. "He's not coming," she said, pointing to Logan with her free hand. He opened his mouth to speak, but she cut him off. "Logan has been through enough because of me."

Trenthom looked at him for confirmation, but before any could be delivered, the door opened. "Mr. Trenthom? There is another gentleman here to see you," said the girl from the front desk. Her professionalism didn't conceal her obvious curiosity. It couldn't be usual for him to have this many visitors at the club.

"Did he give you a name?" Trenthom asked.

"Omar Nazaryan."

Lacy gaped at Trenthom. Oh shit. Had they made a mistake? Was Trenthom in on this whole thing? Logan touched her shoulder. She turned to him, and he gave a small shake of his head.

"Tell him I'll be right there, Michelle."

She nodded and closed the door.

Trenthom turned back to them. "I have no idea what this is about, but I doubt it's good. I want you two to stay here a moment." He got up to leave and turned back. "Just be prepared to run if this doesn't go well."

"WHAT DO YOU THINK?" she asked as soon as Trenthom closed the door behind him.

"We should do as the man suggested and get ready to run."

He got up and hit the lights, then walked over to the window. There was a good view of the parking lot, and he could see Alexey and two of his cronies waiting by an SUV. He opened the window, hoping he might be able to hear what they were saying, and then moved back so he couldn't be seen.

"Doesn't look like they're here for us. Maybe they're just here to see what Trenthom knows. As head of the investigation into Markus's death and your disappearance, he'd be the man to ask. What's interesting to me is, where is your father? Why isn't he here demanding to see Trenthom?"

"My father wouldn't ever demand to see Trenthom. He has people in the police department who tell him what's going on. You have to remember that outsiders see me as another one of my father's employees. No matter how concerned he is personally about my disappearance, he can't ask around about me."

He watched her for a minute before looking back out the window. "This is really hard on you." His hands clenched into fists. Here she was making excuses for her father after everything he'd put her through, intentional or not. He had to take a deep breath and grind his teeth to keep from telling her what he thought of Armand. The man was an ass. What kind of father treated his daughter like an employee in the name of protecting her? If he really wanted to protect her, he would keep her the hell away from his arms dealing business. Hell, if he really loved her, he wouldn't *be* an arms dealer in the first place.

He kept watch out of the window until he had something to report. "Omar is back by the SUV with Trenthom," he whispered. They both fell silent, waiting, listening, but they could only hear a few mumbled words now and then.

Finally, Omar threw down his cigarette and ground it out with his boot heel. He must have said something to Trenthom because Trenthom nodded and proffered his hand. Omar shook it before getting into the SUV and driving off.

Logan savored her sigh of relief. She came up to stand behind him, close enough that he could feel the heat of her body. Electricity danced across his skin whenever she was close. It made it hard for him to concentrate. Made other things hard, too.

The door opened, and Trenthom stood outlined in the light. "You two, come with me now." He turned and walked away. Logan took her hand once more, and they followed Trenthom out to the parking lot. He kept his eyes open. He wasn't completely convinced that Omar and his friends were gone.

Trenthom climbed into a sedan and gestured for them to follow. Logan got in the front seat. He wanted access to Trenthom just in case he tried anything. He made sure Lacy was in the back, as far from Trenthom as possible.

They left the parking lot and headed back the way they

had come. "Where are we going?" Lacy asked from the back seat.

"That shack I was telling you about."

"But Logan needs to leave," she insisted. "Can we drop him off at the police station or somewhere safe first?"

Logan started to protest, but Trenthom beat him to it. "Unfortunately, there's no way that can happen." Trenthom's statement was blunt and a bit of a shock, not that Logan disagreed with it, but he tensed in the front seat, ready to fight Trenthom if he whipped out a gun.

"Omar is looking for both of you. The assumption is that you two are a couple. If we drop Logan off now, they'll just find him and take him again." He glanced at Logan. "No offense, but I don't think you're really set up to fight them off."

"I've held my own so far," he challenged.

Trenthom glanced at him. "Yes, you have, but I have a feeling they're more desperate at this point. We need to keep you both alive. I think going your separate ways will make things harder."

He could see Trenthom's point. He'd already decided it was too dangerous for them to go back to their original hotel to get their passports. He could go back to the company suite and try to wait it out, but chances were good they'd circle back around looking for him sooner rather than later. Besides, he didn't trust Trenthom enough to leave Lacy with him.

"So, what's the plan?" he asked quietly as he looked out the window. They were passing a small town. It had a few shops and a restaurant right on the highway.

"Like I said, I'll drop you two off at the shack and make some calls. Miss Carmichael, you need to start thinking about the best way to reach your father and get the news to him."

"Can't you pay him a visit and manage to get the message across?" she asked. "Don't you have a way of contacting one another?"

Trenthom shifted his gaze to the rearview mirror. "Omar knows we are in contact and have a mutually beneficial relationship. I'm not sure I can get word to Fontaine without him knowing."

Something clicked in Logan's head. "Wait, if Omar knows about your relationship with Fontaine, then he has to know how valuable Fontaine is to you. He approached you, didn't he? It would only make sense he'd want to maintain the same deal with the CIA. He wouldn't want the CIA to get nervous. You could stop him or take him out."

Logan turned in his seat, preparing to tackle Trenthom.

"Is that true?" Lacy asked from the backseat. "Did you already know he was planning on killing me and my father?"

Trenthom hesitated. "Yes and no," he finally answered. "Omar approached me about possibly taking over Fontaine's business. I didn't know whether Fontaine had decided to retire. He's been making noises about it for a while, especially in light of his health issues. Yes"—he glanced in the rearview mirror at Lacy—"I know about your father's diabetes. Not a death sentence, but he does have to be much more careful.

"Omar didn't elaborate on how he was going to take over. You have to understand that from the CIA's perspective, it doesn't really matter who it is as long as the relationship is maintained."

"You son-of-a-bitch," she hissed. She started to move forward in her seat.

Logan's hands curled into fists. He turned so he could see her over the back of the seat and shook his head slightly. His hatred of the CIA was proven once again. He didn't trust Trenthom as far as he could throw him, but he couldn't let Lacy get hurt. She needed to be calm and not do anything stupid. They were in a moving car, and currently the only thing he could see were trees and inky darkness.

"Wait. Hear me out," Trenthom demanded. "I said that was true from the CIA's perspective. I think Omar is a loose cannon and a hell of a lot more unstable. He'll be very difficult to control.

"Your father is a reasonable man. Even when he does what he wants instead of what we ask, he always has a good reason. And nine times out of ten, it works out for the best. Your father is very smart and very cautious. I pointed all this out to my superiors. They agreed to wait it out and see what happens.

"I told Omar that we would not support a takeover. But privately my bosses insisted I not fight him on it either. I don't know if Omar has a mole on the inside, or if he simply realized we weren't going to fight. Either way, he decided to move ahead with his plan. He didn't tell me about Voloshyn, though, which is not surprising. He was smart enough to know we wouldn't be pleased."

Logan wasn't sure he believed what he was hearing. It might be close to the truth, but he was sure there was some spin on it to make Trenthom appear like a good guy. CIA agents were rarely good guys as far as he was concerned.

Trenthom turned off the main road onto a dirt lane that was full of potholes. "Voloshyn has some pretty nasty friends, so it's not in our best interest to arm him and his people." He looked at her again in the mirror. "Your father has always known the risks. He knows exactly where he stands with us —and with everyone else for that matter. He is definitely an asset, one we'd like to keep, but he knows he's not irreplaceable.

"I honestly tried to get a meeting so I could give Armand a heads up." Trenthom paused for a moment as he navigated a large pothole that ran the width of the road. "I know you don't believe me, but I consider your father a friend. We have helped each other out of a jam or two over the years, and I certainly don't want to see him killed.

"We were supposed to meet on Friday, but it never happened. Your father canceled. I don't know why. I'd like to think your father already knows what's going on, but I really have no way of knowing for sure."

Lacy said, "I arrived on Friday, and he wouldn't see me either. He told me to come Monday and not before."

All this information was making Logan's brain hurt, and each time they rolled over a pothole, his ribs ached. It was hard to know what was real and what was a lie. The CIA excelled at lying. He did believe Trenthom about one thing —Armand Fontaine was a smart man. It was a safe bet he had known what was going on well before it started, which explained why he wouldn't let Lacy come on Friday and why he canceled the meeting with Trenthom.

Trenthom said, "What I do know is this; apparently, your father's health has deteriorated. Rumor has it he's been in bed for the last week or so. His doctor comes and goes, but nobody knows much about the situation beyond that he doesn't want to be disturbed.

"It's hard to tell if it's just a setup. Omar plays his role of right-hand man to a tee. When he asked about you tonight, it was with great concern. Went on about how he wants you to see your father since he is so sick. That has been his angle with me. He hasn't admitted to being in the middle of a coup."

"You think Omar is waiting to see what happens?" Logan asked. "If Fontaine has a lot of friends out there, then it would be better for him if Fontaine dies of natural causes… Or at least if it's perceived that way." He glanced back at Lacy. He couldn't see her face, but he knew she was suffering.

"That's certainly what I am hoping for. It'll give Armand

more time to work out whatever he's planning." He looked again at Lacy in the mirror. "I really don't think your father's ill. I think Armand has put some kind of plan in play, but for the life of me, I don't know what it is, and I have no idea how to find out. I've tried calling, but he doesn't answer. I've even tried to talk to Armand's doctor, but he was called out of town rather suddenly after his last visit with your father. I have no idea where he went, but he's no longer on the islands."

They pulled off the dirt road onto a very narrow unpaved track that was only slightly wider than the car. The trees were surprisingly thick here, and the headlights barely pierced the darkness. Suddenly, a building appeared out of the trees.

Shack was a good word for it. It was hard to tell because of the lack of moon, but the building appeared crooked. Like a good wind could knock it down. To say it was a downgrade from where they'd been staying was a huge understatement.

Logan climbed out of the car and circled around to help Lacy. He took her hand and led her in the direction Trenthom had disappeared. He still wasn't sure about Trenthom, however given their options, they had no choice but to trust him.

A light went on in the shack as he approached the door. He opened it cautiously, revealing a place that was as ramshackle inside as it was out. There was a cot against the right wall, and on the opposite one there was a kitchen area equipped with a tiny stove, a small fridge, a sink, and a water cooler. Between the cot and the kitchen area stood an old wooden table and four mismatched wooden chairs. There was one door on the back wall that presumably led to a bathroom, and that was it.

Trenthom was leaning against the stove. "It's not much, but you'll be safe here. No one knows about it, and it's not easy to find." He turned around and pulled a box off one of the shelves.

Logan couldn't see what Trenthom was doing. He tensed up in case Trenthom was about to try something, but when Trenthom turned around, he handed Logan a burner phone.

"I'll call you on this once I have a better idea of what your next step should be. There is some food in the fridge, and there's water. Extra blankets are in the cabinet in the bathroom. I should be in touch in a few hours." He reached back and removed a gun from his pants.

Logan jumped in front of Lacy, but Trenthom just smiled.

"Here. Just in case." He moved around Logan and handed it to Lacy. She automatically checked the clip, sighted it, and then gave him a nod.

Way to go asshole. Nothing like being jumpy. No wonder Trenthom gave the gun to Lacy. Logan had no reason to be surprised she was familiar with guns. Hell, he'd seen her with one at the house where they'd squatted, but it still seemed wrong somehow. Not that he didn't want her to know how to handle herself, just that he didn't want her to *have* to handle herself that way. Another thing he would like to take up with her father.

Trenthom gave them a wave and disappeared out the door. Logan heard the car start, and then the sound of the engine faded away. Lacy still had the gun in her hand.

CHAPTER FIFTEEN

"Well," she started as Logan walked around the shack, "I guess I owe you yet another apology. I really wanted you to walk away from my mess. Hopefully, we can get this sorted in short order. You can go back to your life, and I can go back to mine."

Fat chance. He sighed. There was no going back for him. He knew he wasn't going to be able to forget her just like that.

Somewhere between the hotel and the club, he had realized he wasn't going to leave Lacy with Trenthom. Or with anyone. He could dress it up and say it was because he still had to find out the truth about Drake. He could tell himself he was staying because it was the right thing to do. But he knew the truth.

He was falling in love with Lacy Carmichael.

She had been talking for a while now, and he had no idea what she was saying. He had been so busy thinking about her, he had failed to listen to her. Not good. But he couldn't help himself. He was scared for her. Scared of losing her.

He walked over to her, cupped her head, and captured

her mouth with his. Pulling her against him, he deepened the kiss. And he didn't stop kissing her until the icy fingers that had closed over his heart when Omar showed up had melted away.

When he finally pulled back, he gazed deep into her beautiful green eyes. "It will be fine. Everything will be OK." She nodded a little breathlessly. He hugged her close and breathed in the smell of her, that unique citrusy fragrance that heightened all his senses. If only he could hold her this close constantly, protecting her from everyone who wished to hurt her.

He let her go more abruptly than he'd intended. He needed to get his head on straight if they were going to figure this out. And that wouldn't happen if they started taking each other's clothes off.

"I'll go get some extra blankets. It's a bit damp." He walked into the bathroom and took a deep breath. He stared into the mirror and knew he didn't have a choice. "You can do this." He needed to keep it together even if it was only long enough to make sure Lacy was safe. "Focus," he said aloud and then headed into the main room with the blankets he had found in the cupboard.

"I'm going to make up the cot. Why don't you see if there's any tea?" Logan started spreading out the blankets.

"Tea? I didn't know you liked tea."

"Sometimes." *Like now when I need time to get my shit together.* He sighed as wrestled with the blankets, listening to her bustle around the kitchen. Within minutes, they were both finished with their tasks, so they sat down at the table to drink their tea and plan.

"TRENTHOM THINKS your father is still at the house. What's the best way to reach him?" Logan asked.

She took a sip of tea and stared at the far wall. She was trying to figure out a plan. "I think the best way forward is to pretend we don't know about Omar. I walk straight up to the gate like I would at any other time and go in. I can apologize if I caused any distress. I can tell them someone killed Markus, then some man tried to kidnap me, and I didn't know who to trust. It's the truth. I should be able to see my father. No matter who is behind all of this, Omar is not going to immediately shoot me. He's going to pretend everything is normal at first. We'll just have to make sure that we have a way for my dad and I to escape."

"And me," Logan reminded her. "Don't forget I'm going with you. You're not going alone." She scowled at him but he continued, "There is nothing you can say to change my mind on that. You are not walking into that trap without backup." His voice was gruff, and there was steel in his gaze.

"Fine." She gave in. Truthfully, she was glad he was going to be beside her. She was scared. "We'll say we spent the weekend together recovering from the kidnapping. It will seem more real to them that I didn't seek Omar out if we were together. They just have to believe we're really into each other."

His voice was soft. "That shouldn't be too hard."

Heat rushed up her cheeks. She cleared her throat. "So"—her voice sounded odd so she cleared her throat again—"how do we get my father out?"

"I don't know. Maybe figure out a way to get to the airport?"

"The fastest way off the island is by water."

"Good point." He nodded. "So airport is a second choice."

"The thing is," she clarified, "my father has his own jet. I think if he could have left that way, he already would have. Maybe he couldn't make the arrangements to fly out without Omar knowing." She took a breath. "We should assume my father knows his people have turned on him. I think he's faking the extent of his illness to buy himself time and privacy." She took a sip of tea.

"We could insist on taking your father to the hospital." Logan leaned forward in his chair, warming to the idea. "Once we're on the road, we can have Trenthom's officers take us all in for questioning about Markus's death. Armand can insist he has to come along. Omar knows you're his daughter so that would seem normal to him. If he wants to have a cover story, Armand can make noise about how he's already lost one employee and doesn't trust Trenthom. And I have to go as your lawyer. Omar can't shoot at the cops unless he wants to be hunted down by every law enforcement officer in the Bahamas.

Logan stood up and got the teapot. He refilled his cup and offered more to Lacy. She shook her head.

"Once Trenthom's people get us away from Omar, I'm sure we can come up with a way off the island," Logan said as he put the teapot back on the stove. He sat back down. Maybe your father or Trenthom will come up with something. Your dad can round up Omar and his pals later." He tried to gauge her reception to his idea.

When she didn't say anything, he continued, "Might work, but we'll have to take Omar with us. There's no way he'll leave us alone once we're all together. I think there's a good chance he'll go for it. It would be the perfect opportunity for him to arrange for his friends to ambush us."

She tapped her finger on the table. "For not having much experience in the workings of the underworld, you're pretty good." He was better than good. If Logan Callahan ever decided to go rogue, he'd be a smashing success. It didn't surprise her in the least. He was the best at everything he did.

"Thanks. I think."

"You know, we do have a bullet-proof ambulance at the house."

He paused, his mouth gaping open. "Why do you have —" He stopped. "You know, I don't think I want to know the answer to that question."

She smiled. "Once my father realized his health issues were somewhat serious, he bought the ambulance. The thing that worries me is if Voloshyn wants revenge, he must already have some sort of plan to exact it."

"I'm inclined to agree," said a voice from behind them. Logan jumped up and placed himself in front of Lacy.

"Relax. It's just me." Trenthom opened the screen door and walked in. "Sorry to sneak up on you, but I thought it was better to leave the car back on the dirt road than drive it down the path again. I don't want to bring attention to you two being here." He was wearing dark pants and a dark shirt. With no moonlight, it would have been very difficult to see him outside. "I agree with what you were saying. I think there is a plan in place. Whatever it is, they want both you and your father alive for it." He leaned against the door jamb. .

Logan relaxed and sat back down. "We were trying to figure out the best way to approach tomorrow." He glanced at her and then said, "We think it would work if we go up to the gate like Lacy normally would. Pretend to have no clue that Omar is involved. Do a whole song and dance about being kidnapped."

Lacy piped up, "I can tell them that I thought the kidnappers were disgruntled would-be customers. They grabbed me to get my father to give them whatever arms they were trying to buy."

"Omar will ask why you didn't come to him sooner," Trenthom pointed out.

"We tell him the truth. We were hiding out from the kidnappers. We did go to town to meet Omar, but we saw the kidnappers. There was no way to get to Omar without alerting them, so we went back into hiding."

"That works," Trenthom said. "So, that should get you in, but how do you plan on getting out with your father?"

Lacy swallowed some cold tea and grimaced. "We're going to insist on taking Dad to the hospital. We thought you and your police officers could intercept us on the road under the guise of taking us in for questioning about Markus's death. Omar won't like it, but he isn't going to try and stop the local cops from taking us in. We might need further help, though, to keep Omar distracted and get us off the island. We thought maybe your CIA people could help. I'm sure my father will want to deal with Omar in his own way at a different time, from a safer location."

"I see." Trenthom looked back and forth between them. "It could work. The officers will follow my lead so that's not a problem, but let me check about getting help with Omar and getting you all off the island. See what my contacts have to say. I'll let you know first thing in the morning."

"Lacy, if I could have a few words with you…" Trenthom folded his arms across his chest and glanced at Logan.

"Sure," she said and then stared pointedly at Logan.

"No problem. I've gotta call my brothers anyway." He got up and went outside.

Trenthom dropped his arms and leaned back against the stove. "You know, I've been keeping tabs on you for a while now. You are a very impressive young woman. Smart, quick-thinking, good under pressure, and you have backbone. Balls, if you will pardon the expression."

She had the distinct feeling he was buttering her up.

What was he playing at? "I'm smart enough to recognize you're blowing smoke up my ass, so why don't you just come out with it?" She leaned forward and put on her best court-room face.

"I said before I think your father is faking the extent of his illness, but he is ill. He needs to retire and take better care of himself."

She nodded. "Agreed."

"That would leave a large power vacuum in the arms-dealing world. It could"—he paused—"destabilize things. My bosses and I would like to avoid that. It would create too many difficult situations across the world."

"I'm sure you'll figure something out." Where was he going with this? She had an uneasy feeling in her stomach. Something told her she didn't want to hear what he was about to say.

"We already have."

Trenthom's stare said volumes. She knew what was coming.

"We want you to take over your father's business."

She tried to school her features, but she knew Trenthom had caught the dread that had flitted across her face.

"We need someone like your father to step into his shoes. Someone who will listen to reason and weigh all the available information before making any decisions on selling the weaponry. Someone who understands the bigger picture and isn't just in it for the money. Someone who will not be corrupted by power. Yes, we could go with Omar, but Omar is not that person. *You* are that person."

"What makes you so sure?" She was puzzled and strangely flattered at the same time.

"As I said, we have been watching you for a while. As Fontaine's daughter, you are obviously a person of interest. But you distinguished yourself right away by exceling at school and then at your first law firm. You seem to have slowed down a bit at this new firm. Perhaps law isn't your thing?" he asked and watched her for her reaction. She was determined to keep a calm face this time. No need to tell him he was correct.

Trenthom continued. "You're similar to your father, but you have your mother's quickness of thought. Your father is sometimes a wee bit too methodical for our taste."

"In other words, you think you can influence me into making quicker decisions."

"As I said, you are very smart. And the added bonus is that many of the people who matter in your father's world consider you the natural choice. They have worked with you when you set up delivery of their orders, so they know you and trust you. Some are aware you are his daughter. It would make the transition much smoother."

"Well," she said as she stood up, "I hate to disappoint, but I think I'll pass on the job offer. Although I enjoy logistics, selling arms is not my life-long dream. I mean, just look at the problems it's currently causing, not to mention the fact that my mother died because of it. So, no, I'm not interested. I'm sure you'll find someone suitable for the position after my father retires." She turned to walk outside. She needed to see Logan.

"I don't think you understand."

His words stopped her in her tracks.

"I'm not offering you the position. I'm telling you that you have to take it."

"You cannot force me to take over my father's business. I'm not interested," she said in an icy tone, turning back to face him.

"Oh, but I can. Do you want to get your father out of this situation? Do you want him to live a long, healthy life after he does retire? Do you want to get yourself and Logan out safely?"

Her jaw dropped open.

"If you don't agree to take over," Trenthom continued, "you'll be forcing us to go with Omar. Which means you'll walk in there tomorrow without any backup and no way out. I will find out what contingency plans your father has in place and make sure they don't happen. I have people working on it right now."

"You wouldn't," she hissed as she took several steps toward Trenthom. "You—you said my father was your friend."

"I said it because it's true, but it is more important to have a sane, reasonable person in charge of the major arms deals that occur across the globe than it is to have a friend."

"You mean someone you can control." Her knees were weak. She felt for the table, stepped back and sat heavily in her chair.

"Yes. You're starting to see the whole picture. Your father gets to retire and take care of his health while you run the business, consulting him as needed, but mostly doing our bidding. It's a win-win. He's been training you to take over anyway. Your father mentioned as much to me. This Omar-Voloshyn situation just sped the plan up a bit."

"But...but it wasn't carved in stone. Now you're telling me I don't have a choice."

"I'm telling you the position you have been groomed for has just become available. Take it so you, your father, and Mr. Callahan can live long and prosper."

CHAPTER SIXTEEN

The door opened, and Logan walked back into the room. He looked back and forth between Trenthom to Lacy. "Is everything OK?"

"Yes. Fine." Lacy tried to flatten out her already smooth chestnut hair.

Her tell. She was lying. He knew it as sure as he was standing there. Trenthom's face gave nothing away.

"I'll be on my way," Trenthom said as he stood up. "Get some sleep, both of you. I'll be back at dawn so we can go over our final plan." He made his way to the door. "Be safe," he said, "and think about what I said." Then he was gone.

"What did he mean by that?" Logan asked. Judging by the look on Lacy's face, Trenthom was talking about her, and she didn't like it.

"He suggested my father should retire. I told him I agreed. He has some ideas about how to make that happen."

Whatever those ideas were, Lacy didn't like it. There was a lot more to the story. She wouldn't even meet his gaze. The knots in Logan's gut tightened. Surprises made him nervous.

This situation was untenable to him. He wanted to grill her, but he knew her well enough by now to know she wasn't going to say anything she didn't want to. Pressuring her would just piss her off. He sighed.

"He's right. We should get some sleep." Logan glanced at the flimsy cot—smaller than a twin bed. "You sleep there. I'll move the kitchen chairs around a bit and use them."

"Don't be ridiculous. We've been sleeping together for the last few nights. We'll both sleep on the cot."

"Actually, we haven't," he said. He was having trouble keeping his voice normal.

"We haven't what?" she asked.

"Slept together. We've done a lot of other things together, but we haven't slept."

Her cheeks went pink. She cleared her throat. "Well, then tonight will be the first time." She turned her back and pulled off her white tank. Then she shimmied out of her pants and crawled under the blankets on the cot in just her bra and matching thong.

Her control was enviable. Logan sure as hell didn't have it. He took his time getting undressed. He tried to marshal his thoughts to anything except the woman lying on the cot in front of him.

After thirty seconds, Logan knew two things. One, he wasn't going to get much sleep, and two, he was going to be hard as a rock all night. He put the heels of his palms on his eyes and tried to block out the images of Lacy naked from his mind. He went through the conversation he had with his brother again.

Gage said Drake's programmer was being followed and someone made a grab for her, or at least she thought someone tried to kidnap her. *How does that work?* Logan wasn't sure how that was possible but after this little adventure he wasn't ruling anything out. That meant Gage had to get over to Europe ASAP.

He told Logan he would send a couple of the guys down tomorrow to help Logan and Lacy stay safe and figure a way off the island, but when Gage asked Logan where he wanted the guys or what he wanted them to do, Logan had no answers other than obtain new passports for him and Lacy. He added her father to the list, but he knew that would prove difficult. He wasn't even sure what country's passport her father held.

Logan had no idea what was going to happen tomorrow, but the feeling of dread was so intense, he was having trouble breathing. He didn't trust Trenthom. The CIA never did anybody any favors without a reason, and often their favors turned to shit. He'd seen it often enough in the navy.

He must have made some sound because suddenly he was aware that Lacy was awake beside him, watching him.

"WHAT ARE YOU THINKING ABOUT?" She rolled over to face Logan, who was lying on his back.

"Nothing. Go back to sleep."

"Liar. Your whole body is tense, and you're grinding your teeth. Are you worried about tomorrow? Logan, you don't have to go with me."

He rolled onto his side to face her. "I'm not letting you go by yourself, so get that out of your head."

She wanted to weep when she gazed into those beautiful blue eyes. What the hell had she done? It was bad enough she was in this mess, but she had dragged Logan in with her. If she had just gone with Markus in the first place, Logan would be safe and sound in New York right now. Of course, she'd probably be dead, but there was a distinct possibility that would happen anyway. At least he would've been out of harm's way. And she wouldn't be in love with him at the worst possible time in her life.

She had fallen for him the first time she'd seen him, but that had been lust. Now, it was different. It was real, not just a hot fantasy. She had hoped that after all this was over, they could go back to New York and try to build a real relationship. Go on dates like normal couples. Help each other pursue their dreams.

But that was no longer in the cards. Trenthom had made it perfectly clear that if she didn't agree to take over the family business, he would essentially let Voloshyn kill them. And if she tried to back out later, she didn't doubt for one second he would have her father killed. Hell, he might even do it himself, friend or not.

Maybe Logan could work with her? He certainly had a knack for it, and it wouldn't take her long to bring him up to speed. There was no doubt he was a quick study. She mentally pictured them side by side, flying around the world, making deals.

Then reality crashed her dreams. There was no way he was going to want to be with her once she took over her father's business. It was a miserable life with no break from fear. Body guards always around, no time to just be. It was a prison, a gilded one, but still a prison. She wouldn't do that to him. She could barely make herself do it, and she had to take on the job to save her father.

There was no future for them because her future had already been written for her without her input. The tears were building behind her eyes, but she tried to blink them back.

"Hey! Please don't cry. None of this is your fault." He

gathered her up in his arms, and she clung to him in desperation. "Look"—he pulled back and wiped her tears—"I'm
here because I want to be here. There is nowhere on earth I'd
rather be right now than here with you. And Lacy, we are
going to be fine. I need you to believe that."

She stared at him as he stroked her cheek with his fingers.
Needing to touch him, she put her arms around his neck and
buried her face against his chest. Desire was building from
her core, but her heart was also breaking.

He claimed her lips in a swift kiss that he quickly deepened. God, he tasted so good. So right. She tangled her
hands in his thick wavy hair and kissed him like she'd never
kissed a man before. She poured her soul into that kiss. She
wanted him to know what she was feeling. She wanted him
to feel it, feel her love.

He broke off the kiss and started to say something, but
she claimed his mouth again in a bruising kiss. Words weren't
what she wanted or needed at the moment. She needed him
inside of her. And she wanted it now. She rolled over onto
her back and brought him on top of her. She moved her
hands down over his shoulders to his back. She explored
every ridge, every ripple of muscle, trying to memorize him
so she could re-live this moment again and again. If this was
their last moment together, she wanted to sear it into her
memory.

He sucked, nibbled, and stroked her tongue with his,
eliciting moans of pleasure from her. His hands were on her
breasts, first through the fabric, rubbing her nipples, and
then his hands snaked behind her back and had her bra off in
seconds. The cool air puckered her nipples. She shivered in
anticipation.

He lowered his head to one nipple and sucked while his
fingers played with the other. He ran his knuckles over the

bud, making her growl. He kissed his way to the other nipple and ghosted his hand lower across her belly and dipped inside her thong. He slid a finger inside her wetness. She almost came right there. Her hips bucked forward, and she moaned.

She reached for him, pushing his underwear down over his hips. He withdrew his fingers and then shifted his weight to help her. She took his cock in her hand and stroked it.

He groaned his pleasure at her touch. "You're so hot and wet. I want to be inside you."

She shifted her legs so they were wrapped around him and he groaned again as his cock wedged against her wetness. She moved her hips so she slipped up and down the length of him.

"You've got to stop that," he said his voice rumbling out of his chest. "I don't have a condom."

"I'm clean and on the pill. If you're clean—"

"I am," he growled. He slid down her body until his mouth was level with her core. He put his mouth over her clit and sucked hard. She twisted her fingers into the blankets and balled them into fists. She pushed her hips up so her core was against his mouth. He teased her with his fingers and his tongue. He took her to the brink and then stopped.

She fisted her hands in his hair and pulled him back up her body. Groaning, he claimed her mouth in a fierce kiss and moved his hips so his cock rubbed against her wetness. She lifted her hips. "Now, Logan. I need you inside me now."

He entered her slowly. She bit her lip at the exquisite pressure his cock caused. She lifted her legs higher on his back, urging him deeper. He obliged, filling her up and then withdrawing and doing it again. She moved her hips to speed up his rhythm. She wanted it primal and pounding. Logan increased his pace. Sweat broke out across her whole body.

She needed this, needed him. "Faster. Harder," she demanded.

The pressure was too much; she was losing her grip. She bit her lip, trying to hold on, but the orgasm overtook her. Euphoria filled her limbs as she fell into oblivion.

CHAPTER SEVENTEEN

Lacy lay on Logan's chest. Her heart rate was just coming down from the stratosphere. Sex with Logan was unlike anything else she'd ever experienced. She tightened her arms around him. She didn't want to give him up.

"We should get some sleep. Dawn will be here soon," Logan said and then yawned.

She didn't want to think about it.

Logan pulled back from her so he could see her face. "I have something for you."

She swallowed. "What do you mean? Like a gift?" she asked, totally puzzled.

He nodded and eased her from his chest. He sat up and reached for his jeans. He stuck his hand into his pocket, bringing out a small box.

A small *jewelry* box.

"I made a deal with Cecil to get some money since I thought we may need some cash to escape. I bought something and charged a bit more to the room. Cecil got his cut, I got us some cash, and you, you got a present."

She smiled and sat up. "And here I was just thinking what a stand-up guy you are. Trustworthy and honest."

He grinned back. "I was a stand-up guy before I met you. Now, maybe not so much. You're a bad influence."

Her smile faltered.

"Hey, I'm teasing you. I promise I'll pay the company back for it. You don't have to worry."

"I know you will." Her throat was clogged with emotion, so it came out as a whisper.

She took the box from him. She opened it slowly since her hands were shaking. All at once, the world spun. She found it hard to breathe.

The earrings were gorgeous. Drop emeralds surrounded by tiny diamonds. Her eyes filled with unshed tears. They were exactly right. Perfect for her. Her heart exploded into a million tiny pieces in her chest.

She loved Logan, but she couldn't have him. Being with her would mean he couldn't have his restaurant, his dream. It would mean he would constantly be in danger. She could not let him do that. It would destroy her. Her belly twisted and lurched—she wanted to scream and cry and rage at the world. But she knew, with her heart smashed to bits, it was time to do the right thing.

She had to set him free.

"Oh, Logan."

He was smiling at her.

"Logan, these are beautiful."

He opened his mouth to say something, but she cut him off with a hand motion. She took a deep breath. "I need to make something clear to you. We've been having...an adventure, but every adventure has to come to an end." The words were coming out of her mouth, but her heart, her soul, was screaming at her to stop talking.

His face registered hurt, but the emotions passed with

little more than a flicker before his face lost all expression. He got up off the cot and pulled on his jeans before he moved across the room.

"I'm sorry if I gave you the wrong impression. I really am." Her mouth was suddenly as dry as the Sahara, and she was having difficulty speaking. "I can't thank you enough for all you've done, but I've decided to work for my father full time when this is over. There is no future for us." Her heart physically hurt in her chest.

He turned and faced her. "What about your dream? You said you wanted to be an event planner," he demanded, his voice full of outrage. You're willing to let that go without a fight? You're going to let someone else decide your future for you?"

She saw her dreams disintegrating. The images of parties she wanted to plan, Pinterest boards she wanted to create, joy she wanted to bring…all turned to dust. Blinking hard to stop her tears, she knew she didn't get to have Logan or her dreams. But she got to save her father, and that had to be worth it.

"It's just that, a dream. My life has been planned out for a long time, and as much as I have enjoyed our time together, it doesn't change anything." Physical pain roared through her body. She put the box down and tried to surreptitiously twist her hands in the sheets so she wouldn't cry out.

"I see," Logan paced across the confined space. "You've decided this is the life you want? Being shot at and kidnapped, running from crazed zealots? An adventure, isn't that the word you used?"

The heat of his anger scorched her from across the room. His eyes were icy blue as they radiated hurt and hatred toward her.

NO! I want a life with you! Every fiber of her being

screamed at her to tell the truth, but Lacy bit her tongue to hold the words back. The taste of blood filled her mouth.

"While we're on the subject of crazed zealots, why don't you tell me who's behind the whole Drake debacle?" Logan snarled.

"What? Drake? What are you talking about?" *What the hell?* She's dying, and he wants to talk about Drake? What did Drake have to do with anything?

"You wrote a coded email mentioning Drake and the prototype when you were at our offices. Who did you tell about it? Who hired you? Was spying on your best friend always part of the plan, or was that a happy accident?"

His words kicked her in the chest like taking a hit in a Taekwondo class. "You read my emails? You *promised* me complete security and privacy if I stayed at your office!" Rage rolled through Lacy's veins. She grabbed the blanket and struggled to wrap it around herself as she got up off the cot.

"Yeah, well, turns out I wasn't the only one who lied. What was in the email?" he demanded. "Why are you in the Bahamas?"

"I don't have to answer that," she spat. *No way in hell was that any of his business.*

"Actually, yes you do. It's why I'm here in the first place. I came to Nassau to follow you and find out how involved you are in this mess, and I'll be damned if I'm leaving here without an answer after all I've been through," he growled as he moved toward her.

She stood her ground as best she could, holding the blanket to her. *She would not cry.* Logan was here to *follow* her? *She was his job?* Her knees threatened to give out. Bile rose in her throat. Humiliation and rage vied for control over her tongue. Rage won. She would not give him the satisfaction.

"I would never betray Alex's trust like that. Not ever. I

would've thought you'd know that by now. Why would I want Drake's prototype?"

"You're an arms dealer. Drake's prototype would be worth millions to your clients. So," he goaded her, "are you a corporate spy, too? Are you involved in trying to steal the prototype?"

"My *father* is an arms dealer. *I* am a lawyer. And, no, I'm not a spy."

"Why should I believe you?"

"I don't give a shit if you believe me. I'm telling you the truth. I wrote an email to my father to ask for his help with it. I thought he could ask a few people and see if he could find out who's behind it."

"Sure. And it didn't occur to you once that your father could make a lot of money if he had the prototype himself?"

"No, it didn't!" She was yelling now. "I came down here to see my father because I missed him and he's sick and I just wanted to spend some father-daughter time before I had to work on the logistics of the next deal with him. Someone took some shots at us in the park, and I wanted to see my father. Is that OK in your world?"

"You'll have to forgive me if I don't believe you. Hell, I thought you— It doesn't matter what I thought. Clearly, I was wrong." His voice was ice. He turned on his heel and slammed out the door.

She hated the fact that she'd lost control and yelled while Logan became calmer and colder with every word. She lost control and he seemed to find it. She sat down hard on the cot. Did he really think she could betray her best friend like that? She couldn't believe it. That he would think that way about her. Her eyes stung and tears overflowed, slipping down her cheeks. *Where had it all gone so wrong?*

She got up and clutching the blanket tight, she went into the bathroom. She threw cold water on her face. Standing upright, she studied herself in the small mirror. Her face was red, but at least her eyes didn't look puffy. It wouldn't be good if Logan could tell she had been crying. She wouldn't give him the satisfaction.

"Get your shit together, girl." There'd be time for grief later. When she walked out that door, they were going to her father's house. They were going to rescue him, and life would go back to normal.

Well, not normal. A new normal. She rolled her shoulders. She was stronger than this. Crying was for other people. In the past, she had always managed to keep it together in tough situations. *That was before Logan*, a little voice reminded her. And wasn't that the truth? The tears threatened again.

Enough. She straightened her shoulders and walked out of the bathroom.

Logan was back from where ever he'd run off to. He looked at her with narrowed eyes but said nothing.

The door opened and Trenthom walked in. "Ready?"

Lacy nodded, but Logan just walked out the door. Trenthom raised an eyebrow in question to her, but she ignored it and followed Logan out. It was none of his business what was going on with her and Logan.

Trenthom's cell rang as they climbed into the car. After a few monosyllabic responses, Trenthom hung up.

"Voloshyn's guys, Alexey and Vladimir, finally gave up on the stakeout at your hotel and tossed your former company's suite. They already did the same at your first hotel, and I understand Voloshyn has people waiting at the airport."

A muscle ticked on Logan's jaw, but he merely nodded. She absently noted that Vladimir must be Hairy.

"So, are we ready?" Trenthom asked.

They both nodded.

"Let's review this one more time." Trenthom glanced at Lacy in the rearview mirror.

Lacy sighed and repeated the plan back to him.

"Right. We'll get all of you to safety and then my associates at the CIA will grab Voloshyn and Omar. They have some questions about things that happened in the Ukraine." Trenthom sent her a quick look. *We'll get you out as long as you hold up your part of the deal.*

Message received.

Barely a minute had passed when Trenthom pulled to the side of the road. He turned and hooked an arm over the back of the passenger seat. "Look, I know you can do this."

She nodded. Whether he meant today or taking over her father's business, she wasn't sure, but it didn't really matter either way.

"We'll be in position when you leave the compound for the hospital," Trenthom said. "You do your part, and I'll do mine."

Lacy nodded. The deal was struck. She would take over her father's business, and Trenthom would help her. She also knew he would rain hell down on her and her father if he even remotely had a doubt she would keep her side of the deal.

She got out of the car. As Trenthom did a U-turn and took off, she stepped around Logan. He grabbed her—

"Wha—?"

—and kissed her hard enough to take her breath away.

"Thought I might as well get in a good-luck kiss." His voice was iron.

"Fuck you! Touch me again, and I'll hurt you!" she snarled. She moved past him and started off through the brush.

It wasn't easy going without a set path, but they made good time. Ten minutes later, she said, "We're coming up to my father's place. There are cameras in the trees, so they'll know we're approaching."

He nodded, looking around. "You ready for this?"

"Yes," was her curt reply. *No, not really.* She discreetly wiped her sweaty palms on her jeans.

He gave her a nod, and they stepped out of the woods and approached the gate.

She was reaching for the call button when the gate silently swung open. "They already saw us." They moved through the gate and heard a car coming down the drive. She wanted to reach for Logan's hand and gave it a squeeze. She needed reassurance, but that wasn't going to happen. She snuck at peek at him. Granite was softer than the expression on his face. This was going to be harder than she'd thought.

CHAPTER EIGHTEEN

A second later, a Jeep came into view with Omar at the wheel. After it rolled to a stop, Omar crawled out, wearing black cargo pants and a black T-shirt. His dark eyes scanned the surroundings.

"Omar! I can't tell you how great it is to see you!" She caught him in a big hug.

She was good at this, Logan had to admit. Very convincing. She'd fooled Logan, but then he'd believed she cared about him, so he shouldn't be surprised. He ground his teeth and refocused on what was going on around him.

Omar hugged her back. "Lacy. Girl, where have you been?" he asked as he set her down. "Your father... We've all been so worried."

"It's a long story. I'll fill you in, but I need to see Dad first."

"Of course. Hop in." Omar gestured to the Jeep as he walked over toward Logan. "You must be Callahan. We heard you've been keeping Lacy safe." He offered his hand. "I can't thank you enough."

He nodded and shook the proffered hand, his stomach

curdled like he'd just drunk sour milk. How he hated this man. He hadn't realized how much until now. Voloshyn was bad enough, but this man, this supposedly trusted employee made Voloshyn's plan possible. This was the man who'd betrayed Lacy and her father, who'd set them up to be murdered.

He had his best poker face in place, though. Omar had no way of knowing how much he wanted to reach out and kill him as he walked around the Jeep to get in. Still, he made a promise to himself that Omar would pay, and pay dearly.

Omar made a U-turn and drove back up the driveway. As he rounded the last curve, a huge sun-drenched mansion came into view. It made the house where they'd hidden out on the island seem like a cottage. "Wow," he mumbled in the back seat.

"Yes. It's quite something," Omar said conversationally. "Armand had it built so that it would serve not only as a house, but as a place of business. He often has parties for three hundred or more, and many of the guests stay onsite."

He could believe it. The place was monstrous, but it was somehow still beautiful. Whoever designed it had done it with a keen eye for detail. There were little flares and touches everywhere that made the house at once grand and yet inviting. The amazing gardens that were planted out front provided a tantalizing riot of color and tropical scents. The statuary usually seen in a place like this was notably absent, which made it less formal. It was certainly a site to behold, but it also felt like a welcoming friend.

Omar pulled up the round drive and came to a stop in front of the stairs leading to the front door. Lacy hopped out and ran up, disappearing from view in two seconds flat. Cursing silently, he took off after her, trying not to lose her in the huge house.

"Armand?" he heard her call out as he came around the

corner into the foyer. *Armand?* The fact that she couldn't call him dad, even in a time of crisis pissed him off even more. Who was this man who made her life so difficult? Who would do that to their kid? Logan tried to shake that line of thinking and take in his surroundings.

There was a large marble table in the middle of the entryway with the largest vase of flowers Logan had ever seen. The foyer itself had to be about thirty feet high and was done in travertine tile with large marble columns. It ran half the depth of the house to a huge open doorway leading to a room in the back.

Lacy took the stairs to the second floor two at a time. Before he could start up, Omar called out from behind him. "Lacy, he's not in his room. He's in the salon." He gestured to the room at the end of the foyer. She turned and started back down the stairs. Logan waited at the bottom.

"I thought…"

Logan shook his head slightly, and she stopped speaking.

Omar looked at her and raised an eyebrow.

"I thought he would be in his upstairs office. Where's the rest of the staff?" she asked.

"Your father gave them some time off."

"Right. He just mentioned how busy he was last time we spoke. I thought he might have kept the staff here," she murmured on the way down the stairs.

Omar just nodded and waited until they passed and walked toward the salon. He stepped in behind them to follow.

A tingle started in Logan's gut. *Something's off.* It was the same reading he got when he walked into a boardroom for a negotiation and the opposing side had a surprise in store for him. He gave Lacy a look and braced himself for what was to come.

When they walked into the salon, the view immediately

stole his breath. He could see a balcony separated from the Caribbean Sea by only a short stretch of grass. All that turquoise loveliness was sparkling in the sunshine. So inviting. At any other time, he would have immediately continued outside, but instead he studied the room.

He felt rather than heard her sharp intake of breath. There was a man sitting on a couch behind a coffee table. The man had to be Armand Fontaine. It was clear where she got her eyes and her hair color.

Fontaine had a black eye and a cut lip. He also noticed that the man's left-hand ring and pinkie fingers were bent at unnatural angles.

"Daddy," she croaked and started to move toward him, but when Fontaine shook his head ever so slightly, Logan grabbed her hand. When she turned to get her hand free, her eyes went wide at something over Logan's shoulder. He froze.

"Good morning, Mr. Callahan, Ms. Carmichael. Or should I say, Ms. Fontaine? How nice of you to join us."

Fear unfurled in Logan's stomach as he watched her face drain of all color. *Voloshyn. Shit.* Her eyes met his, and he knew they were thinking the same thing—if Voloshyn was already here, there was no way they could get her dad off the grounds. They couldn't contact Trenthom, which meant he couldn't help them. They were screwed. His stomach knotted. Would he ever see his brothers again?

He turned and winced. His ribs twinged sending pain skittering across his body. "Mr. Voloshyn." There was no point in hiding the fact they knew his true identity. Their plan was a bust. They would have to make a new one. The wheels started turning. "I would say how nice it is to see you, but we both know that would be a lie."

Voloshyn smirked. "You two have caused me great trouble." His smile turned into more of a baring of teeth as his eyes narrowed. "But no matter. You are here now, and I will make you pay for wasting my time." He ran his eyes over Lacy, leering at her in an unmistakable way.

Logan started to move forward, but he suddenly dropped to his knees. Omar had hit him in the kidneys and followed up with a hit to the backs of the knees.

"Omar, you son of a bitch!" She started forward, but Logan staggered to his feet and stopped her. Still not able to speak after that hit, he just shook his head.

Omar laughed. Logan could tell Lacy wanted to kill Omar, but she understood there was no way to make that happen at the moment.

"Good choice." Omar's sudden laugh echoed in the room. "Although I would have loved to see you try." His dark eyes glittered with hatred. "I have spent years indulging. you and your father. I would love the chance to make you bend and scrape for a change."

Logan ground his teeth, but he schooled his features to remain neutral.

"My, oh my. What shall we do about the three of you?" Lacy remained silent, and Logan took the opportunity to ease her slightly behind him. Omar had caught him off guard once. He wouldn't let it happen again.

"Come now, Callahan, you cannot protect her. Surely, you have realized by now that I no longer need you. I have both Fontaines in one location, and they will do whatever I want them to do because they don't want to see each other get hurt. You are now extraneous to this little adventure."

Logan felt Lacy's hand on his arm, and he moved her a little farther back from the men. "What's your plan, Voloshyn? I admit to being curious. I figured there was more to the story then just wanting some guns, but why don't you fill us in on the details?" Logan asked.

Of course, they already knew the answer to that, but he needed time to think of some way out of this mess. The thing was, he had nothing to offer. There was nothing he possessed that made him valuable to Voloshyn.

Voloshyn smiled slightly as he started wandering around the room. He picked up a glass figurine and watched to see if Lacy reacted. Logan had a feeling if Lacy showed any interest, Voloshyn would have broken the figurine. He was looking to hurt Lacy and her father any way he could.

He stood tensed, waiting to see if Voloshyn would start bragging about his ludicrous plan, about how fucking brilliant he is. *Come on*, he begged silently. *Show off to me. Let your ego have full reign.* Wasn't that what Voloshyn wanted? A chance to show off? Tell how he was wronged?

Voloshyn gestured toward the couch where Fontaine was sitting. "Why don't we all take a seat?"

Lacy went immediately to her father and hugged him. Logan followed more slowly. He could see tears in the older man's eyes. This had to be hell for him, too. Their eyes met, and an understanding passed between them. They were both going to do anything and everything they could to get Lacy out of this alive.

He immediately felt better. Sure, they didn't have a plan or anything, but he wasn't the only one watching out for Lacy. There was a chance she would get out of this alive, even if he didn't.

Voloshyn sat in a chair on the opposite side of the coffee table. "As I have been explaining to your father, he has really brought all this upon himself. And you, of course." Voloshyn shifted to get more comfortable in his chair. A man walked into the room and placed a cup and saucer of something, presumably tea, in front of him.

Logan glanced at Lacy. Her mouth was a flat line and her eyes narrowed at the man who delivered the tea. Whoever this was, it had to be someone who worked for Fontaine.

"Thank you, Reggie." Voloshyn smiled when Reggie

bowed slightly before moving to stand in the far corner of the room. Definitely one of Fontaine's people. Or Omar's people. Alexey was by the door, keeping an eye on everyone. That made too many people to overpower even if Logan had the opportunity.

"Where were we? Ah yes, it's your father's fault." Voloshyn paused for a minute, his face dark, his eyes flat He picked up the drink but didn't take a sip.

Logan braced himself.

"I came to you in good faith. I had been told you were the best at tracking down the necessary equipment." Voloshyn pointed his finger at Fontaine. "I came to you for help. I had the money, and with your resources, I could have ensured our success. But you said no!" The man's fury was building. His eyes were wide and spitting fire. The teacup clattered against the saucer. "You said you didn't want to get involved in. You didn't agree with our cause!"

Voloshyn's voice got louder and his accent grew thicker. "You, bah—who are you to decide what's right, eh? It is not of your concern. You need to sell the weapons and stay out of it. But no. You decided you couldn't sell them to me."

Voloshyn was in a rage; his body vibrated with it. "And then you called the other arms dealers and convinced them not to sell to me either! Who are you? You are not God! You do not get to decide who wins and loses a war. It was not up to you!" Voloshyn roared. "You killed my Anna and my children! You killed them by not giving me the weapons to protect them! Their blood is on your hands, and you will pay!" His eyes were wild and his hands shaking. There was spittle in the corner of his mouth. Voloshyn was half out of his chair before he seemed to realize what he was doing.

He paused, took a deep breath, and sat back down. Then he reached for his tea. The cup rattled in the saucer, and it took him a couple of tries, but he managed to take one sip and then another. Several moments passed while he got himself under control. No one moved. No one dared to so much as breathe.

This guy was certifiable, no doubt. For the first time ever, primal fear flooded Logan's body. His nerves were on fire with free-flowing adrenaline. His heart was slamming double time in his chest and his mouth had a coopery taste. Had he bitten his tongue? He couldn't feel it. This guy really was going to kill them all. Everything seemed to move slowly, like he was underwater, and his skin felt clammy and cold.

"So you see, Hazel...may I call you Hazel?" He continued on without waiting for a response. "Your father brought this on himself and on you. You have to die just like my children did. Fair is fair." The smile returned. "Of course, I had two children, a boy and a girl. You are only one, so it's still not equal, but it will have to do."

He turned and studied Logan. "Sadly, I...*we* have to wait a bit for the fun to begin. I'm expecting a phone call."

Logan's gut rolled. It didn't look good for them. Surreptitiously, he hauled in a steady breath, trying to keep it together.

Armand frowned slightly but stayed silent.

Logan worked his fingers through Lacy's and squeezed. Maybe this was the break they were looking for? Maybe the delay would give them a chance to create a new plan? At least it bought them a bit of time.

"You didn't mention a delay," Omar growled.

Voloshyn frowned. "A brief delay. I need to speak to some people. Funds need to be moved. It's all in hand."

"We have our own schedule to keep," Omar reminded him.

"I said we wait." Florid red flushed into Voloshyn's face again. His hands were balled into fists.

So there's a bit of a power struggle between Omar and

Voloshyn. Logan caught Fontaine's eye just for a second, but it was long enough to confirm his hunch. *Good to know.* Maybe it could help if he stayed alive long enough to use it. Yeah, they needed a plan, and it had to be sooner not later. Voloshyn was unstable, and chances were good he wouldn't wait long.

The wheels in Logan's head started to turn. He was no longer afraid. Cold calm settled over his nerves. He was in control and strangely accepting of whatever came his way. In the past, he had wondered how his brothers, had managed to stay sane and function when their lives were in such danger. Now he understood. After the blinding fear came a calm, and that was when you planned or moved or escaped. Fontaine started speaking, which startled him out of his revere.

"Voloshyn, I would think killing the young man outright would rob you of a good deal of pleasure. After all, revenge is what you want along with the business, and Logan obviously cares a great deal for my daughter. If I'm not mistaken, I do believe they are even talking of marriage."

Both his and Lacy's heads whipped in Fontaine's direction. Lacy's hand started toward her head, no doubt to smooth her hair like she always did when she was nervous, but her father grabbed it and held.

"Am I right, darling? Have you and Logan been discussing marriage?" Fontaine's eyes bore into his daughters. Then he gave Logan the same intent look.

"Yes," Logan answered. To his surprise, it came off his lips easily, as if it was the most natural thing ever. He truly did want to create some sort of life with Lacy. He was in love with her. Too bad she'd already made it very clear she did not feel the same way.

"See? Two birds with one stone," Armand said.

Omar's eyes narrowed. "What are you up to, old man?"

"Nothing. I'm trying to buy time, Omar. Time for my daughter and her fiancée, time for myself."

"Your time is up, Fontaine. Now it's my turn." Omar smiled. "But I am not a bad person. You want more time for you and your daughter? OK, we will wait for Voloshyn to get his phone call, but only a few hours. This must be finished today."

"Now that we all agree," Voloshyn said, "let's celebrate the wonderful news of your engagement." Voloshyn's smile grew before twisting into something truly evil.

"Alexey, bring us champagne. I'll drink it to celebrate while you throw this bunch in the room I have prepared for them. Bring me the best vintage Armand has on hand. I need to celebrate properly."

As Voloshyn got up, his cell phone rang. Glancing at it, he said, "On second thought, bring the champagne outside. I want to admire the view while I celebrate." He answered the call as he headed out onto the balcony and disappeared from sight.

Alexey motioned to them to stand and Vladamir, aka Hairy, came through the door. The two men marched them through the house at gunpoint, bringing them to a room on one of the upper floors. Logan tried to keep track, but the mansion was enormous, and he got a bit confused as they pushed farther into the house.

When they reached a large door, Alexey motioned for them to stop and instructed Lacy to open it. Vladimir pushed them into the room and then stood outside the door. Alexey told Logan to chain Armand first. Logan's brain scrambled to find a way out. He ran scenarios through his head while he tightened the clamps of the shackle then hooked the links through a loop embedded into the wall. Maybe he could rush Alexey. There weren't a whole lot of options. Once they were tethered to the wall, that was it.

He was the last one. It was now or never. He pivoted and immediately stopped. Omar had arrived silently and was now pointing a AK47 machine gun at Lacy's head. Logan sat heavily, letting Alexey close the manacles around his wrists and bind him to the wall, and then he silently watched the men leave.

CHAPTER NINETEEN

"Oh, Daddy, I'm so glad you are all right." She reached out with one tethered hand and tried to reach her father. The chains stopped her hand about two inches short. "Fuck!" she growled. She was losing it again, only this time it was tears not laughter.

"Relax," Logan grumbled.

She whipped around and glared at him. "Don't patronize me. We're bound to a wall with no help coming, so it's definitely not going to be OK!" A rage was bubbling up that she couldn't control. Logically, she knew it wasn't Logan's fault—far from it—but she was so angry, so full of fear, she lashed out.

"I'm not patronizing you. It's going to be OK." He looked over at Armand Fontaine. "So, what's the plan?"

She frowned at her father in confusion. "What plan? Why does he think you have a plan?"

"Because your father wouldn't let you in here if he didn't have a plan to get you out." He stared at Fontaine, who gave him a slight nod.

"I've been thinking…" Logan leaned back against the

wall and raised one knee. "We weren't sure your father knew what was going on, but we were being stupid. Of course, he knew. If he has spies all over the islands like you and Trenthom say, then he had to know that Omar was planning something. There is no way Voloshyn would land in the Bahamas without your father hearing about it."

He turned to face her father. "So, you knew Omar was switching sides and Voloshyn was here. My guess is you weren't sure when, otherwise you would never have let Lacy come down here in the first place. You must still have people who are loyal to you, filling you in. There has been a plan in place for something like this for a long time."

"Is it true? Did you really know all along?" Lacy asked anxiously. Logan's theory made sense. It would be typical of her father to have back-up plans A through Z without telling her. Until now, he only ever told her what he thought she needed to know. That had to stop. If she was going to take over the business, she would need to be looped in on every detail, no matter how minute.

"So," Logan asked again, "what's the plan?"

Fontaine studied Logan for a long minute and then nodded slightly. "Your friend is correct, honey. I do have a plan." He reached out to try to touch his daughter, then dropped his hand. "I'm sorry I couldn't tell you. Things moved more quickly than I anticipated. I"—he hesitated—"I thought it was better to keep you in the dark until I had more details." He smiled slightly. "That may have been a mistake."

"May have been? *May have been*!" The rage was about to explode from her chest. "If I'd known, I would have been prepared. I could have avoided this whole damn mess and had a real vacation! You think it *might* have been a mistake?"

"You're fine. You had help." He glanced at Logan. "Very good help. And you would have missed the rest of it, too.

You seemed to enjoy the resort. The room you had is fabulous, I hear. The shack on the beach was not so nice, but"—he shrugged—"you made the best of it."

She felt a flush creep up her neck. "You had people watching us? People you trusted? What the fuck? Do you know what I went through not knowing if you were alive or dead? Never mind all the rest—the car accident, the kidnapping, and the escape. Do you know what it's like to wonder if you will ever see your father again? To wonder if you will be alive in twenty-four hours? To wonder if you're going to get the people around you killed?" She glared at her father, incredulous that he would do that to her.

Looking sheepish and a bit sad, he reached for her again. "Sweetheart, I truly am sorry. If there had been another way, I would have done it. Like I said, it happened faster than I anticipated and honestly"—he glanced at Logan—"you were in good hands.

"I didn't expect Voloshyn to grab you and take you to the yacht. I can't tell you the agony I felt knowing you were trapped on there. I had people watching, but there was nothing we could do at that point. If my people had tried to take over the yacht, it would have put you in more danger. There simply weren't enough of them. Once everything started, I had to let it play out."

Lacy closed her eyes and swore long and loud in her head. All her life, her father thought he knew better. Not trusting her to make her own choice. She opened her eyes and glared at him.

"Once I knew you were off the yacht and safe at the hotel, it was…safer to leave you there." Again, he glanced at Logan. "I did everything I could to protect you.

"My old boss," Logan blurted out. "You got him to lend us the suite, didn't you?"

Fontaine nodded. "My people did reach out and suggest

it would be wonderful if he were helpful to you. I do a fair amount of business in New York and I am always looking for legal help besides my beautiful daughter." He smiled.

"And Cecil. You got him to help me with the money at the hotel."

Fontaine nodded. "Yes, little things, but they were as much help as I could give you at the time. But, you are here now, and we're together. That's what matters." He smiled at his daughter again.

"What matters? I'll tell you what matters! We are never doing this again. Ever. I'm going to take over the business, and you're going to retire to take care of yourself. There will be no more secrets." She heard Logan's chains rattle, and when she glanced in his direction, she saw a look of something, pain? Hurt? Disappointment? A shadow crossed his face. Then his expression went blank. Completely blank.

Turning back to her father, she took a deep breath. In a calmer voice, she said, "Uh, what is the plan?"

He smiled slightly at her. "All in good time." She opened her mouth to protest, but her father lifted his chin toward Logan. She turned to look and saw Logan had his eyes closed. "We're all exhausted, and we have time before anything happens. Let's rest up a bit. I have some thinking to do." She narrowed her eyes at her father, but he shook his head slightly. She sighed and closed her eyes, trying to get more comfortable against the wall.

Men. Honestly. They sucked. She fervently wished she didn't love the two of them so much. Life would be easier that way.

LOGAN TRIED to sit still and relax, but his mind kept going back to the statement Lacy had made. He still couldn't believe she was choosing this life. It was so unsafe, so volatile. What the hell? Her father couldn't possibly think it was a good idea.

He tried to take a deep breath. Relax. He had to accept her choice. After all, when it came down to it, most people would choose their family over a new romantic entanglement. Except for him. When push came to shove, he had chosen Lacy rather than do the job he was here to do.

He took his eye off the ball for the first time in his life, and look where it got him? He was never going to do that again. He was never going to fall so easily for someone. When he got back to New York, if he got back, he was going to keep his head down and focus on work.

He must have dozed off because he woke with a start. As he looked around wildly, it all came crashing back—where he was, why he was there. He glanced at Lacy, but she had also dozed off. When he switched his gaze to Fontaine, the older man was watching him. And then it hit him, like a lightning bolt, why he had woken up. His brain had knit the pieces together as he slept.

"You have a way out of this, but only for you and Lacy," he stated, barely above a whisper. "That's why you wouldn't tell her your plan." Logan needed to know the truth. Or, rather, he knew the truth but needed it confirmed. Fontaine nodded.

"I am sorry. I…I didn't think you would come here with her. Stupid, now that I think about it. A man who stayed through everything you've endured wasn't likely to leave my daughter in a life-threatening situation by herself." He smiled a little ruefully.

"This contingency plan has been in place a long time." He took a deep breath. "I have been sitting here wracking my brain for a solution, but there is no way to alter it and guarantee…" he stopped.

"And guarantee that you and Lacy get out safely." He finished the sentence for Fontaine. "I get it. You can't risk her life, and if you aren't with her, she'll face a world of trouble once she gets out of here."

And he did get it. Somehow, he was still calm. It was like before in the study—the fear had passed, leaving a calm energy in its place. Now he would be able to think. There would be a way out. There always was. He just had to figure it out. "Tell me your plan, and I'll share ours with you. Maybe we can come up with something together."

Fontaine cocked his head. "You are impressive."

His brows knit together. "I don't think so. My brothers are impressive. If they were here, they would already have a great escape plan in place, and they'd take down all the bad guys on the way out. Me, I am going by the seat of my pants. Impressive is not the word I would use."

His voice got tight when he thought of his brothers. He had never before realized how impressive they were. Especially Mitch. He had never given Mitch enough credit. He'd always thought of Mitch as the irresponsible one, the party boy, but if his brother's work was anything like this, the man deserved to party hard. Mitch had been proving himself with the company, too, by bringing in a steady stream of clients. He just hoped he'd live long enough to tell Mitch how proud he was to be his brother. Gage, too.

He cleared the lump that had suddenly sprung up in his throat. "So, we were planning on taking you to the hospital." He went on to outline their entire plan while Fontaine listened intently.

———

LACY STIRRED and reached out in her sleep. The rattling of chains—chains!—forced her eyes open. Disoriented, she looked around frantically and then remembered where she was. She glanced wearily at Logan.

"You're awake. Good. Your father and I were just going over things. I think we have a plan cobbled together." When she glanced at her father for verification, he nodded.

"I—" he jolted to a halt at a sound on the other side of the door. The heavy wood panel suddenly swung open, admitting Reggie. Logan hopped to his feet, but Reggie immediately set to work undoing Fontaine's chains.

"Your inside man?" Logan speculated.

Fontaine nodded and smiled.

Soon they were all on their feet. Reggie said, "Voloshyn has been on the phone all afternoon with the Russians. Although they want to rule Ukraine, they are refusing to pay more money. Not enough bang for their buck. Voloshyn spent too much on this whole situation, and now he doesn't have enough to buy the guns and pay Omar. He's been drinking the whole time, so he's getting a bit sloppy. We have to move now before he decides it's time to torture all of you." He unlocked Lacy's chains and made his way to Logan.

Fontaine nodded. "Is everything ready?"

Reggie nodded once. "All is in place."

"Good, but we have a change of plans."

Reggie's expression turned sour. He wasn't pleased. He finished unlocking Logan's chains. Armand said, "You need to go with Logan and open the gate for him. He'll drive the ambulance out. Do you think you can manage that and still get away?"

Reggie hesitated before nodding again but his mouth was set in a firm line. "I'll set off the sprinklers to cause more of a commotion," he said. "Should buy me enough time."

She piped up. "We're still going in the ambulance?"

"No. You and I are going out through a tunnel. I have

scuba gear waiting for us because we'll be in the water for a bit before we're picked up."

Her heart stopped for a beat and then started slamming against her ribs. She and Logan would be separating! She wanted to reach out to him, wanted to beg him not to risk himself, but she couldn't. She nodded.

Some emotion flickered in his eyes. Fear maybe? Sadness? She wanted to say something, but what was left to say? They had two separate paths to take, and that was just the way it had to be. Besides, he didn't trust her so what was the point. "Good luck." She reached out to touch him but stopped herself. Touching him wouldn't help her walk away. She said a prayer—*please keep him safe*—and disappeared through the doorway.

CHAPTER TWENTY

H e couldn't believe what had just happened. Lacy, the woman he had fought to protect for days, the woman he'd come to love, had just dismissed him with a quick "good luck." Seriously?

Fontaine turned to face him. "You go with Reggie. He'll lead you down to the ambulance and help you get to the gate. After that, you're on your own." He reached out and offered his hand. Logan took it and they shook. Fontaine squeezed his hand. "Like I said before, impressive." And then he let go. "Good luck."

"You, too," Logan said, but Fontaine was already gone.

Reggie nodded at Logan. "Look, I knocked out and tied up the guards up here, but there are at least eight more inside the house and an unknown number outside on the grounds. No one here except me is loyal to Armand. Omar sent everyone else away or possibly killed them. I'm not entirely sure. So, if you get lost or left behind or captured, no one is coming for you. Are we clear?"

"Crystal," Logan said. If he didn't focus, he was dead. There was no backup. Message received.

Reggie led him down the hall and around the corner, down one flight of stairs and down another hallway. It took no time at all for him to be completely and utterly lost. There was no way in hell he could get out of this one on his own, so he held on to the fact that Fontaine clearly trusted Reggie with his life.

The trip through the house confirmed for Logan that he was not cut out for Special Ops. They almost walked into one of Voloshyn's men, and another stood in a hallway facing away from them when they snuck by. It was too much. His gut ached with adrenaline overload.

They finally came to a stop before the door to the garage. Reggie turned to face him. "The keys for the ambulance should be in the box at the end. They're clearly marked."

Reggie handed him a two-way radio. "Here. When I give you the signal, drive out and head down the lane as fast as you can. The ambulance can plow through the garage door, but not the wrought-iron gate protecting the drive. I'll get the gate open for you, but don't dawdle. I can't guarantee how long I can keep it open."

He turned away and started down the hall. Then, turning back, he said, "It's your job to be the distraction so Mr. Fontaine and his daughter can get to the tunnel. Make sure you're a good one."

"Understood." He put his hand on the knob of the door and then turned back to ask Reggie where he was going to be, but the man was already gone.

"OK, then." He opened the door a crack and checked the interior. Seeing no movement, he entered the room and closed the door softly behind him. He was about a quarter of the way along the side of the first car bay. He slid along silently to the end. Now that he was at the corner of the garage, he could truly appreciate its size. It had to be what, eight, nine, no ten bays. A ten-car garage. Of course, it was.

The ambulance was third from the end, but the box of keys was at the very end.

Wasting no time, he set off at a trot along the back wall to find the keys, but he quickly came to a halt. "Holy shit!" He was staring at a Bugatti. It was beautiful. He reached out and ran a hand over the rear quarter panel. Stunning. He had passed a couple of Ferraris and a Lambo, but the Bugatti was by far the most spectacular car in the garage. He contemplated using it to make his escape. After all, if he was going to die, he might as well do it in his dream car. Then his practical nature took over, and he started moving again.

Fontaine had said the ambulance was bulletproof, so using it would increase his chances of survival. Plus, he would hate to see the Bugatti riddled with bullet holes. *Still*. He sighed as he reached the box with the keys. Sometimes he hated his pragmatic side.

It took him a full minute to realize the keys to the ambulance were not in the box. Reggie had failed to mention that all the keys for every vehicle on the estate were in this tiny box, not just the ones in the garage, so it took him precious minutes to realize they were missing.

He trotted back over to the ambulance and looked in. The keys were hanging from the ignition. He tried the door handle, but it was locked. He made a circle of the vehicle, but all the doors were locked.

He was trying to figure out where else the key could be when his walkie-talkie squelched. "Thirty seconds," someone squawked. Thirty seconds until what? Until go time or until the gate closes? He froze for a second.

"Ah, problem," he said into the walkie-talkie. Silence greeted him. "Ah, hello?"

"What!" came the hiss from the other end.

"The keys are locked inside the ambulance." He frantically searched for another set of keys, but there was nothing. The Bugatti was looking better and better.

"Check the front wheel well," Reggie whispered through the radio. "Ten seconds."

He searched the wheel well and found the other set of keys. He unlocked the door and jumped into the seat. He started the ambulance, but the engine wouldn't catch. Cursing, he tried again. This time the ambulance roared to life.

"Now!" Reggie yelled.

Logan hit the gas and crashed through the garage door, bouncing over it on the way out. He started hitting buttons, but he couldn't make the lights and siren go on. "Fuck!" Finally, he managed to hit the right buttons. The lights lit up the sky and sirens wailed to life. The vehicle went up on two wheels as he took a sharp right. He flew down the driveway. Despite the flashing lights, the road was hard to see. He frantically searched the dash for the headlight, breathing a sigh of relief once he got them turned on.

"You're going the wrong way!" Reggie voice shrilled through the walkie.

"What?" He couldn't pick it up to ask the question, but when he looked around frantically, he realized nothing was familiar. "Shit!"

He whipped the wheel of the ambulance, and it swung around in a wide arc. He went over the grass as the first bullet hit the windshield. It was rapidly followed by at least a dozen more. He ducked, bobbing and weaving, every time he heard a bullet hit, not trusting the ambulance was really bulletproof.

He came down hard off an embankment and floored the vehicle back the way he had come. It had never occurred to him to ask which direction to go. Most driveways weren't miles long!

He drove wildly, weaving back and forth as bullets hit

him from all sides. He could see the muzzle flashes of the gunmen as he flew past. There were dozens of them. Swarming like ants. Where the hell were they all coming from?

Suddenly the place lit up like the Fourth of July. He blinked against the afterburn on his retinas to see a huge crater formed in the driveway ahead of him. Logan swerved and almost hit a tree. "Fuck!" There was no way the ambulance was missile-proof. He was driving over the grass when it started pouring. No, not pouring. It was the sprinklers.

"Thank you, Reggie!" But that also meant no more help because Reggie would need to escape, too.

He put his foot all the way to the floor and shot off the grass. The tires screeched as they bit into the pavement. He came around the corner and rocketed toward the gates. Thank God. He wasn't getting shot at anymore, but he was sure it was only a brief reprieve. Voloshyn's men were undoubtedly getting in vehicles to chase him. As he neared the iron barrier, he realized the gates were moving away from him. They were closing!

"Fuck!" he screamed as he leaned forward jamming his foot harder against the accelerator but it was already on the floor. Shots started hitting the back again as he raced up on the gates. It was going to be close. Very close. He lined it up as best he could and went for it. He closed his eyes. Then he heard the sound of crunching metal and shattering glass.

LACY FOLLOWED her father through the rabbit warren of hallways until they reached an outside door. After checking to make sure it was clear, he gestured for her to go. She ran to the nearest tree and stayed in its shadow. Her father did the same. He pointed to an area covered by bushes. She raised her eyebrow at him. It appeared to be a bunch of A/C units, but her father gestured again, so she shrugged and ran over to the units, pushing through the bushes. Her father joined her seconds later. He led the way through a few more bushes, and she suddenly found herself next to a drain cover.

Her father removed the drain cover and reached in and flicked on a lantern hanging just on the inside of the drain. She could see a ladder.

"Go on. Climb down. I'll keep watch."

She nodded and started down the ladder, then waited at the bottom for her father. He had carried down the lantern, which he used to lead the way down the tunnel.

The sound of waves ebbed and flowed in the dimly lit corridor. Water lapped at her feet. The space filled with the tang of sea air and the faint perfume of flowers. After a few more twists and turns with the water level rising, they came to the end of the tunnel.

The tunnel opened onto a group of trees that were on the edge of the sand. The tang of salt and the scent of tropical flowers was overpowering. "Now," her father said, "there should be…yes. There they are."

She looked over and saw scuba gear hidden in the undergrowth.

"We'll use this to swim out. There's a spot around the point where someone will be waiting to take us to safety," her father said.

"Are you sure about this, Daddy? Are you sure you can do it?" She had been watching him this whole time, and he didn't look so good. He was out of breath for sure. And, although it was hard to tell in this light, he looked a bit gray.

"I'll be fine. Don't worry about me." He gave her hand a reassuring squeeze before turning to pick up one of the tanks. Then he stopped. He brought the light closer to it and inspected it closely.

"What is it? What's wrong?"

Whatever he had been about to say was lost in the sound of nearby gunfire. They both automatically hit the sand. The bursts of gunfire continued, but the sound receded. Logan. Her heart thumped hard in her chest. It was as if the life was being squeezed out of her.

Her father put his hand on her shoulder and squeezed again. They both got to their feet but stayed in a crouched position. "I think the tanks have been tampered with. There are holes in the regulator hoses. We can't use them." He studied her face. She tried to remain calm as she considered other options.

"Shit." She couldn't believe what she was about to suggest, but she didn't think there was another choice. "If you can, I think we should still swim for it. It's a dark night, so it'll be hard for them to see us in the water."

Her father nodded and then reached over and gave her hand a squeeze. "You are a brave girl. I am very proud of you."

She smiled back. "OK, let's move."

They crept out of the undergrowth and waited. There was more gunfire now. A lot more. She tried to keep calm and not think about Logan, but it was almost impossible.

"On my count," he said.

She nodded. Her father held up three fingers, and at the count of one, they waded into the ocean. Shoulders hunched around her ears, she kept waiting to get shot, but it didn't happen. The waves were bigger tonight than when she and Logan had taken their late-night swim to safety, but the water wasn't as cold. Her father was close behind her.

Suddenly, there was a rumble in the water. She stopped moving and her father pulled up next to her. They listened in the darkness. "Jet skis. Two of them," she said in a near whisper. "Are they your people?"

She saw her father shake his head. "Voloshyn's men would be my guess. They must have known we would escape this way. They sabotaged the tanks so we couldn't be underwater."

It was dark, which helped hide them, but it also hid the jet skis. They treaded water for another minute. She started to worry. They couldn't stay in the water too long, and they still had a long way to swim.

Without any warning, someone grabbed her arm. She started to scream, but a hand covered her mouth. Kicking, hitting—she fought with everything she had, particularly when she saw her father had been grabbed by another man in scuba gear.

"Just relax," said a voice in her ear. She tried to struggle some more. "Relax." It was a command this time. The voice sounded strangely familiar, and she tried to place it. The instant it clicked, she gasped out loud. "Mitch?"

She turned toward her attacker as he pushed his mask to the top of his head and grinned at her. "Thought you might need some help."

"Oh, my God!" She threw her arms around his neck. "I don't think I've ever been so happy to see someone." She turned back toward her father. Gage had removed his face mask as well.

"I'm assuming you know these two," her father said.

"Yes. They're Logan's brothers. And he's Alex's boyfriend," she said, pointing to Mitch. "How did you know we were here?"

Gage smiled. "We ran into a guy on the grounds and asked him a whole lot of questions and then we listened to his radio. Some guy named Omar ordered two guys out here on jet skis to scoop you all up when you came this way. We just borrowed some extra scuba gear we found in your boat house. Nice setup by the way." He nodded to Fontaine.

"Anyway, we waited 'til we saw you and then came out to meet you. We also called a friend who's waiting in a borrowed speed boat."

"I don't mean to break up this reunion, but we should go." Mitch looked around. "Where's Logan? I thought he was with you."

"Um, it didn't work out that way." They were all treading water, and Lacy turned toward the shoreline. The sharp crack of gunfire echoed toward them, and then a huge explosion lit up the sky.

"Logan!" she yelled and started swimming to shore. Her heart was a solid blockage in her throat, and her only thought was that she needed to get to him.

Mitch held her fast. "Going back is not going to help him. He'd want you safe." He and Gage exchanged looks. "Let's go. The sooner we get you to safety, the sooner we can help Logan." She still reached toward the shore, she couldn't help it, but Mitch tugged her away. She turned and swam after Gage and her father. Mitch brought up the rear. Soon they were pulled aboard a speedboat.

"Where's Logan?" asked the man on the boat as he helped Mitch climb onboard.

"We don't know," Gage replied. "Get us to shore, Jake, so we can go help him."

"Will do, boss man." He turned on the speed boat, shoved up the throttle and sped toward safety.

Fontaine asked, "Do you have a cell phone? I have to send a text?"

CHAPTER TWENTY-ONE

The ambulance lost both mirrors to the gate and the rear windows to the hail of gunfire. It was bulletproof for only so long, apparently. Logan risked a glance in his rearview mirror as he whizzed down the road, heading back in the direction he and Lacy had come from earlier in the day.

Voloshyn's men had arrived at the gate, but it was still closing. They had to wait for it to open again, but they still fired in his direction. Muzzle flashes lit up the rearview mirror. He'd be lucky to get a minute head start.

He drove like a maniac, his foot all the way to the floor, praying that Trenthom was waiting for him somewhere along the road. He was glad there was no traffic. He didn't think he could weave around other cars at this speed.

Gunfire interrupted his thoughts, and the dashboard computer exploded next to him. Sharp pain seared his face as he was hit by shards of plastic. Ignoring the fiery sting, he fought to keep the ambulance upright and on the road. He managed to get it back under control, but the blood dripping down into his eye, making it hard to see.

He saw something reflected in his headlights as he rounded a curve, but there was no time to react. He went over the strip of spikes, and suddenly all his tires went flat. He lost control of the ambulance and it went over on its side. He was tossed to the passenger side as the vehicle slid along the ground, and he banged his head, arms, and legs on the dash and the door before the airbags exploded and knocked him around some more.

When he opened his eyes, he found himself staring into the dark, deadly barrel of a pistol.

"Get out," a voice growled. He couldn't recognize it because his ears were ringing. The gunman was crouched down in front of him where the windshield used to be, totally concealed by darkness. Logan groaned and made an attempt to move. After an eternity of struggling, and fierce battle to control his nausea from the pain of his head injury, he finally cleared the vehicle and stood. He staggered a few steps and then walked in front of the headlights and came around the other side.

There, lit up by the headlights of four vehicles parked in a circle, stood Voloshyn, Omar and Trenthom. There appeared to be other gunmen behind them, but they were outside the scope of the lights, so it was hard to tell. He had no idea who was in charge of the scenario. Or whether this meant Trenthom was against them after all.

"Where are Fontaine and his daughter?" Trenthom demanded.

"I have no clue." He ran a hand down over his face, feeling all the cuts while wiping some of the blood away. Now that he was standing, all the hurts on his body roared in a blazing cacophony of pain. His ribs and one leg were killing him, his shoulder was bleeding profusely from a bullet wound, and his head was about to explode. Only his force of will kept him from gagging.

"Come on, where are they?" Omar raised his gun and pointed it at him.

He shrugged and then immediately winced in pain. "I don't know. We split up back at the house. They didn't mention their plans. Just that there was no room for me."

"Liar!" Voloshyn howled. "You will tell me!" He started forward with his hands outstretched, obviously intent on strangling answers out of him, but Trenthom brought up his gun.

"Stay where you are, Voloshyn."

Voloshyn stuttered to a stop and stared at Trenthom with venom in his eyes. "You will not stop me. I *will* have my revenge. Where are they?" He started forward again. "They must pay. They must—"

The sound of the gunshot was so loud in the otherwise quiet night that Logan jumped. He watched as Voloshyn crumpled to the ground. He stared at Trenthom, but the CIA agent was staring at Omar.

"He was becoming annoying." Omar shrugged. "He promised me money, but it turns out he didn't have it. He stole his people's money to chase his revenge. There wasn't enough left to buy weapons. The Russians won't help. I suspect Fontaine had something to do with that." He gestured to Voloshyn. "He was no longer of any use to me, and quite frankly, I was tired of listening to his ranting and raving."

Logan swallowed. Hard. That answered that question.

"Now, Trenthom, what do you say we get down to negotiations, hmm? I am taking over Fontaine's business now that he's dead."

Logan must have made a sound because Omar turned his attention to him. "Yes. Fontaine and Lacy are dead. Did you think I didn't know about the tunnel plan?" He smiled. "I know everything. I had men on jet skis waiting for them after

I had them wreck the scuba gear." Still loosely pointing his gun in Logan's direction, Omar turned back to Trenthom.

Logan's heart was ice. He couldn't breathe. She couldn't be dead. There was no way. He would know…wouldn't he? Surely, Fontaine had been one step ahead of Omar. He must have had another plan. He tried to rein in his fear. His body started shaking. Deep breaths. Deep breaths, but Omar's words were echoing in his mind, making it hard to focus.

Omar stated, "I know your people don't care who's making the deals as long as they can call the shots when they want to. I want in. I will be happy to work with your people. I know Fontaine didn't always do what you wanted. He always had too much of a conscience for this business. Fortunately, I am not burdened with such a thing. I will—"

Omar's head exploded into pink mist. The sudden sound didn't startle Logan as much this time. He was too caught up with the notion that Lacy might be dead. He fell against the ambulance. He slid to the ground and stared up at Trenthom.

Logan gasped. "What the hell?"

Trenthom grimaced. "Sorry about that, but plans change, and Omar had to go."

Logan was two beats behind everyone else. What the hell was going on?

Trenthom must have realized this because he nodded and said, "It's not important for you to understand, just for you to keep your mouth shut. Your life will go much more smoothly that way."

He sat stunned, but the message had been received. It was all so surreal. He tried to speak, but his tongue wouldn't work. He took a second and tried again. "Is Lacy still alive?" His heart was double tapping a staccato rhythm against his aching ribs, but it stopped beating altogether when Trenthom paused before answering.

"Yes. She and her father are fine. Fontaine contacted me as soon as they were clear of the house."

Logan's breath came out in a whoosh. He tried to get up, but his legs couldn't hold him. He was dizzy with relief. He was saying a prayer of thanks when he realized Trenthom was still standing over him. Men were coming out from behind the vehicles and carrying the bodies away.

"Uh, are you going to kill me?"

"Should I kill you?"

Logan shook his head.

"No," Trenthom said, "I will not be killing you today. There's no need." He gestured toward the men disappearing in the night with the bodies. "There's no proof of anything anyway."

Logan blinked.

"Are you coming?" Trenthom offered him a hand. He nodded and took the help up.

CHAPTER TWENTY-TWO

Logan raised his glass toward the bartender at the Ocean Beach Resort. After receiving the man's nod of acknowledgement, he tilted his head back and poured the rest of his drink down his throat.

"A little early, don't you think?" Mitch sat down on the barstool next to him.

Logan shook his head. "I've never understood that."

"Understood what?"

"Well, it's eleven am. If I was drinking Bloody Marys or mimosas, that would be fine, but because I'm drinking"—he stopped and looked down at his electric blue drink—"whatever this is, it's too early. Why is that? It doesn't make any sense."

Mitch shrugged, and when the bartender put another drink in front of Logan, he said, "I'll have what he's having." He turned to face Logan, who was eyeing him. "What can I say? You made a convincing argument."

Logan stared down at his drink for a moment, then lifted his gaze to meet his brother's. "I've been through hell these last few days, Mitch, and I have to tell you, I have a whole lot more respect for what you do."

Mitch laughed. "How many of these have you had?"

"Not enough, but I'm being serious. Mitch, I've never really given you credit for being a SEAL, for being the first one through the door, for always putting your ass on the line and not buckling under the weight of fear."

"Thanks, Logan. You could have done it, too. Hell, from what I hear, you did it over this weekend."

"Maybe, but I am nowhere near as good at it as I think you must be, and I have no desire to improve my skills." He grinned and took a long haul of his drink.

Mitch laughed. "Don't blame you there. Some days my line of work really sucks."

"Tell me about it."

There was the sound of approaching footsteps, and Gage said, "I'll have what they're having." He sat down on the other side of Logan. "What *are* you having?" he asked as he frowned at the wild concoctions in front of his brothers.

"We don't know," replied Mitch.

"Cool."

Mitch glanced around the pool area. "I can see why you picked this resort, Logan." The aqua water was sparkling in the sunshine, and the pool was surrounded by bikini-clad girls.

"Yeah, well, I think I'm kind of done with women for the moment."

Gage put a hand on his shoulder and gave it a squeeze.

"That just leaves more for Gage." Mitch smiled at a dark-haired beauty who was walking past them. "I like this vacation thing. We need to do it more often." Both brothers turned to stare at him. "What?" he asked, feigning innocence.

"Mr. Callahan?" said a voice behind them. The three brothers turned on their stools.

"Which one?" asked Gage.

"Mr. Logan Callahan?" The speaker was a bland-looking man of average height and build. He had a slight British accent.

"Yes?" Logan wondered what fresh hell was about to unfold. His attitude had not improved after catching up on sleep and food. He couldn't stop thinking about Lacy, and it didn't help the whole Drake thing was still hanging over their heads. He didn't need any more shit in his life.

"Mr. Callahan, if you could please come with me, sir? Mr. Fontaine is here," he said, gesturing toward a few private cabanas beyond the pool, "and he would like to speak with you."

Logan sat there for a solid minute before climbing off his stool. He would like to tell the guy to go to hell, but he still wasn't totally sure where he stood with Trenthom after the way shit had gone down. Maybe Fontaine could fill him in. And, there was always a possibility he'd catch a glimpse of Lacy.

His brothers exchanged a look and then immediately got up and stationed themselves at better vantage points around the pool area.

The man walked him over to a private cabana. All the tent sides were down, so he had to push a flap aside to step in. It took a moment for his eyes to adjust to the dimmer light. Disappointment ran through him when he realized Lacy wasn't miraculously waiting inside.

Armand Fontaine was the sole occupant. The man was short and sported a large belly that reminded Logan of Santa Claus. He shoved the ludicrous thought aside and finished his evaluation of Fontaine. His hair was the same color as

Lacy's, but he had the fringe effect going and his bald spot was well tanned. He was sitting at a small table with a bottle of water in front of him. He was wearing a cream-colored suit that was still crisp in the suffocating heat and shoes that had been polished to a high shine.

"Would you like some water?" He gestured to the water, then reached into the ice bucket beside him and pulled one out. "With all those drinks you've having at the bar, you should probably have one of these." He handed it to Logan and then gestured toward the chair opposite him.

Logan sat, opened the water, and took a swig. "So, what can I do for you, Mr. Fontaine?" He leaned back in the chair, biting the inside of his cheek to stop begging for news about Lacy. He had his pride, such as it was.

"Lacy told me what you did for her. And, of course, your brothers are the ones who got us away from my home alive. Your brothers' arrival was well timed. I am very grateful. Lacy is as well. She is fine by the way. No worse off for the ordeal."

He tried to school his features, but the alcohol was starting to take effect. He didn't want the man to know how much he cared, but he was pretty sure it was written all over his face.

"I owe you and your brothers a great deal. To pay that debt, I took the liberty of asking around about your little problem, or should I say Jameson Drake's problem? It's interesting. There are not many things in life that I do not succeed in but finding this buyer is one of them."

"Great. Still a mystery. Why am I not surprised? Things have had a way of going sideways ever since we took Drake on as a client."

"Mr. Callahan, it is very odd that I did not turn up any information. I asked a great many of my sources. Sometimes they chose for one reason or another not to share information with me but," Fontaine leaned forward and tapped the table with his finger to emphasize word, "not once in my entire career did they truly not know. This is very disturbing and distressing to me." His gaze locked with Logan's. "Whomever this buyer is must have an incredible amount of power and resources. They are not someone to be trifled with."

A coldness wrapped itself around Logan's heart. He recognized it for what it was—fear. If Fontaine took the lack of information this seriously, then whoever or whatever was after the software was far more dangerous than they ever imagined.

"I still owe you for saving my life. Please don't hesitate to ask, if you need my help," Fontaine said as he stood.

"What will happen with Trenthom?" Logan blurted out.

Fontaine looked slightly confused. "What do you mean?"

"Well, you know, Omar, Voloshyn, what's he going to do about the whole thing?"

Fontaine shrugged. "Have you not seen the news today? There was a nasty shoot-out between drug kingpins last night. Whatever is this world coming to?" His smile didn't quite make it to his eyes.

"As for Trenthom? It will all be handled. If you are worried he will come after you in the future, fear not. There is no threat to you. There is nothing for him to gain by bothering you. Especially now that he has what he wants. You can rest easy, my friend."

Fontaine got up from the table and offered his hand. Logan reached out and shook it. "Until we meet again, Mr. Callahan." He gave a little bow and disappeared out the back of the tent.

Logan wasn't sure how long he sat there until the front flap moved and Gage walked in. He caught a glimpse of Mitch standing watch outside the cabana before the flap slapped back into place. Gage sat down in the seat Fontaine had vacated.

"What did he want?" Gage asked.

"Fontaine wanted to say thank you, but I think we're in a lot more trouble than we thought."

CHAPTER TWENTY-THREE

Three weeks later

"Good crowd last night. Must have been because you weren't cooking," Mitch said.

Logan threw a beer cap at his youngest brother. Mitch dodged it and laughed.

"I did cook last night, and the food was popular, wasn't it, Carol?" The waitress nodded as she wiped down the tables in the back. Logan went back to looking at the paper in front of him. It was next week's menu.

"Popular with the women. I'm sure they are begging for something, but I'm guessing it's not your food."

"When are you going back to Europe?" Logan demanded.

The smile slid off Mitch's face, and Logan could have kicked himself. Mitch had just gotten back last night. Things with Drake were tense. They still didn't know who was behind the push to steal the prototype software. Mitch only came back to regroup and make sure one of his guys was OK. There had been an exchange of gunfire last week, and Mitch's guy had taken a bullet to the gut. He lost his spleen, but he was going to recover.

"We've got to talk about how we're going to handle this," Logan said. "Gage is busy trying to find the programmer, so you and I have to come up a game plan." They hadn't heard from Gage directly in days. They were both on edge.

"You're right, we do," Mitch said as he moved over so he was sitting directly in front of Logan. "But we agreed tonight we would just celebrate the fact you are now cooking at the pub. Gotta say, it's convenient being downstairs from the office. With you cooking, we don't have to order in as much. That's got to be saving us money."

"Maybe," Logan said. He wasn't ready to go that far. "We'll see how it goes." Ever since he came back from the Bahamas, he'd been working on the side to revamp the pub that was on the first floor of the building next to their office building. Their father bought the building years ago but Connor Bennett had been renting the space for the pub well before that. It used to do well in the old days when the Irish mob ran Hell's Kitchen. Now, it was a dive that only the most steadfast of locals went to.

Logan had talked Connor into letting him be a partner and make some changes, which included doing some of cooking. In truth, Connor hadn't made the rent in months, but the brothers had agreed to let it slide. Connor had to be seventy if he was a day. They didn't want to see him on the street.

Within days of Logan making a few changes, not the least of which was putting decent tables on the sidewalk and calling it a patio, people had started coming. The beer was cheap and the food was good. It wouldn't be long before it was a raging success. Logan could feel it in his bones, but first they had to deal with the Drake mess. He was still CEO of Callahan Security. Cooking relieved his stress but it didn't solve his problems.

"Pour me a beer, brother, we need a chance to catch up."

Logan was reaching for a glass when he saw a flash of daylight in his peripheral vision. "Sorry, we're closed," he said. He turned around to pull the tap for Mitch's beer, looked up and froze.

"I, AH—" Lacy stopped speaking once she saw the look on Logan's face.

Mitch turned to see what had spooked Logan. "Lacy, what a surprise," he said.

"Hi, Mitch." She approached the bar.

Mitch stood up. "Why don't you take my stool. I was just heading back to the office anyway. I'll catch you later, Logan." He gave his brother a wave. "Nice to see you, Lacy." He nodded in her direction, then left the bar.

She sat down on Mitch's stool. Words failed her. She'd planned a persuasive argument that would make Supreme Court Justices sit up and listen, but Logan looked so damn good standing there that the words stuck in her throat. The blue button-down shirt with rolled-up sleeves emphasized his stunning blue eyes.

The muscles in his arms rippled under the fabric as he wiped the bar down. It was a relief to see for herself that he was back on his feet and healing nicely. It made her want him all the more and she hadn't thought that was possible.

"Carol, can you go downstairs and continue the inventory?" Logan said. "I'm almost finished. It shouldn't take you long, and it'll give you the chance to sit before the supper crowd comes."

"Sure," she chirped. She smiled at him as she passed. "Thanks for the thought, boss."

The hairs on Lacy's arms stood up. The chirpy waitress was in love with Logan. She watched as Logan smiled back at Carol. She wanted to rip the girl's lips off.

Logan moved back to lean on the counter behind him, arms crossed in front of his chest.

She frowned. "Alex told me you're cooking here now. That's great. How's it going?"

"Fine."

"That's awesome. You're living your dream."

"Uh huh." He just stared blankly back at her.

"So, I um…guess you are wondering why I'm here?"

He just stared at her with a cocked eyebrow. Damn. He was making this as difficult as possible. Could she really blame him? After everything they'd gone through together, she'd treated him like shit.

"Pour me a drink?" she asked, licking her dry lips. She saw his gaze follow her tongue. Well, that was something at least.

He turned around to pour her a glass of white wine. She was moved by the way his faded jeans molded his fine ass. Heat crawled up into her belly from her core. God, she wanted this man. Now more than ever. He turned again and plunked the wine down in front of her before returning to the position he'd assumed before.

She reached out and took a big swig of the wine, then put it back very carefully. *Here goes nothing.*

"Logan, I owe you an apology. I treated you horribly. I was scared. It's not an excuse, but it's the truth." She watched his face but didn't see one flicker of emotion. She licked her lips again and continued, "I get why you had to check me out over the email. It was pretty stupid to send an encrypted email while I was at your office. It was only going to make you suspicious." She toyed with a napkin on the bar.

"I wanted you to know Trenthom was blackmailing me into taking over my father's business. He said if I didn't take over from my father like Dad had wanted, he wouldn't help any of us. He actually threatened to…hurt us."

She looked into his eyes, saw nothing there, and started playing with her napkin again. "We didn't use the scuba gear, by the way. My father got there and said there were holes in the regulator lines, so we just went into the water straight off the beach and swam for it, but I guess you already knew that.

"I turned back when I heard the explosion, but your brother got a hold of me and wouldn't let me go. He said the last thing you would want was for me to get killed trying to help you."

She kept searching his face for a sign. Anything that might give her hope, but it was still blank. His posture was just as unyielding. She took another sip of wine, fidgeting in her seat a bit.

"Did Alex tell you that my father retired? He realized I was serious about it, so he got out. Well, he's getting out. There are a couple of loose ends to tie up, but in a month or so, he'll be free. He says he's going to spend the summer here in New York with me, but we'll see."

"I thought you just said you had to take over or Trenthom would hurt you?" Logan's tone was terse.

"Well, um, the truth is Trenthom just wanted to work with someone he could trust to do the right thing. Dad suggested Reggie. Reggie has been with us for years, longer than Omar, and he knows the business almost better than anyone. So Trenthom worked out a deal with Reggie, and now I don't have to go into the business anymore."

She watched Logan's face closely and prayed for a sign. "I

can follow my dream now, like you did…" Her voice trailed off. Glancing at him again, she twirled her wine glass.

The silence grew around them until she finally couldn't take it any longer. "Look Logan, the truth is, I panicked when you pulled out the box." She touched the earrings as a nervous gesture. She wore them almost all the time. "I was already in love with you, but I knew that I had to agree with Trenthom's demand. I couldn't ask you to stay with me. It would have meant asking you to give up your dream. Give up all of this." She waved her arms around. "I couldn't ask you to live that life for me." She stopped speaking, and the silence settled once again.

"It's all different now." She glanced into his eyes, but all she saw was an unbreachable ice blue wall. "I love you. You heard that part, right? I have been totally miserable without you. My father made me admit it. He realized it was tearing me apart not being with you. He knew I was unhappy as a lawyer, but he thought bringing me into the family business was a great solution since I love logistics so much. I finally told him about my dream. He understands, and he is totally supportive of me. So, I came back here to start up my life again, hopefully with you in it. There, I said it. That's the truth."

She chanced a glance at his face, which was still impassive. *So that was how it was going to be.* Well, she didn't have the right to expect anything else from him. Taking a deep breath, she stood up from her stool and bit her bottom lip as she brought a hand up to smooth her hair. Her heart was splintered like tempered glass did when hit by a bullet. She had to get out of here while she still had a modicum of control. In about thirty seconds, she was about to burst into tears, and she didn't want him to see her like that. She didn't want him to know how much his rejection was killing her.

"Well, now you know where I stand and where to find

me," she said while looking at her shoes. She straightened her shoulders and brought her head up to give him one last chance to say something to her, only to find herself alone. He wasn't behind the bar. "Well, shit." She sighed.

It had only taken him two seconds to disappear after she'd confessed she loved him. Message received. Her shoulders slumped as she turned around and walked right into Logan's chest.

"Oof."

"Seems to me, this is right where we started," he growled, his voice gravel. She gazed up at him. His eyes were the color of a stormy ocean. The color they turned when…

She blinked. "You love me," she breathed.

"Of course, I love you." He put his arms around her. "I will love you no matter what hell you put me through. No matter what you do for a living. No matter what adventures you drag me on. We were made to be together, always." He swooped down quickly and claimed her mouth with a scorching kiss. And that was exactly how the chirpy Carol found them some twenty minutes later. Totally wrapped up in one another.

ABOUT LORI MATTHEWS

I grew up in a house filled with books and readers. Some of my fondest memories are of reading in the same room with my mother and sisters, arguing about whose turn it was to make tea. No one wanted to put their book down!

I was introduced to romance because of my mom's habit of leaving books all over the house. One day I picked one up. I still remember the cover. It was a Harlequin by Janet Daily. Little did I know at the time that it would set the stage for my future. I went on to discover mystery novels. Agatha Christie was my favorite. And then suspense with Wilber Smith and Ian Fleming.

I loved the thought of combining my favorite genres, and during high school, I attempted to write my first romantic suspense novel. I wrote the first four chapters and then exams happened and that was the end of that. I desperately hope that book died a quiet death somewhere in a computer recycling facility.

A few years later, (okay, quite a few) after two degrees, a husband and two kids, I attended a workshop in Tuscany that lit that spark for writing again. I have been pounding the keyboard ever since here in New Jersey, where I live with my children—who are thrilled with my writing as it means they get to eat more pizza—and my very supportive husband.

Please visit my webpage at https://lorimatthewsbooks.com to keep up on my news.

Please stay in touch! You can find me here:

Facebook: https://www.facebook.com/LoriMatthewsBooks
Instagram: https://www.instagram.com/lorimatthewsbooks/
Twitter: https://twitter.com/_LoriMatthews_
Amazon Author Page: https://www.amazon.com/author/lorimatthews
Goodreads: https://www.goodreads.com/author/show/7733959.Lori_Matthews
Bookbub: https://www.bookbub.com/profile/lori-matthews

ALSO BY LORI MATTHEWS

Break And Enter

Smash And Grab

Hit and Run (Coming Soon)

CPSIA information can be obtained
at www.ICGtesting.com
Printed in the USA
LVHW111145311022
731895LV00008B/228